The Innocents

William A. Meis, Jr.

Suffer the little children to come unto me,
and forbid them not;
for of such is the kingdom of God.
Mark 10:14

Published March, 2014
Fallen Bros. Press
6010 South Pacific Coast Highway Suite 9
Redondo Beach CA 90277
ISBN-13: 978-0615976631 (Fallen Bros. Press)

Cover and interior design: © Guillermo Bosch, 2014

For
Sabine
and
George Henry.

The Death of the Holy Innocents, Giotto di Bondoni (1305)

CONTENTS .... Page

The Holy Innocents, Sano di Pietro (c.1470)

Chapter One

The rumor stirs his frantic cry / That One who'd drive him forth is nigh / Cries he: Go, soldiers! take the sword! / Each cradled infant's blood be poured! / But what avails his wicked way? / What mortal can God's purpose stay? / Though many die, all innocent, / Christ safely far away is sent.
Hymn, Matins, The Octave Day of the Holy Innocents.

Little Iggy Loyola's life began again when the cooper's hawks arrived to roost in the magnolia tree outside the front door of our Jesuit home in Riviera Beach.

I was reciting Matins during my usual early morning walk when suddenly something fell from the sky and landed at my feet with a hollow clunk! It was a stark white corpse. Picked clean. Head and chest and legs intact.

The corpse was a large bird, maybe a seagull, perhaps a crow, hard to tell stripped of its flesh and feathers. I stumbled backward. Startled. Perplexed.

I looked up into the branches and there among pale wax blossoms, two young hawks were scuffling. Dark brown spotted wings flapping. Scimitar beaks bobbing. Talons frantically grasping to hold onto a teetering branch.

Suddenly they both swooped down right in front of me. The quicker one grabbed his ghoulish prize and lifted off toward a Chinese elm. His combatant following in hot pursuit.

I watched the two birds wrestle each other before I went

1

inside the rambling, weather beaten house on Dolorita Avenue that served as our province's way station for priests removed for one reason or another from permanent assignments and those not yet delivered into the arms of our Lord and Savior Jesus Christ.

I inhaled the familiar dusty, musty odor of a wood frame beach cottage built in the 1920s. Never renovated.

I walked through the dining room and nodded a good morning toward our skeletal old Father Thomas huddled over his morning Los Angeles Times which rustled and shook in his palsied hands. Half deaf. Also Parkinson's.

He ignored me. He had spilled his coffee again and our housekeeper, Angela, was cleaning up around him while mumbling under her breath a stream of French expletives that would have shocked Father Thomas if he understood them.

I understood her, but I never let on that I spoke her language. In fact, I tried to avoid any contact with her.

She was trouble. For me.

Angela was a tall, dark-haired, ex-Ursuline nun from Quebec City. She left the convent and came to the United States hoping for a husband, children and prosperity. She struck out on all three, perhaps because she had a 4-inch angular scar that ran from just below her right brow down and across her upper cheek to the chin of her otherwise very attractive face.

Such imperfections are not taken lightly in Southern California. So, she eventually ended up at 1215 Avenue Dolorita where for ten years she watched over bad boys and old priests who came in the front door and stayed until their dead bodies rolled out the back.

I was one of the bad boys. Older but not old. Not old

enough to die anyway. Yet.

I passed through the dining room and climbed the creaking stairs carpeted with threadbare harvest gold to my room on the second floor. My space was pleasant enough. Roughly 15 feet by 30 with bay windows facing south overlooking Dolorita and the cooper's hawks in the magnolia. The windows were large. The light was good for reading and for painting in oils, a hobby to which I had become addicted after the Society removed me from teaching Canon Law at Edmund Campion University.

I had a narrow single bed with a hard mattress. A gray metal writing desk that was surely rescued from some bureaucratic government office. A Herman Miller desk chair with a loose arm. A Baxton overstuffed leather club chair that was losing its stuffing. Three IKEA particleboard bookcases. A Santa Fe II double-masted studio easel standing near the windows and an antique L Wolff cast iron corner sink with a rusting towel rack. My one luxury was a Turbo boosted MacBook Pro with 17-inch screen, maxed-out memory, a massive Iomega external hard drive and HD graphics.

I also had a Samsung Android smart phone, but since my forced removal from teaching, no one called me. I only bought it because I used one essential app—my breviary that made it convenient to follow my daily prayers wherever I happened to be. So I was startled when, as I sat in my club chair and tapped into the Divine Office to finish Matins, my phone chirped. I let it go to voicemail, and then it bleeped to indicate that whoever called left a message.

I finished quietly reciting: "O God, whose praise the martyred Innocents did this day proclaim, not by speaking but by dying…may our lives also proclaim thy faith, which our tongues profess."

Then I checked the call log that indicated the caller's ID was blocked. Curious, I tapped into my voicemail and heard a long silence, then a faltering voice. Sex indeterminate. Speaking, what sounded to me like repetitive gibberish.

"Yaaaaabbbbbbbaaaaddddddabah," pause, "Yaaaaabbbbbbbaa aaddddddabah," pause, "Yaaaaabbbbbbbaaaaddddddabah." Then a beep as the caller broke the connection.

I pocketed the phone in my jeans and went back downstairs. Thomas was still trembling, still reading his paper.

Charles-David, who used to chair the Classics Department at Edmund Campion until heavy drinking and old age dulled his memory, joined Thomas in the dining room. Charles-David was reduced to teaching Latin and Greek part-time at St. Aloysius Country Day where students taunted him by calling him Father Chunky. He yearned for a civilized life. He hated teaching. He hated adolescent boys. He hated being called Chunky.

He sat, dressed in one of his worn, threadbare cassocks, hunched over at the other end of our 8-foot long burled walnut table. His big, round head was covered by his fat swollen fingers. He was obviously suffering from another night nursing a 3-liter jug of Mont LaSalle Chateau Des Fréres sacramental wine.

"Charles-David," I said, "I want you to listen to this."

He groaned. "Not now, not before coffee."

I ignored his hangover and pulled out my Samsung. I played the message. I asked him what he thought.

"It makes no sense. It's nothing. Leave me alone."

Angela placed a chipped brown cappuccino bowl next to him. He gripped the handle gratefully and brought it to his fat lips. "I don't think it's a real language, Peter."

"What's not a real language?" asked Andrew as he also joined us.

Andrew was blessed with curly black hair, cursed with an unruly black beard. He had sharp blue-gray eyes. He was, like me, one of the bad boys, too young for retirement, but he was suspended from active involvement in church affairs because of his passionate commitment to preaching liberation theology. He was being investigated by the dogmatic Bishop Freibourg, prefect of the Vatican's Supreme Tribunal of the Apostolic Signatura, but he had great hope that the new Pope Francis would reinstate him.

"All sounds are an attempt to communicate," said Andrew, "and therefore real language. Let me hear the message."

I played Andrew the voice mail. "Weird," he said. "Very weird. I'll have to think about it." He hesitated. "By the way, you know your so-called smart phone was assembled by 12-year-old Asian slave labor don't you, Peter? Wouldn't have one myself."

"I have my breviary on it," I said. "It's convenient."

Andrew glared blankly at me. He never said his daily prayers anymore.

Charles-David took his coffee and wandered off toward the small study at the front of the house. Andrew picked up the international news section of the Times from the pile of paper next to Thomas who'd stopped reading and was staring off into middle space.

I sat down and was eating a single piece of toasted European black bread when I heard a loud crash. All of us, even Thomas and Angela turned toward the front of the house.

Seconds later Charles-David came staggering into the dining room. He held a large round, mottled gray stone in his right hand. His left hand was holding his forehead where blood dripped from a cut near his temple down onto his cassock. "Call 911," he screeched, "Call 911." He let the stone fall from his hand.

"What the hell happened?" asked Andrew while Angela grabbed a wet cloth and began cleaning the blood from Charles-David's face.

"I was sitting there with my coffee when this rock," he pointed toward the stone on the floor, "this rock shattered… shattered the window next to me."

"The stone hit you?"

Charles-David looked confused. "No, I don't think so. The blood…window…glass, window glass, I think."

Angela examined his wound that had stopped bleeding. "It's a small cut," she said. "It's not serious."

"Good," said Andrew, "let's not call 911. The popo always bring trouble."

We moved into the sitting room to investigate what happened. The front window was indeed shattered. Shards of glass littered the moth-eaten Persian carpet. Curious, I walked to the front door and opened it. I didn't see anyone. Then I looked down.

There on the stoop was a large wicker basket filled with stained, dirty rags. "Well, what do you make of this?" I asked the others.

We stood, dumfounded, looking at the strange basket when Angela screamed, *"Criss de tabarnak!"* She dropped to her knees next to the basket, rummaged through the filthy rags and pulled out a tiny naked body, limp and blue. *"Jésus, Jésus, Jésus,"* she moaned, *"Il est mort, Il est mort."* She was crying. "He is dead, no?"

The pathetic little fellow, for the baby was clearly a boy, was not breathing. His tiny body was covered in blood and mucus. His skin, wrinkled and puckered. His eyes closed. My heart went out to him. The poor little guy never even had a chance.

Then Father Thomas tottered over to Angela. He hovered over the child. Suddenly he stumbled forward and wretched the baby out of Angela's arms with his cramped arthritic hands. He stared at the infant's closed eyes. The infant's silent purple lips.

Thomas mumbled the old Latin words of The Eucharist, *Corpus Domini nostri Jesu Christi custodiat animam tuam in vitam aeternam.* (May the Body of Our Lord Jesus Christ keep your soul unto life everlasting.) He pressed his lips over the boy's mouth. He pinched the infant's nose as he breathed deeply, once, twice, three times. Nothing. Then again. Nothing. Again. And again.

Then there was a soft mewling. Jerking arms and legs. A tremendous wail. Thomas smiled and handed the child back to Angela who squeezed him to her breast as fresh tears ran down her face.

"Well, now we should call 911," I said.

"No!" said Angela, "No! This baby is a gift from God. He is my baby. I will never let him go."

I was astonished. "But Angela…" Angela stared at me with a look so fierce and determined I was forced into silence.

Everyone's eyes turned to the child. He gurgled and cooed in Angela's arms. Father Thomas made the sign of the cross on the child's forehead.

The cooper's hawks whistled from their roost in the highest branches of the magnolia.

The Holy Family, Icon

Chapter Two

Praise the Lord, O ye his servants… He maketh the barren woman to keep house, and to be a joyful mother of children.

First Vespers, Evensong, Feast of the Most Holy Family within the Octave of Epiphany.

Once the baby arrived, Father Thomas stopped reading newspapers. Each day he sat with the child in his lap. His hands did not shake when he was holding the baby, and he refused to let any of us except Angela touch the child.

She kept the baby in her room at night and Thomas sat in a chair outside her door keeping watch. For whom or from what, I didn't want to know.

Angela loved being a mother. Her harsh voice grew soft when she spoke to the child. Her eyes were wide with excitement observing Iggy's jerky wiggling and twisting. She was tolerant and infinitely kind when he fussed and cried.

A few days after our foundling was brought back to life, Angela walked down to the Bank of America branch in Riviera Beach and emptied out her meager savings.

She left the bank and walked to the corner of Avenue H and Catalina where she caught the Beach Cities Transit #104 bus heading south. At Torrance Avenue, the bus turned east away from the ocean and headed toward the endless shopping centers and mini-malls on Hawthorne Boulevard.

She exited the #104 at Hawthorne and Del Amo Circle,

just outside the three million square-foot Del Amo Fashion Center, and boarded the Torrance Bus Lines #8 for a short ride past the Audi and Honda car dealerships to the corner of Hawthorne and Del Amo Boulevard where she treated herself to a small frozen yoghurt at Penguin's.

Then she walked past Payless Shoes to Babys R Us where she bought: A Sorelle crib. Two Halo sleepsacks. Five organic cotton swaddling blankets. Munchkin PBA free feeding bottles. Similac Advance Organic formula. She piled the lot into a new, ash wicker Moses Basket.

As things turned out, the formula wasn't altogether necessary because Angela also put the child to her nipples and after a week of dry suckling, her milk inexplicably came in. Her full breasts and gentle demeanor complimented her in unexpected ways and she was utterly transformed by her virginal maternity into an even more beautiful, more attractive woman.

But I was growing increasingly concerned that we shouldn't, and probably couldn't, continue to keep the child a secret. We had to let the police, or child care workers or somebody in authority know about the baby, but I couldn't bring myself to reveal our secret unless the others agreed. The baby's arrival actually was pretty miraculous. Perhaps we were meant to have him. I kept my mouth shut and prayed for divine guidance.

It was Charles-David who finally broke our little community's reluctance to face reality when, after dinner and half a bottle of Mont LaSalle St. Benedict, he grew angry and annoyed when the baby cried. "So what are we going to do with the little brat?" he shouted. Along with his antagonism toward adolescents, he also didn't like babies. Especially crying babies.

The scar along Angela's chin shown iridescent red. She handed the baby over to Father Thomas. She leapt out of her chair and headed for Charles-David ready to lay him out if she had to.

Andrew put out an arm to restrain her, but she easily brushed him off. "Our baby is not a brat," Angela yelled at Charles-David.

"Hold on, hold on," I cautioned. "Angela! Angela, please!" She hesitated. "Angela, please sit down."

"Tell him to shut-up."

"Please, Angela."

She slowly returned to her chair.

"Charles-David is right," I said, "What are we going to do?"

No one answered. Then Andrew said, "He's obviously been abandoned. We can't just turn him over to the authorities. What will happen to him once he's swallowed up by our fascist government's bureaucracy?"

"I'm sure they'll find a good home for the little rascal," said Charles-David. Then he hiccupped. "We're not fit to raise a child." Another hiccup.

"Speak for yourself, Father Chunky," said Angela as she struggled to regain her composer. Charles-David glowered.

Andrew focused on me. "Peter, we do need to know more about the child. You should find out where he came from."

"Me?"

"You know the law."

"Canon law, Andrew. I taught Canon law, church law. What does that have to do with finding a child's parents?" They were all staring at me. "Anyway, I wouldn't know where to begin."

"Yes you would," said Angela. She gave me a knowing glance. I had no idea what she thought she knew. I ignored her.

"You might start by cranking up that over-priced, useless machine you keep in your room," said Andrew.

"Well, yes," I agreed. "I could do a basic search. Find out about missing babies. That kind of thing. But beyond that…"

My phone chirped. I glanced down. A text message. I looked up and around the table. "I should read this," I said.

"Not now," said Angela. "He's is more important."

"Who's more important?"

"Our baby."

"Why do you keep calling him our baby," said Charles-David. "He's not our baby."

"He is our responsibility," said Andrew, "therefore, he's our baby, at least until we find out who he belongs to."

"Whom," mumbled Charles-David.

"Ig…ig…natius L-L-Loyola," stuttered Father Thomas. I was astonished. I thought he couldn't hear us. Could he read lips? "His name is Ignatius Loyola."

"This is absurd," said Charles-David. "We're not naming this foundling Ignatius Loyola. It's an insult to our order. I'll not be party to that."

"Moses, Moses Loyola," offered Angela, "We found him in a basket."

"No," said Andrew, "no lawgivers, no false prophets offering false promised lands."

"Moses, was a false leader?" questioned Charles-David.

"Richard," I suggested. "He certainly has a lion's heart." I looked to Father Thomas for approval. "Richard Loyola?"

Father Thomas appeared to think for a moment. He shook his head, no. "Ignatius, Ignatius Loyola," he said, firmly.

The baby cooed. He liked the name.

"Okay," I said, "then, his name is Ignatius Loyola, at least for now."

"Oh, for God's sake," Charles-David whined.

"Exactly," Angela huffed.

I was annoyed.

I went upstairs to my room. I opened my messages and read the text: *"Fiant aures tuæ intendéntes: in vocem deprecatiónis meæ."* Latin. It took me a minute to translate: Oh, let your ears pay attention to the sound, no, the voice, yes, the voice of my begging? No, not begging, supplication, supplication, or something like that. Hmmmm?

I spent a few minutes lost in thought. The words seemed familiar. I opened the breviary app and scrolled to Vespers for that evening, the holy day of Sts. Tiburtius and Susanna, Virgin Martyrs.

The text message was taken from that day's Vespers, from Psalm 129. It went on to read: "For with Thee there is merciful forgiveness, and by reason of Thy law, I have waited for Thee, O Lord... Because with the Lord there is mercy, and with Him plentiful redemption."

Were the phone messages meant for me? If so, what voice in supplication? For that matter, what supplication? What forgiveness? Were these messages connected to the baby? I put my phone on my desk. I shut down my computer.

I walked over to my window and stood in front of my easel in order to study the painting mounted there.

The oil was meant to be a realistic depiction of the warring cooper's hawks and their prey picked clean. The hawks' images weren't working. The tree. The leaves. The branches. They all looked real enough. I even captured the peculiar texture of magnolia blossoms. The corpse was as I remembered it.

But the hawks weren't turning out right. I painted over them three times, but their expressions were unnatural. Very generic. I looked closer. One of the two birds had a dab of Venetian Red in the lower left quadrant of his right eye. I didn't remember putting it there.

I flicked the wet oil with my thumbnail, but the color remained. That was odd. I used my painting knife to scrape the canvas. There was still red. The color seemed to be a stain infused into the canvas itself. Pentimento? Couldn't be. I'd never used that canvas previously.

I studied the painting. The sky outside went from evening to nightfall. I turned on a light. I heard Ignatius Loyola fussing downstairs. He called out twice. Then I didn't hear him again. The house was quiet. The street outside was quiet.

I took off my clothes and climbed into bed. Naked. In that half suspended space between full consciousness and true sleep an erotic vision appeared to me. Part Angela, part distant memory. I could feel myself aroused. Excited.

Startled. I forced myself back to full awareness. Why now? I shuddered. I blinked four or five times. I remembered I hadn't recited Compline. I left my bed. The cool night breeze softened my erection.

I retrieved my phone and opened my breviary. The words comforted me. As I finished my recitation I whispered the words repeated so many, many times before: "May the souls of the faithful departed, through the mercy of God, rest in peace. Amen. Our Father, who art in heaven, Hallowed be thy Name. Thy Kingdom come. Thy will be done, on earth as it is in heaven..." And then I fell off into a deep sleep. Delivered from temptation.

St. Anthony, El Greco, (1577)

Chapter Three

O let no evil dreams be near, / Nor phantoms of the night appear / Our ghostly enemy restrain, / Lest ought of sin our bodies stain.
Compline, The Hymn. Feast of St. Anthony

Despite numerous searches through various databases, I could not find any record of a missing baby who matched the description of our baby.

The search itself was depressing: Thousands of missing infants, most with pictures. Pictures of African-American babies. White babies. Latin babies. Asian babies. Native American babies. Some babies were crying, some cooing, some smiling. Some expressionless. Blank as if they were dead. All gone somewhere. Most never to be found.

I stumbled onto one website featuring "Missing Angels," pictures of stillborn infants who, unlike our little guy, had not been brought back to life by the Breath of Christ. I could only bear to look at a few of the pictures.

Why would parents want to post those images on the internet? These stunted souls would linger in Limbo until the Final Judgment. Which reminded me, we needed to baptize Ignatius immediately. Odd that Thomas hadn't pushed for a christening.

Since I found nothing on the internet. I decided to try the police. Risky, but what else could I do? I closed my computer, left my room and walked north on Dolorita.

I turned left at Avenue "A" toward the Pacific Coast Highway, then north again on the PCH to Knob Hill, then west to Broadway and then once more north.

Broadway is a very wide street filled with tall palms, shady eucalyptus trees, magnolias, small cottages, apartment buildings, a fire station and a great many churches. As I walked north toward City Hall, the First Church of Christ Science was on my left, neat, low-rise New England meeting hall and reading rooms.

Then Christ Church Episcopal, a classic small white wooden chapel with a peaked roof. Then the Seventh Day Adventist Church, modest solid stucco. Then the suburban Bay Cities Community Church.

There was a break in churches as I passed our Riviera Beach main fire station where a flaming red hook and ladder truck was parked out front getting a good washing from the firemen. Then back to the churches.

The imposing bell tower of the United Methodist Church that boasted a bright blue banner proclaiming Hallelujah in bold white letters. The homey, tiny Child Evangelism Fellowship. The nondescript First Congregational Church.

The combined congregations of South Bay Christian Church and Southgate Korean Christian Church. Praise Chapel which looked like a small office building except for the prominent cross on the roof.

Then the back parking lot of St. James Roman Catholic Church where we Jesuits were sometimes asked to fill in to celebrate early morning masses when the diocesan priests were otherwise occupied.

These were the churches I passed on my walk.

If I had turned east on Knob Hill, I would have passed the

Immanuel Lutheran Church, The Church of Jesus Christ of the Latter Day Saints and St. Katherine's Greek Orthodox Church.

There were so many logical places to abandon a baby. Why had Ignatius Loyola landed on our doorstep?

I arrived at City Hall, a collection of modest, one-story buildings that resembled an elementary school. They were far less impressive than the adjoining glass and steel Riviera Beach Library which dwarfed the municipal offices and hid them from cars passing on the Pacific Coast Highway. In my opinion, that spoke well for the city.

I reviewed my strategy. How was I going to question the police without hinting why I was concerned about a missing infant?

I opened the heavy glass doors at the entrance to the police department. The reception area was unintimidating— an outdated, wood paneled room with a linoleum topped counter to my right. The counter ran across the width of the room. Behind the counter were a half-dozen desks. There were two people in uniform sitting at two of the desks. The rest of the desks were empty.

The youngest officer, a pretty girl with dark hair and deep brown eyes, raised her head. "Can I help you," she asked.

"Yes, well maybe," I said, "I'm Father Peter Paderewski. I live in the Jesuit residence over on Dolorita."

The young girl got up from her desk and approached the counter. The nameplate pinned at her left breast identified her as Officer Linda Alvarez. She looked somewhat skeptical. "You're a priest?"

I tried to see myself as she saw me, bald, scruffy three-day beard, paint spattered tight t-shirt and torn blue jeans, toeless huarache sandals.

I smiled. "Perhaps I should have worn my collar?"

"Perhaps," She didn't smile back, "So, what do you want, Padre?"

"I, um, well, I'd like to speak to someone about missing children."

"Children?"

"Well, an infant, actually, a baby."

"A missing baby."

"Yes, exactly."

"Well, Padre, we don't have many of those around here. Not in Riviera Beach. People here keep pretty good track of their babies, you know."

"Well, yes of course, I was just wondering if, perhaps, someone, someone in the area reported, a…a baby, a new baby, missing."

"Hmm." She studied my face. My clothes again. "Just a minute." She left the reception area.

After a few minutes, she returned with a fleshy man in his mid-50s, sandy thinning hair, sandy moustache flecked with white, a mournful face, full belly, tan chino slacks, and a navy blue Brooks Brothers blazer with frayed cuffs. He wore a white shirt and a striped maroon and yellow tie.

He didn't smile as he strode up to the counter. "You the guy who claims to be a priest?"

"I am a priest. Father Peter Paderewski, S.J."

"A Polak."

"Jefferson Park. Chicago."

He finally smiled. "I'm a Polak. Wisconsin, Milwaukee, Lincoln Village. Sergeant Stan Milosz. Come on back. We can talk there. Linda?" Officer Alvarez pressed a button under the top of her desk, there was a loud buzz, and Sergeant Milosz opened a half door in the counter.

I followed him past the reception area down a long, narrow hallway lit by florescent lights into a small room. His name was on the door. In plain black lettering, Sergeant Stanley J. Milosz.

The office was filled with the memorabilia of a suburban family man and involved active citizen. Framed photographs of kids in uniform. Green and white soccer shirts, shorts and knee-length socks. Gold and blue football uniforms, helmets cradled in their arms. Little League outfits with Mesa Monsters blazoned across their chests. A large, black standard bred poodle. Bright happy faces captured looking directly into the camera.

On the corner of his desk, Sgt. Milosz kept a photo of a slightly overweight, round-faced blond. An attractive woman. She was also looking directly into the camera. No matter what their actual lot in life, everyone in Southern California knows how to pose for the camera, even the dogs. It is their birthright. Just in case a producer sees the snapshot. Just in case a director is looking for a new face. Just in case.

"So, Pete, you don't mind if I call you Pete do you?"

"No, I guess not."

"So, Pete, what's your interest in missing children?

"Babies, actually. An infant."

"Uh-huh…?"

I was already feeling uncomfortable. "I was just asking the pretty officer out front if anyone in the area reported a missing infant."

"Why," he chuckled, "do you have one hidden away somewhere?"

I frowned.

He smiled. "Just kidding, Pete, Just kidding. Why would a priest…you really are a priest aren't you Pete?" I nodded. "Why would a priest have a baby hidden away?

I tried to smile as well. Just us guys goofing. "Good question."

"Unless you were trying to stash the child away for future entertainment."

I ignored him for a moment and stared hard at two Rip-It baseball bats and two Wilson gloves resting in the corner next to a file cabinet. I struggled to control my emotions. "That remark is totally uncalled for, Sergeant. It's not funny. It's crude." I stood up. "I'm leaving now."

"Hey, hey, I'm sorry, Paderewski. You're right. Not funny."

He waved a hand toward the sports pictures. "One of those kids, just a kid I coached, your typical sweet kid, altar boy and all that, had some uh, trouble with a priest. We reported the problem to the diocese. The cardinal didn't do a damn thing. Just transferred the bastard to a small parish in East LA where he molested more kids. Then they transferred him to rural San Angel, Mexico."

"I'm sorry," I said.

He hesitated. "Look, we haven't received any reports of missing babies, but we did find a homeless young woman collapsed on one of those concrete benches along Esplanade. You know those benches overlooking the ocean?" I nodded. "EMTs took her to Torrance Memorial, where they reported she'd recently given birth. We never found a baby though."

"Where is she now?"

"You know, Pete, I'm tempted to ask why you want to know?"

I shrugged.

"I'll give you a pass this time. Anyway, no one knows where she is. She left her hospital bed in the middle of the night. No one's seen her since. No one really cares, frankly, except we've been curious about what could have happened to her child. If there was a child."

"What do you think happened?"

Milosz gave me another piercing look. He rubbed his thumb and forefinger along his moustache. "You know, Pete, you're just way too curious about this woman."

He paused to see my reaction.

I didn't react.

He shook his head. "Okay. Well, personally, I think she drowned the child in the ocean. That's what I think. What do you think, Pete? As a priest. A man who's supposed to know the human heart. Would a woman really drown her newborn?"

"If the poor woman is mentally ill, I suppose she might toss him into the ocean."

The Sergeant frowned. "You said 'him'. Why did you say 'him'?"

He got me. I worked to make my face an empty mask but I'm sure he caught a tell. "Him, she, it. Habit, I guess."

Milosz slapped his hands down onto his desk. "Well, so I guess the whole mystery may never be solved. But you'll let us know if you hear anything?" He gave me that damned stare again. "You will won't you, Pete…? You will let us know won't you?"

"Of course," I said. "If I hear anything."

"Even if you heard something in confession, right, Paderewski. I mean, you wouldn't have to tell us everything.

You could just give us hints, right?"

"If that were to happen, we might be able work around the seal of silence. But it's not going to happen, Sergeant. I don't hear confessions. No active roles at all."

"I didn't think priests were ever deactivated."

"Deactivated?" I smiled. "Interesting way to phrase it. Sometimes we are."

"Why? Your choice or were you a dirty old man, Pete?" That stare again.

He was becoming a real pain in the butt. "Nothing you'd be interested in."

"Everything interests me, Pete. Everything."

"That's why you're a policeman."

I left the station. Didn't immediately return to the house. I walked south to Esplanade and sat on one of the benches. Maybe the very bench the mystery woman was lying on when the police found her.

I stared at the waves pounding the shoreline. The sky was clear, a perfect bleu de France. The light was golden, warm. A slight, cool on-shore breeze blew in off the water. Paradise. "Paradise to live in or to see." Woody Guthrie. I felt blessed by the Lord to live in such a place.

Milosz' questions shook me. Was I a dirty old man? No, really, truly I wasn't. Getting old? Well, yes. Sort of. But not dirty. Certainly not interested in children. Not in that way.

I reached into my right pant's pocket, took out my phone and opened my breviary. I started the familiar recitation for None, softly chanting: "O God, make speed to save me. O Lord, make haste to help me. Glory be to the Father, and to the Son, and to the Holy Ghost. As it was in the beginning, is now, and ever shall be, world without end...." when a cold chill ran down my spine.

I looked up from my phone. Nothing had changed in the sky, but everything appeared darker. Nothing had changed in my soul, but I was suddenly afraid.

I repeated the opening prayer: "O God, make speed to save me. O Lord, make haste to help me..."

For some reason, I started to cry.

St. Agatha, Guidoccio Cozzarelli (c.1480)

Chapter Four

Lo, on thy handmaid fell a twofold blessing, / Who, in her body vanquishing the weakness, / In that same body, grace from heaven obtaining, / Bore the world witness.
Matin, The Hymn, Feast of St. Agatha, Virgin and Martyr

Little Iggy Loyola's baptism started as a joyful celebration on a glorious Southern California morning. After three days of rain, high winds and pounding surf, the sun rose cream white in an azure blue sky. There were no clouds. Not a speck of smog. The air fresh and clean. The ocean at low tide actually was pacific, lapping the sand in gentle waves as the hulking yellow LA County tractors raked away the detritus washed out to sea from the city's storm drains into Santa Monica Bay where the tides brought it back on shore. Nature's payback.

I walked along the beach reading Matins: We sing of courage which was never daunted, / By cruel bondage, nor by death through torture; / We sing of blood shed which thou hast rewarded, / O King of Martyrs. / Fountain of mercy, hear the sweet petitions, / Of thine own Blessed whom today we honour; / Cleanse our defilements, so that we may praise thee / Meetly in heaven....

Back at the house, Andrew insisted we write our own text for the Baptism, one that fit with Iggy's unique arrival and unusual situation. That was okay with me. There was nothing in Canon law that explicitly forbade us from doing so.

In fact, it has long been the tradition of the Church that any pouring of water upon the child's forehead while reciting the words, "I baptize you in the name of the Father…" and so on, is a valid baptism that cleanses the newborn's soul of original sin and allows the baby to enter the kingdom of heaven.

But Thomas would have nothing to do with Andrew's creativity.

So Andrew argued that we could at least remove any references to Ignatius being born with sin staining his consciousness. He scratched his thick beard and grimaced. "That whole original sin concept's so medieval."

"No," said Father Thomas.

"And the salt and the oils? Come on now! We don't need Roman voodoo."

"He…does," said Thomas looking toward Ignatius sleeping in Angela's arms.

"Then I suppose we have to talk about devils as well?"

"Yes," said the old man his eyes determined, his voice weak but steady.

"I won't have anything to do with this barbarism," huffed Andrew as he stomped out of the room. I remained silent. It was clear Thomas would not be moved.

"We need godparents," Charles-David said. "Where will we find godparents for our boy?"

He actually said "our boy." Angela smiled. Charles-David was coming around.

Father Thomas pointed a long, scrawny finger directly toward me. I shook my head. "No…no," I pleaded. "I can't."

"Why not?" asked Angela.

I hesitated. "It doesn't matter."

Angela persisted. "Why not, Peter?"

"I am not worthy. I am a bad priest."

There was embarrassed silence all around. Then Thomas again pointed toward me. "You," he said. There really was no moving the man.

"Alright," I said. "I'll do it." I turned to Angela. "And you will be his godmother?"

"No," she said. "I am his mother. I cannot be his godmother."

Again silence. "Well," I said, "you're not really his…"

Charles-David interrupted in a quiet, trembling voice: "I will be his godmother."

No one knew exactly what to say.

"I've been wanting to…to, you know," said Charles-David. "Now seems as good a time as any."

I was dumbfounded. I looked over at Thomas, expecting to see disgust and revulsion in his eyes over Charles-David's revelation. Instead there was peace. He nodded assent, and my jaw dropped.

"Well, well," I said. "I guess we have godparents."

Father Thomas went to his room to don his ecclesiastical robes. I changed into a clean white t-shirt and my one pair of jeans that weren't spattered with paint.

Angela went to fetch Ignatius from his basket. She dressed him in a white cotton gown she'd cut and sewn the night before. Then our little group assembled in the front room, joined by Andrew who had apparently changed his mind and decided to attend. I raised a skeptical eyebrow. "Wouldn't miss it for anything," was all he said as he nervously ran his fingers through his thick hair and managed a wry smile.

Father Thomas reappeared wearing a magnificent red and

purple raw silk stole stitched with gold and silver thread. I had never seen such a deeply colorful, beautiful drape even in photos of the Holy Father or the paintings of El Greco or Rubens.

Charles David brought an antique Swarovski crystal cruet filled with Evian water. He also ground up small crystals of pink Himalayan salt into fine granules and produced a bottle of cold-pressed, virgin almond oil he'd hidden in the back of our pantry.

He poured the pink salt onto a Thomas Forester & Sons, gold-trimmed tea saucer, and the almond oil into a Seiko Minegishi *guinomi* cup. Suddenly, Charles-David was full of surprises.

Thomas began the age-old, traditional ceremony in Latin, *Quid petis ab Ecclésia Dei?* But switched to English when he realized that for all of us except Charles-David, our Latin was at best rusty. Charles-David held Ignatius. I handled the responses. Thomas began again in his weak, quavering voice, "What do you ask of the Church of God?"

"Faith," I answered.

"What does Faith offer you?"

I hesitated, then sighed. "Everlasting life."

Thomas blew his old man's breath three times across Ignatius' face. I thought the sour odor would upset the baby, but Ignatius only blew an air bubble. "Depart from him unclean spirit, and give place to the Holy Spirit, the Consoler," intoned Father Thomas with an urgent edge to the words.

We proceeded through various prayers and responses that came back to all of us as we wove our way through memories of our early training. Then Thomas blessed the salt and placed a pinch on Ignatius' lips. Iggy grimaced at the taste. Thomas continued, "Receive the salt of wisdom. May it win for you mercy and forgiveness, and life everlasting."

More prayers, and then Thomas made the sign of the cross on our baby's forehead. "Then never dare, accursed devil, to violate this sign of the holy cross which we are making upon his forehead. Through Christ our Lord."

More prayers and responses. Then Thomas took spittle from his mouth and touched Ignatius' ears and nose.

Andrew groaned. "Oh, come on, Thomas," he whispered, "give the kid a break." But Thomas was not to be dissuaded.

When he touched the child's ears he said, "Be opened." Then the nose, "So that you may perceive the fragrance of God's sweetness. But you, O devil, depart; for the judgment of God has come." As Thomas looked directly into Ignatius eyes, he said, "Do you renounce Satan?"

I knew what I was supposed to respond, but suddenly Andrew blurted out, "This is not the work of Christ, this is paganism," and he stomped out of the room.

I took a deep breath, and then answered for Ignatius, "I do renounce him."

"And all his works?"

"I do renounce them."

"And all his display?"

"I do renounce it."

Thomas dipped a thumb into the almond oil and anointed Ignatius on his chest while making the sign of the cross. "I anoint you with the oil of salvation, in Christ Jesus our Lord, so that you may have everlasting life."

We all, except the departed Andrew, responded, "Amen."

Thomas closed his eyes and inhaled deeply. The emotion

of the moment appeared to overwhelm him as he swayed slightly and I was afraid he might fall. But he opened his eyes; tears rolled down his cheeks. He leaned toward Ignatius. "Do you wish to be baptized?

I answered for our baby, "I do."

Thomas lifted the cruet above Ignatius' head and poured once, slowly, "I baptize you in the name of the Father," he stopped, then he poured again, "and of the Son…"

Little Ignatius' face scrunched up as the water dripped into his eyes and mouth. Father Thomas poured a third time, "…and of the Holy Spirit."

Ignatius could take no more. He howled at the top of his tiny lungs a plea that resounded throughout the house. Andrew came rushing back in, shouting, "Is he alright? Is he alright?"

Angela took Ignatius from Charles-David and held the baby tightly to her breast. She was clucking and cooing. Ignatius calmed down.

Thomas intoned, "Go in peace, and may the Lord be with you." We answered a joyful, "Amen."

"Well," sighed Charles-David, "I think this occasion calls for the better stuff. I did stash a bottle of Moët et Chandon, Dom Pérignon, 1996, in the back of the fridge."

While Charles-David went to get the champagne, Andrew pulled me over to the window. "That pale blue Ford sedan in front," he whispered. "I'd lay odds it's an unmarked police car."

"You're paranoid, Andrew."

Charles-David returned with the bottle of champagne and glasses. He popped the cork and everyone cheered.

Andrew tugged my sleeve again. "There's a man dressed

like a plainclothes cop getting out of the car." Andrew was very nervous. "Now he's walking toward our door."

I glanced out the window. Andrew was right. The man approaching our front door was Stan Milosz, Sgt. Stanley Milosz from the Riviera Beach police. "Don't let him in," cautioned Andrew. "He needs to have a warrant."

The doorbell rang. "I'll get it," I told the others. Andrew disappeared. I took a deep breath and opened the door. "Ah, Sergeant Milosz, Stan, what brings you here?"

He stared at me. "Can I come in?"

I inhaled two more very deep breaths. Tried to stay calm. I knew I shouldn't let him in. Invited, he didn't need a warrant to search for whatever struck him as suspicious. But to refuse him was probably more suspicious. "Uhm, sure, come on in."

Milosz scanned the room as he walked through the door. At first he didn't make eye contact with any of us, then he asked, "Having a party?"

"A baptism," I said. "My niece, from Canada, uh, from Quebec, uh Montreal is visiting with her new baby. We decided to christen him here in our house since…"

Milosz ignored me and walked over to Ignatius who was cradled in Angela's arms. He spoke to Angela. "Cute little fella', what's his name?"

I quickly interrupted. "She doesn't speak English, Stan." I turned to Angela and spoke in rapid French.

When Angela heard me speaking French I thought she was going to drop the baby, but she recovered quickly. She looked directly at Milosz. "Ignatius," she said in a very heavy French accent. Smart girl.

I spoke to her again briefly in French, and then to the others, "This is Sgt. Milosz from the Riviera Beach police. He wants to talk. Maybe we should move the celebration into the dining room. I'll join you in a minute."

I turned back to Sgt. Milosz. "So, what's new?"

"We found her."

"Her?"

"The young woman who fled the hospital. The one who gave birth to a baby."

"Oh," was all I could manage.

"She's dead."

"Oh no."

"Murdered most likely."

That required more than an "Oh." I looked perplexed. Then I asked, "That's terrible, but why do you want to talk to me?"

"You're the only one who has inquired about a missing baby."

"Stan, look, I told you that was a question I was asking for someone else."

"No you didn't."

"Well, it was."

"What?"

"Someone else asked me to check if there were any reports of a missing child."

"Child? You asked about infants. Babies."

"Yes. Children, infants, babies."

"Who asked you to check?"

"It doesn't matter."

"It might, Pete. It might matter. You said we could work around certain issues. Confession and all that. You might be able to help."

I remained silent.

"Would you like to see the mother? She could use a prayer or two."

"Now?" I didn't want to see a dead woman who might possibly be Ignatius' birth mother. But I decided to leave with Milosz. "Let me tell the others."

I found our little group huddled in the kitchen. Andrew was holding something in his hand. At first I thought it was a toy pistol, but when I looked into his eyes, I knew it was real. I looked more closely. A Beretta Model 21 Bobcat. Tiny but lethal.

My neck ached from the tension. "What are you thinking?" I whispered. "Have you lost your mind, Andrew? For God's sake put that thing away."

"For God's sake I'll keep it handy, Peter. No popo's gonna' take our baby." Thomas nodded in agreement. Angela was rigid, catatonic with fear.

"Save me a glass of champagne," I said loudly so Milosz could hear me.

As we walked toward his car, Milosz said, "Nice looking girl, your niece." I said nothing. "Very attractive except for the scar. Where did she get that scar, Pete?"

"I honestly don't know," I said. That was the truth; I didn't.

As we climbed into the blue Ford, he frowned slyly. "Very fit too. Great body. You wouldn't think she just gave birth."

"Women today. They like to stay fit while they're pregnant."

"Hmmm," he said as he started the engine and put the car in gear.

We didn't go far. He turned left on Pearl Street and went straight down to Veteran's Park. The pretty uniformed officer I met at the station, Linda Alvarez, was guarding the entrance to the parking lot that was filled with numerous police cars and an ambulance. She saw Milosz and waived us through.

"The dead woman's over by the old library building," said Milosz as he pointed toward a 1930s Mission Spanish-styled building with graceful arched windows overlooking the tourist restaurants, beach bars and fishing boats in King's Harbor. "She's under that big tree, curled up against the base." I saw the Moreton Bay Fig—an Australian import with gnarled roots that extended out from the trunk above the ground.

As we approached a dozen uniformed and plainclothes officers milling around the library, I could see the body slumped against one of the larger roots wrapped in filthy clothes, wearing a torn yellow watch cap. There was a shopping cart from Albertson's grocery store parked next to her. Milosz carefully walked up to the body and signaled for me to follow in his footsteps.

I was horrified. She was young, very young, too young to be homeless. She might have once been beautiful, however her face was badly gouged and shredded. But the most disturbing shock came when I saw her eyes. She didn't have eyes. Her empty sockets were a bloody mess. Pieces of flesh, jagged nerve endings. Bile rose in the back of my throat, but I was able to contain it. Barely. I turned away.

"Can't look?" said Milosz.

"I'll be alright," I said.

I turned back and saw that her filthy rags were actually numerous layers of dresses, sweaters and jackets. I looked more closely. The top-layered skirt was a Comme des Garcons, one of her tattered sweaters was Nordstrom's cashmere wool, her ripped and torn maroon jacket was a Cole Haan lamb leather ¾ length coat and her shoes, muddy, stained, Rag & Bone Newbury Classic ankle boots.

"Her clothes are very expensive," I said.

"I wouldn't know," he deadpanned.

"What happened to her?"

"Look closely. She was shot directly through the heart. Small caliber bullet. Most likely a .22 or a .32. No exit wound. Not much bleeding. That at least was merciful."

I look her over again. I shuddered. "But her face?"

"That happened after she was already dead. Birds. Gulls most likely. Could have been hawks."

"Hawks?"

"Those damned cooper's hawks. They love to pick apart carrion. Eyeballs. Exposed flesh. I've seen them pick a dead animal clean."

"So have I," I blurted without thinking.

That remark earned me that Milosz stare. Then he shrugged. "The early morning walkers who found her remarked that they heard hawks whistling in that big silver eucalyptus over there." He pointed toward the far end of the park near the concrete block Senior Recreation Center, "Around dawn. They were walking over to see the birds when they discovered the body."

I looked at the tree. A Eucalyptus caesia, Silver Princess. Another Australian import. There were no birds there now, only the fiery red, wispy flowers that hung from the tree's branches.

I knelt down next to the young woman and forced myself to look into her ravaged face. It took all my willpower. I prayed for her soul.

It was obviously too late for Last Rites so I recited a Prayer for the Dead: "Dear Lord, accept this prayer which I offer You, merciful Father, for this woman who has died, whose faith in this life was known to You alone. Have mercy on her soul and bring her into Your kingdom of peace and light without end where You and Your saints live in the happiness which she has not known in this world and which this world cannot give. Amen."

Someone next to me echoed, "Amen." I turned. It was Milosz.

I stood.

"So, you did know her," he said.

"No, I've never seen her before, but I'm sure I won't forget her."

"Hmm," he mumbled.

I looked down toward the harbor and watched a small motorboat, a 17 ft. Boston Whaler Montauk, churning through the waves as it passed inside the breakwater into the calmer waters of the harbor.

"You're coming with me," said Milosz.

As we left the crime scene, my Samsung chirped. I glanced at the screen. A text. In Latin: *Et fílius iniquitátis non appónat nocére ei*. Hmmm, I was beginning to remember more Latin then I cared to: "Don't let the son of evil dare harm him" or something like that. Close anyway.

I was pretty sure I wouldn't get to finish my champagne.

St. Titus, Icon

Chapter Five

This meek Confessor of thy Name, / Today attained a glorious fame; / ...Earth's fleeting joys he counted naught, / For higher, truer joys he sought... .
Lauds , The Hymn, Feast of St. Titus, Bishop and Confessor

Sgt. Milosz's office was the same as it was the last time I was there. Except the baseball bats and gloves were gone. In their place were two taped Easton wooden hockey sticks and a couple of badly chipped, hard black rubber pucks.

"Hockey in Southern California?" I asked.

"There's a rink in the shopping center up on the hill. You played?"

"Goalie...before masks."

"Tough guy, huh?"

I smiled. "No, no not really."

Milosz told me to sit down.

I said. "I'm not a suspect am I?"

"Well, tell you the truth, Pete, I don't know. Perhaps a person of interest." He considered. "Yes, definitely a person of interest. That's why I want to talk. Just the two of us. Informally. No lawyers. No recordings. Just you and me, Pete."

I nodded cautiously. "Alright."

Milosz placed his notebook on his desk and flipped through the pages. Without looking up he said, "Seems she was only nineteen years old. Shot through the heart with a

.32 caliber bullet. Fired from very close range. Probably held directly on her chest."

"A .32 not a .22?"

"Yes. Why?"

I shrugged as if it didn't really matter, but I was relieved to know it couldn't have been Andrew's gun.

He continued. "Her name was Masha, Masha Bentz. Does that mean anything to you?"

"German?"

"She was Russian actually. Probably Jewish with that German last name. And her family emigrated when not too many Russian Russians were getting out."

"Whatever… her name means nothing to me."

He looked up from his notebook. "You're sure about that?"

"Yes."

"I ask because we found a folded piece of torn notebook paper in the pocket of one of her sweaters. It has your address on it."

"You mean the address of the Jesuit residence."

"Let's not split hairs, Pete. Remember, we're just talking. Just two guys talking."

I shrugged.

"So, tell me why she might have your address, Pete."

"This is about me, then?"

"I don't know. Is it? Who are you really, Father Peter Paderewski, S.J.? I know you're involved somehow."

I said nothing.

"Who am I talking to, Pete? Besides being a priest. Besides being an ex-university professor. Besides being a painter. Besides…"

"Whom…whom am I talking to."

The Milosz stare. "Don't be a jerk, Pete."

I was angry. "You've obviously been checking up on me. Why are you asking what you already know?"

"You sound like a lawyer, Pete, but then that's your training isn't it?"

"Canon law, Stan. Church law."

"Don't patronize me, Pete. I know all about church lawyers. Trust me. All about them."

He didn't add anything. We sat in silence for two or three minutes. Then his cell phone played the opening riff from "Bad To The Bone."

It startled both of us. He glanced at his Blackberry's screen. "I need to take this outside," he said, then, "I'll be back." He tried to deliver his parting words as an imitation of the actor Arnold Schwarzenegger's catch phrase, but his accent failed miserably.

I took out my Samsung and linked to the prayers for midday—Sext, the sixth hour. Psalm 55. "Be merciful unto me, O God, for man hath trodden me underfoot; / all the day long he hath afflicted me fighting against me. / Mine enemies have trodden upon me all the day long / for they be many that make war against me. / From the height of the day I shall fear, / yet put I my trust in thee."

I tried to stay focused on my prayers, but my mind wandered. Milosz was actually right.

I was involved. Somehow. The rock thrown through our window. Baby Ignatius' arrival on our doorstep. The mysterious calls and texts appearing on my phone. The dead homeless woman, dead girl, just a girl actually.

But what was going on? I needed to get back to my computer. There were so many mysteries. I wanted a few answers.

Milosz returned and said we would have to talk another time. He seemed distracted. Said he needed to deal with new developments. He didn't say what they were.

When I returned, our house was deserted. There were half empty glasses sitting on the kitchen table. The empty bottle of Dom Pérignon. Father Thomas' fine stole was draped over the back of a chair. Accouterments from the Baptism. Everyone clearly left in a hurry. Together.

I sat down in front of my computer and Googled the name, Masha Bentz. Google asked me if I meant, Mercedes Benz.

I scrolled down past dozens of Southern California Mercedes dealers. Finally there were a few Bentzes. But no Masha Bentz.

Then Google started giving me Mashas. Clearly a Russian name because there were plenty of Mashas with many, many Russian surnames. There was also one entry that indicated the name Masha could be Hebrew. Perhaps, after all, she was Jewish as well as Russian. The entry indicated the name in Hebrew meant 'bitter'. That brought an ironic smile to my face. Then I thought about the dead girl's face and my smile quickly vanished.

I entered just Bentz, no Masha. There was an Amelia Bentz, a German woman from Dresden who around the turn of the 20th Century invented the coffee filter.

Then a very American Bentz who taught English at a Christian university and wrote Christian books. A couple of CPAs, a real estate broker, a California state legislator, a pharmacist, a soldier in Nazi uniform and finally, a commercial and recreational boat manufacturer in Lewiston, Idaho.

Then I discovered an entry for Edward Wilhelm "Eddie" Bentz, an American bank robber and Depression-era outlaw who was associated with Machine Gun Kelly and eventually ended up in Alcatraz. That Bentz seemed properly sinister, but he was definitely not Russian and he died in the 1970s.

I was ready to give up when I saw a listing for a textile designer, Tsilia Bentz, owner of Truly Bent Fabrics, a business in Lomita, California, in an industrial park a few miles inland from Riviera Beach. She had a website, www.tsiliabentz.com, but when I clicked on it, I received the dialogue box, "Server not found." I clicked on the "try again" button, but Firefox still found nothing. Curious, I entered Tsilia Bentz into Google search.

There was a Wikipedia link for Tsilia Bentz, and when I clicked on it, there was a very short narrative with the notation that more information and verification were needed. And a picture. I was stunned. A photograph of an attractive middle-aged woman with dark hair streaked gray, wide brown eyes, high cheekbones and a pointed chin.

It was her. I didn't know Tsilia Bentz, but I did know the woman in that picture. I knew her very well. She was the reason I was living in a Jesuit residence in Riviera Beach rather than teaching Canon law at Edmund Campion University.

I left my Mac and walked very slowly over to my easel. I took down my still unfinished painting of the cooper's hawks in the magnolia, leaned the canvas against the wall, went into my storage closet and removed another unfinished painting from years earlier. I rested that painting on the Santa Fe easel, stepped back from it and admired the portrait. It was the best work I'd ever done.

My Madonna was painted from memory. She was nude, at

least in my mind, but from the back, with her neck turned so that she was looking over her left shoulder. Looking over her left shoulder at me. Looking at me looking at her face and her naked body. Antonia Lucia Belladone. How did she become Tsilia Bentz? I went back to the Mac, but further searches revealed no additional information.

It was getting dark when I removed Antonia Lucia's portrait from the easel and replaced it with the cooper's hawks. I picked up my Holbein Japanese steel spatula and repositioned some Van Dyke brown in the corner of the one Hawk's eye that was stained Venetian red.

Then I lost all natural light so I put the my paints away, and started Vespers, Psalm 129, "O let Thine ears be attentive / to the voice of my supplication. / If Thou, O Lord, shalt observe our iniquities, / Lord, who shall endure it? / For with Thee there is merciful forgiveness: / and by reason of Thy law, I have waited for Thee, O Lord."

As absorbed as I was in prayer, I did not hear Andrew approach my room. My door was open. I was startled when I realized he was there. He stood in the doorway holding the Bobcat in his left hand, waiting for me to ask him to enter. There were bags under his sunken red-rimmed eyes and his curly hair was matted on top. His voice was hoarse. "What are we going to do, Peter?"

"What's with the Bobcat, Andrew?"

"It isn't…it wasn't loaded."

"You could have been killed anyway. Maybe Ignatius as well."

"Maybe all of us," he said nervously. "Maybe that would be best, Peter. Safe in the arms of the Lord and all that."

I ignored his little suicidal melodrama. "Where are the

others, Andrew?"

"Downstairs. I wanted to take them into the mountains. But the mountains...I got lost. On the freeways. I really had nowhere to take them. Except back here. Back home. I'm not a very good guerrilla fighter, Peter. I failed."

We went downstairs. Little Iggy was sleeping. Thomas was cradling him in his arms. Angela was cooking. Charles-David was drinking.

Andrew began pacing back and forth on the kitchen linoleum. I gently lifted Ignatius from Father Thomas' arms and hugged him tightly to my chest with his head nestled against my neck. Wisps of his straight, dark brown hair tickled my earlobe. His gentle breath blew softly against my collarbone.

Then I held him out in front of me and carefully studied his face. He was gradually filling out from a wrinkled, scrunched-up newborn into a real baby person. He had recognizable features. I stared at his long eyelashes, his pug nose, his curved, sensuous mouth, his full pink cheeks.

Against my will, I remembered the mutilated face of the young woman in the park. Was she his mother? I couldn't make a connection. That woman was damaged beyond recognition. Iggy was beautiful. So beautiful.

Angela finished cooking dinner. Complete silence around the room except for the occasional hiccup from Charles-David as he nursed his Mont LaSalle.

Thomas wouldn't eat until Angela finished. Then she took the baby, opened her shirt and put him to her left nipple. Thomas picked at his food. Just a peaceful family evening around the kitchen table. That illusion held until my phone chirped.

"Pete?"

"Sergeant?"

"We have another body."

"Another body?"

"That's what I said, Pete."

"Connected to the girl in the park?"

"He sure is, Pete. Her father. Vlad 'The Count' Bentz."

"Her father." I was relieved. Not that the man was dead. That this Vlad was the girl's father.

"Pete?"

"Yes."

"No reaction?"

"I will pray for his soul as I already pray for his daughter's."

"I'm sure you will, Pete. I'm sure you will. Meanwhile, any thoughts?"

"How did he die?"

"In a fire. At his loft apartment in downtown LA. Burned to a crisp. Not a pretty sight."

"A fire. So it wasn't murder?"

"Hard to tell."

"Just a coincidence then?"

"I don't believe in coincidence, Pete. You religious types, you believe. Coincidence, spirits, mysterious forces, gobbledygook. No such thing as coincidence, Pete. No such thing." Neither of us spoke for awhile after that remark. Then, "So where were you this afternoon, Pete."

"Here at the house. Working on my computer. And painting."

"The others, the other priests, they will of course confirm that?"

"No, I was alone."

"Well, well, alone…at least you're honest to tell me that. Or an accomplished liar."

"If you want to put it that way, Sergeant."

"I do. Come see me tomorrow. We need to have another talk." He broke off.

Andrew eyed me suspiciously. "Are they going to take Iggy away?"

"I don't know," I said. "For the moment, Sergeant Milosz seems more interested in me than the child.

"Why you?" mumbled Charles-David.

"He seems convinced I know something about a murdered girl and her dead father."

Angela smirked, but said nothing, only holding tighter to Iggy still sucking at her breast.

Andrew frowned. "Do you?"

I didn't feel like sharing. "No," I lied, but it felt like a venial sin, perhaps only a mental reservation. I didn't know if the dead Bentzes were related to my Antonia, but I was pretty sure they were.

I was dizzy. Lost in a fog. I didn't clearly understand anything at that point.

Back in my room. I shut the door. I went to my Mac and returned to the Tsilia Bentz link. I finally admitted to myself that the woman's photo in the Wikipedia entry had to be Antonia. An older, even a gentler, less stressed Antonia, but the resemblance was too strong. It had to be her. So I did know something.

As I began to search the internet for any other information I could find out about Tsilia Bentz, I heard a soft knocking at my door. I clicked out of Firefox and went to the door. It was Angela.

She spoke in French. "I want to talk to you." She used the informal *tu*, not the formal *vous* we'd been using since we started speaking French to each other.

I replied using the familiar form as well. "About Ignatius?"

"Yes." Angela didn't hesitate. She was very direct: "You are Ignatius' father, aren't you?"

"Angela! Of course not."

"He was abandoned at our door for a reason, no?"

"God knew we would take care of him."

"But old, old Thomas could not be his father. Nor poor, confused Charles-David. Nor crazy, angry Andrew. Who else but you?"

"Angela. I'm an old priest."

"But a bad priest," she spoke softly, "and not so old, Peter." She kept her head slightly bowed and shuffled her feet. "I see the way you look at me. I feel your eyes caress my breasts, my buttocks." Her words were very sexy, especially in French. "You are still a man."

I was speechless. I assumed she had never noticed me looking at her.

Then she raised her face to me. Her eyes were moist. "But never my face, Peter. Your eyes never caress my face. Is it my scar? Am I so disgusting to you?"

Then she stepped forward, wrapped her arms around me. She let her head rest against my chest. She began to cry.

"Angela," I said, "Angela, please...don't." I tried to gently push her away. "If I have been...if I..." I couldn't budge her. "Angela, you are an attractive woman...I mean...a very attractive woman. Really you are, but I cannot...would not...."

I stopped pushing her, hesitated and then said, "I can't let these feelings out…again."

"Again?"

"You don't understand."

"You won't allow yourself to have feelings? Even for Ignatius' sake? Even to save our baby?"

"Angela, what are you talking about? You're not his real mother, and he's not my son. You know that."

"He is my baby. And I am certain you are his father."

I pushed her back from me again. That time I succeeded. "Angela, this is crazy. You're distraught. I…look, we can talk in the morning, but for now, you need to take care of Iggy. Please, for…for both our sakes, Angela. Please leave me alone now."

She left, but not before firing a final shot. With snot running down from her nose and defiance flashing from her wet, dark eyes she jeered, "You are really full of shit, Father Peter Paderewski, S.J. You don't know who you are, what you are or what you want. You're just full of shit!" Then she slammed my door and probably set everyone else in the house to wondering about what was happening in my room. Except Thomas couldn't hear. Charles-David was drunk. Andrew was lost in his visions of revolutionary conspiracies.

And Iggy was sleeping soundly, the deep sleep of the innocent.

St. John of Matha, Fresco

Chapter Six

Today if ye will hear his voice, harden not your hearts, / as in the provocation, and as in the day of temptation in the wilderness / when your fathers tempted me, proved me, and saw my works… .

Matins , Psalm 94, Feast of St. John of Matha, Confessor

The following day I awoke very early, locked my door, recited Matins, replaced the cooper's hawks painting with my painting of Antonia, and set to work finishing her portrait.

It took all day. I didn't eat. I didn't answer knocks at my door. I didn't answer my phone. I didn't read text messages. I didn't go on my computer. I peed in the sink and fell onto my bed that night completely, utterly exhausted. The following day, I resolved to track down Tsilia Bentz in Lomita.

I first had to figure out how to get to Lomita without attracting undue attention. We owned a house car, a 1987 dull gray Chevy Astro minivan, badly rusted, with one broken window on the driver's side that was replaced with a clear plastic bag attached to the frame with silver duct tape. We received it as a charity donation—a tax deduction for a retired school teacher in Hermosa Beach.

We hardly ever used the van because we could go most anywhere we needed to go by walking and Angela couldn't drive. So the vehicle sat in the driveway near the front door, filthy, rusting, increasingly splattered with white guano from the cooper's hawks and seagulls, an embarrassment for the rest of the neighborhood.

We also owned a bicycle, a used, rusting, women's Tahiti pink, wide-tired beach cruiser with a kid's rider seat mounted on the back. Angela picked it up in a garage sale for twenty bucks. She planned to take Ignatius on rides when he was older. Once she figured out how to explain his existence to the neighbors.

The bike was parked in back of the house next to our sun-bleached lawn chairs and a broken umbrella destroyed by fierce blasts from the occasional windstorms which blew in from the ocean. Rust and wind and sun were endemic to Southern California. Those combined elements slowly wore away the surface of everything. And everybody.

I could take a taxi to Lomita, but that would be prohibitively expensive. And the driver would know every stop I made just in case someone else wanted to know. Just in case.

Then there were the buses. I checked on the internet, and I found I could simply walk down to the Pacific Coast Highway at Avenue C and board an LA Transit orange and gray bus #232 heading south toward Long Beach, ride to Vermont Avenue where I could leave the bus and walk a few blocks north to 253rd Street, turn left and walk three blocks west to Petroleum Avenue, turn right and walk north four blocks to 251st Street which placed me somewhere very near Truly Bent Fabrics. I decided to take the bus.

As I travelled south on the Pacific Coast Highway, the road moved further inland behind the steep hills and luxury homes of the Palos Verdes Peninsula. At that point, the highway was no longer a coastal road at all, but instead was a suburban thoroughfare jammed with traffic. There were endless mini-malls, gas stations, fast food restaurants and car dealerships.

Bored, I recited my breviary, Lauds, the words near the end of the prayers were words of supplication to Mary Queen of Heaven, words that jumped off the page: "so by the help of her intercession we may die to our former sins and rise again to newness of life." That's what I sought from Antonia although she was no Queen of Heaven. I needed to put my old sins behind me. I needed to care for the precious new life with which I'd been entrusted.

It was easy to spot the Vermont intersection, where the giant Kaiser Permanente South Bay Medical Center commanded the high ground next to Ken Malloy Harbor Regional Park and Machado Lake, the lake surrounded by thick greenery where gay men found release and a released alligator nicknamed Reggie swam in the murky water preying on careless ducks and gulls.

I left the #232 Long Beach bus, crossed over the highway and headed north along Vermont Avenue past the Rejoycing Korean Presbyterian Church, then the New Life Center and the Vermont Christian Academy. God bless them all for trying, but the area was depressing.

For all the beauty and magnificence of Southern California near the water, once I go inland to the flatlands, even a short distance inland, there are only miles and miles which were once empty desert and then later irrigated orange groves, later still vast housing tracts for veterans returning from a war in the Pacific seeking a better life. When I walk these streets, I am struck by the complete absence of anything significant, anything that can provide any sort of natural, emotional reaction.

Some have called this wasteland ugly. Some have deemed it destructive. It's neither. It's banal. And if there is evil there, it's the banality of evil, or the evil of banality, the evil of complete indifference to human dignity or the spirit of the human soul. For all the parishes and churches that sprout like weeds everywhere across these vast developments, there are few, if any, which keep faith with the redeeming love of Jesus Christ. Instead they preach endurance.

The minute I turned left and walked west on 253rd Street, the neighborhood evolved into small warehouses with asphalt covered parking lots overflowing with scrap metal, broken, dented RVs, stacks of weather-beaten pallets, shipping containers, delivery trucks.

Petroleum Street was more of the same, although right in the middle of the block, amidst the sheet metal cladded warehouses, there were two tract homes with grassed-in front yards and struggling bottlebrush trees. God bless them for trying.

251st brought with it a sense of dread. The narrow street was no different than 253rd or 252nd except this was the street where I would find Antonia's workshop and possibly Antonia herself.

I walked along the sidewalk on the north side of the street where grass was struggling up between the pavement cracks and thigh-high weeds fought to stay alive next to the curb. When the spring rains stopped, they would die.

On my right there was a sloppily painted green corrugated sheet metal building, a gate and then an open warehouse that appeared to be a maintenance facility for a fleet of trucks. A large red crane in the parking lot next door. The steel fence protecting the lot was strung with gleaming razor wire along the top of the sharply pointed pickets. Not her place. Not Antonia's style.

Then I passed a building that had four large brown pebble encrusted panels decorating the front, but no sign or other identification whatsoever. Also not her style. Another small parking lot. Then a small warehouse with a rather nicely hand painted American flag covering the cinder blocks from the parking area to the roof. There were two forklifts parked out front. That wouldn't be her either.

I knew before I even saw the number on the next building, that this warehouse would be Antonia's. The shop's appearance betrayed a certain design consciousness, a three-foot wide horizontal terra cotta red stripe along the top, followed by a two-foot wide teal blue stripe running beneath the red and the entire lower section of the frontage painted stark, bone white. There were two small struggling decorative palms to the left of the front door.

The doorway itself was flanked by floor to ceiling columns of local Palos Verdes fieldstone—the irregularly cut rocks randomly embedded in concrete. The front door was a black CECO steel, flush mounted 18 gage door, not even a peep hole. And the four windows were blocked by thick steel bars painted white to appear less foreboding.

I approached the entrance cautiously. I found a small call box next to the door and a notice that directed me to press the button if I wished entrance. I pressed the button.

I waited. No response. After perhaps a minute, I pressed the button again. Still no response. Just to make certain, I tried one last time, leaving my thumb on the button for longer than necessary. There was still no response.

I went next door to the American flag warehouse that turned out to be an industrial tool and die company. There was a pleasingly plump, late middle-aged Hispanic woman behind a dark blue, linoleum-topped counter with her hair pulled back in a bun and glasses dangling from a glittering silver chain. She was working on an older model Dell PC but immediately looked toward me with a big smile as I stood at the counter. "How can I help you?" Very friendly. Only a slight accent.

"About the business next door…"

"Oh, you want to rent the building?"

"No, I…"

"The rent is very cheap right now. The recession you know, and there are two other empty buildings just down the block."

"So, the building next door is empty?"

"Oh yes." She became somewhat pensive, slightly less friendly.

"Truly Bent Fabrics. The woman who ran the business, did you know her?"

Then the woman lifted her glasses from around her neck and put them on her nose. She also became very cautious. "Who are you?"

"An old friend of hers."

"Not police?"

"No why? Was there some sort of trouble."

"Oh no. No, no, no."

"Do you know where she went?"

"No."

"Do you know why she left?"

"No."

"Do you have any idea how to reach her."

"Reach?"

"Phone? Mail? Website?"

"No."

I tried my best relaxed, counseling voice. I smiled my best smile as well. "It seems you weren't friendly with her?"

"No, definitely not."

"You didn't like her very much."

"No."

"Can you tell me anything about her?"

"No."

Interesting reaction.

I left the American flag building, and returned to where Antonia's business was once located. It was clear I couldn't get in from the front. I walked west to the poorly named Marigold Avenue which contained more warehouses but no flowers, marigolds or otherwise. I turned right and after half a block found that there was an alley behind the businesses on 251st Street. Then I backtracked, counted the number of businesses before Marigold, then entered the alley and counted backwards as I walked east.

From the rear, Antonia's building had a small shed attached to the back, and a chain link fence and gate. No razor wire but the gate was covered with green canvas. I peeked through the space between the canvas and the wire fencing. The small parking area was deserted. I looked to my right. No one was in the alley.

Then I looked to my left and saw a tall, gaunt man, dressed in a long black coat, a filthy blue baseball cap pulled down over his eyes, a full curly black beard ran half the way down his chest, floppy unlaced red running shoes on his feet.

He was shuffling toward me pushing a shopping cart. As he approached me, he stuck his right index finger in his nose, seemed to find a booger, pulled it out and popped it in his mouth. He laughed when he saw me watching him. "Got milk?" he asked.

I waited until he passed on down the alley then I climbed over the fence.

My climb got me into the parking patio, but I was still outside the building. There was a garage. The door was a steel Hörmann up-and-over fitted tightly flush to the jam. The back door to the building was, like the front door, CECO steel. I decided my snooping wasn't going to get me in when, just to vent my frustration, I kicked the back door and it flew open.

The clerk in the reception area of the neighboring warehouse was correct—Antonia's building was deserted. Not just deserted, completely empty. My footsteps echoed against the bare cinder block walls and concrete floor. Sunlight filtered in through the barred windows highlighting the dust motes raised by my footsteps. It was eerie.

There was a small reception area just inside the front entrance, a cousin to the reception area next door. I opened drawers and cabinets. All empty. I was wasting my time.

I headed back toward the rear of the building when I noticed there was a partitioned area against the back wall. When I entered, there was a small room to my left with an American Standard white ceramic toilet and a sink. A mirror, cracked in the lower right hand corner. Gray painted floor.

The other room to my right was obviously once an office. There were phone lines and cable outlets for T1 internet access. Nothing else really. Except for a door that appeared to lead into the locked garage.

I couldn't be lucky twice, but I was. Lucky twice. The door was unlocked. In fact, the door had no lock.

The garage was definitely not empty. The space was

crammed full of fabric rolls, but it also contained other equipment.

It was very dark, pitch black really, inside the garage, so I removed the equipment into Antonia's old office space, and when that began to fill up, out onto the warehouse floor.

Once I could see the garage's contents, I quickly realized the equipment was designed for a photography studio: Altman lights, Manfroto stands, various Impact clamps and Pony A-spring clips. Curious, I pulled out one of the fabric rolls that turned out not to be a fabric roll at all, but an Impact black muslin studio backdrop.

I checked the other rolls. Backdrop fantasy scenes, garden scenes, floral scenes, pools, skies, bedrooms, even monasteries and prisons. And many of the rolls weren't cloth at all, but paper: Savage seamless background paper, also in multiple colors, Tulip, Sage, Coral, Blue Mist, Fashion Gray and Primary Red.

Basically, I discovered everything one would need for a small professional studio. Had Antonia shot her own promotional advertising for her designer fabrics? And where were the designer fabrics? Even samples of fabrics? Digital fabric printers? Dyes? Washers? Cutting and sewing machines? There was nothing like that, no indication there was any equipment involved with creating designer fabrics.

Suddenly I realized I was very tired from moving around all that equipment. And thinking. And anticipating. Hours had passed by. I needed to rest. I needed to say my mid-day prayers.

I lay down on top of a Victorian Garden backdrop and used the rolled up Stormy Sky for a pillow while I read from my phone.

I was near the end of my recitation: "O God, who by thy revelation to thy blessed John didst institute the Order of the Most Holy Trinity for the redemption of captives from the power of the infidel; grant, we beseech thee; that at the intercession of his merits, we may by thee be delivered from all bondage both of body and soul…" when I was delivered unto the blessing of sleep.

When I awoke, the wild man who earlier passed by me in the alley was standing over me, threatening me with a broken wooden broomstick, its sharp edge not more than six inches from my face. "Where are the girls?" he asked, his body tense, his voice trembling.

I was still groggy. "Girls? What girls?"

"I said, where are the girls!" This time he was screaming. He jerked his stick back and forth, ever closer to my face. That woke me up.

Trying to stay calm, I said, "I don't know. Where do *you* think the girls are?"

Throwing the question back at him put him in a different mood. He removed his stick from in front of my face and leaned against it as he considered his answer. Then he said, "Hmmmm…Maybe…maybe they're coming later?"

"Yes," I said as I stood up next to him. "That seems right. They're coming later."

His confusion lifted. A big smile crossed his face. "I like the girls. They are very pretty. I like it when they take their clothes off."

"They do?" This was new territory. "Why do they take their clothes off?"

His smile grew even bigger. He tipped his blue hat and did a little dance in his floppy red running shoes. "So they can rub against each other and make noises while the lady takes pictures of them."

"That sounds like fun." I ventured.

"It is. It is so much fun." He stopped dancing. "I like to watch. The lady says I can watch if I protect her building with my spear." He held up his broomstick, threw it the length of the room and then ran to retrieve it. He yelled back at me. "I keep the bad guys away."

His rambling monologue made it pretty clear what had been going on in the warehouse, but under further questioning it was also clear he had no more information for me. I left him playing with his stick.

Maybe he would build a fort with the backdrops. Maybe he would actually keep the bad guys away. Maybe he would dream about girls for the rest of his life. I was plagued with the same problem even though I had vowed, literally, as a priest, not to dream about them.

But I did anyway.

St. Cyril of Alexandria, Icon

Chapter Seven

Oh, may our hearts be pure within, / No cherish'd madness vex the soul; / May abstinence the flesh restrain, / And its rebellious pride control.
Prime, Hymn, Feast of St. Cyril of Alexandria, Bishop, Confessor and Doctor of the Church

The next morning Angela asked me to keep an eye on little Iggy. He still slept most of the time so there wasn't much to the task. Thomas lingered nearby as he always did. Charles-David hadn't made an appearance. Andrew was sulking and mumbling while reading his latest copy of the International Socialist Review.

The more time I spent with Ignatius, the more I fell in love with him. He was truly beautiful, very even-tempered, smiling and gurgling and looking about, turning his little head this way and that. Very attentive to sounds. Very actively wriggling and moving his arms and legs. And when he was hungry, very loud in his demands for the breast. Altogether a very happy, healthy little boy, and that was a miracle in itself, considering. Considering how he'd started. Considering where he came from.

I gathered him up in his white swaddling blanket with the tiny long-necked giraffes and carried him on my shoulder through the back door into our yard.

There wasn't much of a garden. Charles-David made a few desultory attempts at planting flowers and decorative shrubs.

Most died, although there was a thriving, expanding bed of bright red and yellow nasturtium blossoms that, thankfully, threatened to take over from the crabgrass. And the gardenia bushes produced highly scented, ivory white blooms each spring despite their lack of care.

Iggy scrunched up his nose when he inhaled the fresh, cool ocean air and blinked his eyes when he was annoyed by the glare from the bright white sun. I moved one of the broken lawn chairs over underneath the California sycamore that shaded a corner of our cracked concrete patio.

I wrapped Iggy up tightly and tucked him into the crook of my left arm where he snuggled between my bicep and chest and promptly fell asleep. I used my right hand to pull out my phone and read, for Terce, the words from Psalm 101, "Turn not away thy face from me: / in the time of my trouble, incline thine ear unto me. / In what day soever I shall call upon thee, / O hear me, and that right soon. / For my days are consumed away like smoke…"

I heard rustling in the upper branches of the sycamore. I looked up but I couldn't see anything causing a disturbance so I went back to reading, "…and my bones are grown dry like as fuel for the fire. / I am smitten like grass, and my heart is withered; / so that I forget to eat my bread. / For the voice of my groaning, / my bones will scarce cleave to my flesh…" The rustling sounds from the top of the sycamore grew more pronounced.

I searched for squirrels skittering up and down the trunk, but saw no squirrels. Vague apprehension overcame me as I returned to the psalm. "Mine enemies reviled me all the day long; / and they that have praised me are sworn together against me. / For I have eaten ashes as it were bread, / and mingled my drink with weeping. / Because of thy wrath and indignation; / for thou hast taken me up, and cast me down. / My days have declined like a shadow, / and I am withered like grass…"

Without warning, there was a terrifying SCREECH from above. Startled, I jerked upright, dropped my Samsung on the ground and instinctively held Ignatius tightly against my chest. Thin, curled strips of white and brown bark floated through the branches. I heard a thump! Then another. I saw golf ball sized sycamore fruit—spiked, needle sharp—landing all around us. I flattened my hand over the top of little Iggy's head.

Shocked by the assault, I searched upwards through the foliage and finally recognized the distinctive spotted wings and ripping talons of two birds hiding near a thick branch midway up the tree. Another joined them. Then another. And yet another. They all perched on the same branch and stared down at Iggy and me with piercing, determined eyes.

I completely covered Ignatius with his blanket and held him even closer. The hawks began whistling, fluttering, dancing their talons along the branch, releasing additional bark and seeds aimed at our lawn chair. One of the birds spread his wings and drifted directly toward us. I ducked in time, but I felt his wing tips brush my shoulder.

I was afraid. Really afraid. And confused. More whistling, whistling, that infernal whistling. Their song raising the hairs on the back of my neck. I turned toward the house and ran as another of the birds lifted out of the tree and headed toward us.

Then Father Thomas came stumbling through the back door with a rosary in his hand, making the sign of the cross over and over on his upper body. "Get inside," he urged. "Hurry, hurry, get inside." While I, with Iggy in my arms, ducked and ran into the kitchen, Thomas, with surprising strength, hurled his rosary into the sycamore.

The whistling stopped, and in the quiet I could hear the sound of flapping wings as the birds flew off to roost on a nearby telephone pole and resume their evil sentinel.

Angela met us in the kitchen, visibly angry and waving her finger in my face. She screamed, "You're supposed to keep him safe! I told you never to take him outside."

She had never said that to me, but I wasn't in a mood to argue. Especially with Angela. I was shaking. I handed Ignatius over to her, ignored her yelling, climbed to my room and slammed my door shut.

I opened the Mac and went on-line. I surfed idly until I regained my composure. I Googled "cooper's hawks," but only found the ornithological information I already knew. I entered "bird attacks on humans" and found far more entries than I would have expected, four million, nine hundred and ninety thousand to be exact.

From Houston, Texas, the story of a lawyer being pecked in the face as he walked toward the courthouse. And then, a few weeks later "police had to close down an entire downtown Houston street in late May after gang of grackles attacked pedestrians, knocking some of them down."

In Raleigh, North Carolina, a postal carrier accustomed to being chased by stray dogs, reported that he ran into a new problem: rambunctious birds. "I was ducking this way, then ducking that way, trying to get away," a Mr. Coper said, recalling a few frenzied seconds where beaks flashed like tiny daggers. "I had no idea what was going on."

In upper New York State, a high-strung woodpecker destroyed the rearview mirrors of twenty-three cars, apparently upset by his own image. In Washington, the nation's capitol, hawks were reportedly dive bombing cars.

In the last paragraph of each story, ornithologists usually gave logical explanations for the birds' behavior explaining that the increasing number of people living in bird-friendly habitats created friction between the two populations. Especially during mating season. In the spring. Especially when the chicks were hatching.

Well, it was spring. Still…

I went into my closet and brought out my painting of the hawks in the magnolia. I was relieved to see that the Van Dyke brown still covered the Venetian red in the hawk's eye.

I tried to think logically. I knew I was in an agitated state but I was determined not to abandon reason. Everything was explainable. It had to be. I decided that all the very real, very weird happenings in my life were making everything else also seem unusually spooky. The hawks were just hawks.

Calmer, I returned to my Mac and Googled "Truly Bent Fabrics." The only return was an entry about a Danish jazz pianist's recording of his album "Alley Cat." The pianist's name was Bent Fabricius-Bjerres, but he recorded as Bent Fabric. He played Rag Time and Honky-Tonk. I listened to a bit of his playing. He was very good.

Then I went back to my original "Truly Bent Fabrics" search. Google asked me if I meant fabric stores in Bend, Oregon. I didn't bother to pursue that link.

I entered just "truly bent" and got over 34 million entries. That was no help. I nervously entered "truly bent porno." Only 24 million entries but they all referred to "bend over" with photos of thousands of actual vaginal and anal penetrations. Not helpful. And not very erotic thanks be to God. I was already feeling very discouraged when my phone went off indicating I had another text message.

"Quia defecérunt sicut fumus dies mei: / et ossa mea sicut crémium aruérunt..." scrolled across my screen. I started to translate the passage, and then stopped immediately after the first phrase, "For my days are consumed away like smoke..." That phrase was from the exact same passage I was reading earlier. Under the sycamore. With baby Iggy in my arms. What was going on?

My agitation returned. I shuddered. Who was sending these messages? Was I overreacting? Were things getting even more bizarre? Was my life actually turning very, very scary? Or was some ornithologist going to explain that, after all, given their proximity to humans, cooper's hawks could read? I didn't think so.

When I need to know the answers to complicated questions about computers or phones, information I can't easily find online, like, for instance, how I might discover who was sending me texts from a blocked phone number, I talk to Kenny Johansson.

Ken is a tinkerer, especially when it comes to electronics. He was the one who advised me to buy the MacBook Pro, but he also suggested I get the Samsung Android rather than an i-Phone. He said I shouldn't put all my apples into one basket. I think he meant that comment as a sly joke. Nerd humor.

Except Kenny wasn't a nerd at all. Tall and fit, light brown hair, strong chin, blue eyes, he played hole set on Ignatius High School's water polo team, then went on to play driver on Edmund Campion's regional championship team.

A bit of a straight arrow, Kenny wanted to be a prosecutor so he could "punish the evil doers," and he took my class in Canon Law because he was interested in religion. He was intelligent and curious so I noticed him right away. He was a great guy, but he was unfocused, and a little lazy. I remember he received a B- in my class, and his scores on the LSAT were below average, although he re-took the law school exam three times. Still, we became friends.

With his scores, Kenny couldn't get into a top-ranked law program so he dropped the idea and became a lifeguard. He said the pay was good and the healthy, low-pressure lifestyle suited him. Kenny only had one problem as far as I was concerned: his wife Katie was one of the most beautiful women in the South Bay. Stunning really, in that classic long-legged, tall, blond sort of Southern California way. Just being around her made me very nervous. Get thee behind me, Satan.

I found Johansson inside a sun-bleached blue-gray lifeguard tower positioned just south of the Riviera Beach Pier. I climbed the ramp up to the shack where Ken was eating lunch: Tofu Fajitas take out from his mother-in-law's California beach-styled Mexican restaurant. He offered me a taste. Although I hadn't eaten for the previous 36 hours, I was too stressed out to be hungry. Especially for tofu.

"What's up, Father Pete?"

Thank God for the Kennys of this world and their natural, easy-going smiles. I felt better already.

"I've been getting strange text messages," I told him, "from a blocked number."

"They're spaming cell phones now, Father."

"No. I don't think the messages are spam."

"Sex ads?" He grinned.

Did everyone know about my problem?

"No." I said.

"What then?"

"It's very complicated, Kenny, but it would help if I could find out who's sending these disturbing messages."

"Not likely." He grabbed his Fujinon 7X50 binoculars and slowly scanned the horizon for ocean swimmers, beach surfers and kids playing near the shore. While he was watching, he said, "Someone can send you a text by using an online anonymous website. They wouldn't be required to disclose their phone number. Ergo…meaning therefore…"

"I know it's Latin, Ken."

He grinned, proud of himself. "…a message can be sent to you from an untraceable source."

"Can't I find out which anonymous site and then discover who used it?"

"Possibly, but way beyond my pay grade, Father." He put down the binoculars. "Yours too."

I felt my shoulders sag. I puffed my cheeks and slowly exhaled. No one could help me.

"Tell me what's going on, Father."

"Someone who knows something about my life keeps sending me cryptic messages."

"Threatening you?"

"No, actually, they seem to be warning me…in Latin no less."

This revelation brought another grin. "Texting in Latin?"

Even I was forced to smile. "Yeah, in Latin."

"Maybe it's your guardian angel.

"Huh?"

"Your guardian angel."

"I don't believe...we don't have..." I stopped. I don't really believe in guardian angels. But then I considered. "Hmm, why do you say that, Kenny?"

He laughed. "Hey, I wasn't being serious." He picked up his Fujinons again and slowly swept across the sand from the bluffs of Palos Verdes to the Riviera Beach Pier. He put his binoculars back on the shelf. "You look beat, Father Pete. Why don't you go on back down the ramp, sit on the beach for a while. Watch the waves roll in. Chill. Hang out. Katie's coming bye in a sec. She likes talking to you."

Instinctively I muttered, "Get thee behind me..."

"What?"

"Nothing, Kenny. Nothing. I was just..." I repeated my question, "What made you think of guardian angels?"

"I told you I was kidding." He stared at me and his ready smile faded. "What's really wrong, Father?"

I didn't answer him. I was thinking about guardian angels. I carefully shuffled down the ramp to avoid slipping on the loose sand.

I heard him behind me say, "Father, come on. What's wrong with you?" But I ignored him.

I saw Katie 100 yards down the shore jogging toward us in a string pucker bottom hot pink bikini. I somehow managed to ignore her as well.

I trudged through the warm dry sand until I reached the edge of the paved 26-mile bike path that ran from Riviera Beach up the coast to Santa Monica, dodged a stream of racers in their red, white and blue LA Tri gear, and then plodded up the steep concrete stairway to the top of the bluff.

Terrifically fit men and women, some of them older than me passed me easily, running up and down the steps to get their cardio workout. They weren't even breathing heavily. I was exhausted.

I reached into my pocket for my Samsung. No new messages. I clicked on my breviary and recited Psalm 108, from None as I headed home: "O deliver me, for I am poor and needy / and my heart is troubled within me. / I go hence like the shadow that departeth, / and am driven away as the locusts. / My knees are weak through fasting; / my flesh is changed for want of oil…"

When I turned onto Dolorita, I saw the flashing red lights atop the Riviera Beach Fire Department EMT truck, more red lights from a McCormack ambulance, and red and blue lights from a Riviera Beach black and white. All in front of our house. Iggy. I panicked.

I ran to the door and arrived just as the paramedics were leaving with Father Thomas strapped down on a Ferno 35A stretcher. He looked terrible. His scrawny right arm trembled back and forth across his chest, frail attempts to make a sign of the cross. There was an ugly red and purple bruise forming along the entire left side of his face from his hairline down to his chin. His eyes were blinking rapidly. His lips pouted in and out like a goldfish trapped in a bowl.

Charles-David and Andrew were on the front porch. Angela was inside the house with Iggy. Charles-David volunteered to go with Father Thomas in the ambulance, but Thomas shook his head, no, and kept clawing the air with his feeble hand pointing toward me.

"If you're coming, we're going. NOW!" shouted the young paramedic. I tried to hop into the back of the ambulance. The paramedic said to sit in front with the driver. Father Thomas became very agitated and violently clawed the air again.

I said, "I'm going in back."

The paramedic was upset, but she only said, "Put on your belt! Now! There, there hanging from the side," and off we went, sirens blaring, toward Little Company of Mary Hospital.

Inside the ambulance the paramedic worked frantically. I asked her what happened. "Shut up," she said. "I'm busy." She glanced at me for a second, then changed her mind. "Stroke, I think. They say he fell against a dining room table."

She administered an injection and Thomas' agitation decreased. I leaned over him so he could see and hear me as I began the process of final absolution: "In the name of the Father, and of the Son and of the Holy Ghost, may all the power of the devil over you be destroyed by the imposition of our hands, and through the invocation of the glorious and holy Virgin Mary, Mother of God, her illustrious spouse, St. Joseph, and all the holy angels, archangels, patriarchs, prophets, apostles, martyrs, confessors, virgins, and all the saints together. Amen."

I had no holy oil, but I grabbed a cotton swab from a nearby shelf and wiped it across his eyes. "By this holy anointing and His most loving mercy may the Lord forgive you whatever wrong you have done through sight. Amen."

I wiped his ears. "By this holy anointing and His most loving mercy may the Lord forgive you whatever wrong you have done through hearing. Amen."

Thomas grew agitated again. Clawing the air. Trying to speak. He wanted something. Something from me. I wiped his nose with the swab: "By this holy anointing and His most loving mercy may the Lord forgive you whatever wrong you have done through the sense of smell. Amen.

I tried to wipe his lips, and began: "By this holy anointing and His most loving mercy may the Lord forgive you whatever wrong you have done through taste and ..." Thomas pushed my hand away. The paramedic rolled her eyes and said, "Do we really need all this mumbo-jumbo right now? It's upsetting him."

I stared her down while finishing with his lips, "...and speech."

Father Thomas arched his back and gasped. He made a tremendous effort, clawing and clawing at me: "U mus," he groaned, "U mus..." I placed my ear next to his lips. Pro... te..." Then, as he collapsed onto the stretcher. "...im." His eyes closed.

I finished my prayers, wiping the backs of his hands. "By this holy anointing and His most loving mercy may the Lord forgive you whatever wrong you have done through the sense of touch. Amen."

Lastly, I wiped his feet: "By this holy anointing and His most loving mercy may the Lord forgive you whatever wrong you have done through the power to walk. Amen."

Thomas didn't move. The paramedic got my attention and stared into my eyes. "He's gone."

"No," I said. "I need him."

"Should I try to revive him?"

I hesitated.

She said, "He's very old, and very badly hurt. It would be a greater mercy than your words to let him go."

"Yes," I finally said. "You're right. Let him go."

I held Thomas's hand, and spoke the words of absolution:

"I absolve you from all censures and sins, in the name of the Father, and of the Son, and of the Holy Ghost. Amen."

I added, on my own, *"Procedamus in pace."* Go in peace.

Preparing for Easter in 50 Days, Fresco

Chapter Eight

All His commandments are true / they stand fast for ever and ever: / and are done in truth and equity. / He sent redemption unto His people / He hath commanded His covenant for ever. / Holy and terrible is His Name: / the fear of the Lord is the beginning of wisdom.

Vespers, Quinquagesima Sunday

"The bodies seem to be piling up around you, Pete," said Sergeant Milosz

I shrugged. "Father Thomas was very old. He had a serious stroke. He fell and hit his head. What's that have to do with me?"

"So the others told me. But why now? And why did he die while you were alone with him."

"Coincidence?"

"I told you I don't believe in coincidence, Pete."

"So you think I killed Father Thomas as well?"

"Did you?"

"Of course not, Stan. I wasn't alone with him. Ask the paramedic. If you want to keep having these so-called friendly conversations, then at least be serious."

We were sitting in his office again. This time there was no sports equipment in the corner near his desk. It was late evening the following day after Thomas died. I was bone tired, feeling a bit churlish. Hungry as well. I still hadn't eaten a decent meal for 48 hours.

"Serious? You talk about serious, Pete? You haven't been serious with me since we first met."

"What do you mean?"

"Care to come clean about what's really going on, Pete?"

"I wish I knew, Sergeant. I really wish I knew."

"I think you're in trouble, Pete. I think you need help. Why won't you let me help you, Paderewski, one Polack to another."

For a moment I was tempted to take him up on his offer, but my training made me cautious, careful. I wanted to be in control. I needed a lot more information. I wanted to protect Ignatius Loyola. I wanted to protect Angela. I wanted to protect myself. I needed to protect myself.

I said, "If I have anything to tell, I'll tell you, Stan."

At the time I meant it. I trusted Sergeant Stanley Milosz. I trusted he would do the right thing at least by his way of looking at it. A practical, down-to-earth, logical small town police way of looking at the world.

But my secrets were bigger than that. I doubted Sergeant Stanley Milosz could cope with malevolent birds, Latin text messages and a child brought back to life by an old man's breath. Maybe. Just maybe. But I doubted it.

On Quinquagesima Sunday, two days after Thomas died and the Sunday before Ash Wednesday, the beginning of Lent, Andrew, who seldom attended church anyway, stayed home to help Angela watch over Ignatius. So Charles-David and I attended Mass at St. James Church on Vincent Street, across from Riviera Beach High School, down the street from a Starbucks and right next door to a McDonalds. The pastor's pre-packaged, pre-Lenten sermon fit in well with the neighborhood.

After the service, Charles-David and I walked along the promenade overlooking the beach below Esplanade Avenue. The late morning sunshine sparkled off the waves rolling across Santa Monica bay. Brown pelicans and white gulls drifted through the air. A small pod of sleek silver-gray dolphins cavorted not twenty yards off shore. Children were flying Asian kites depicting multi-colored demons with long trailing tails. God was in His heaven and for a while at least, all seemed right with the world.

Charles-David stopped, turned to me and said, "You know, Peter, I've always wanted to ask you, why did someone like you become a priest?"

His question took me by surprise. "What do you mean by 'someone like me'?"

"Oh, I don't know. You pray a lot, but you don't seem particularly religious. You're smart. You're good looking. You could have made a lot of money. And you obviously like women."

I grimaced. "What makes you say that?"

"Men like me know, Peter." He smiled. "Our antennae are always out. We're always thinking, is he? What about him, is he? It's a matter of self-preservation."

As we resumed our walk, I thought about why I became a priest. "I've always felt a strong sense of God's presence. When I was a teenager, I used to sit in church and talk to God. Just like you and I are talking now. Like He was my buddy."

"Didn't your friends think you were strange?"

"No, not really. I was a normal guy. I played hockey. I dated girls. I smoked cigarettes and drank beer when we could get hold of some. No one thought of me as odd."

"That must be a wonderful feeling."

I thought about his response. "I suppose it was," I said. "You've had a rough time of it, haven't you, Charles-David?"

"Yes."

I thought a little more about his original question. "Well, actually, I don't know that I ever really thought about being a priest. I went to a Jesuit high school in Chicago. I was surrounded by these really great guys who seemed to have something special. I wanted to be a Jesuit more than I wanted to be a priest."

"But why?"

"I wanted to keep talking to God the rest of my life, and I thought the Jesuits were smart, sophisticated, progressive just like Pope Francis. They were also scholars, lawyers, philosophers. They ran universities and elite high schools but took vows of poverty. Being a Jesuit seemed like a cool thing to be."

"Yes, a cool thing to be. I understand that." He was silent for awhile. "Do you know I speak nine languages, Peter?"

"Nine! No I didn't."

"I spoke four of them before I even entered seminary. I was a very odd child, a very odd young man. I thought the priesthood would protect me."

"From whom?"

"From the world."

I had to admit to myself I understood that feeling. Maybe all priests do.

"So I kept learning languages although I seldom spoke to anyone. In any language. I really was odd, wasn't I?"

"But you can speak nine languages. Imagine."

"And all so I can teach a dead language to spoiled kids who

hate it. Who hate me because I'm old and fat and a drunk and…"

"Nine languages! I know a little French…remember some Latin. I envy you."

"Maybe it'll get me elected pope?" He remarked. "I could be the first openly gay pope."

I laughed. "Yes, 'openly'." 'We walked a little further.

"I thought it was very courageous for you to come out for Iggy's baptism."

"To you? To Andrew? To Angela? That didn't take much courage. I was worried about poor Father Thomas, but he didn't seem bothered either."

"These are different times, Charles-David. Even Francis says, who are we to judge. Anyway, Thomas lived in the Church of the Holy Spirit. He was not concerned with earthly matters."

"Did you know he was 101 years old? He would have been 102 in a month."

"No, I didn't."

"The Society sent me his records for the funeral." He gazed out over the ocean "101. I'm not sure I want to live that long."

"That won't be your decision will it, Charles-David?"

We turned east at Avenue C, leaving the beach behind. That was when Charles-David dropped a bombshell. "Peter, do you know Anthony was in the living room with Father Thomas when Thomas fell. He says it wasn't an accident. He says Thomas didn't have a stroke."

"I don't understand."

"I think you better talk to him."

"Can't you tell me?"

"He would only tell me it wasn't a stroke and it wasn't an accident. He won't say more than that to me. He wants to talk to you."

"What do you think, Charles-David?"

"I think I'm scared. I'm Iggy's Godmother," that brought forth a wry smile, "but I'm afraid I'm not doing a very good job of it."

When we arrived home, I found Andrew in his room sitting on his rusting, cast iron Junqui bed. As I entered he attempted to conceal something behind his back.

"You still have the Bobcat?" I asked.

"I need it, Peter. To protect Ignatius."

I sighed and glanced around his room. Hopeless. There were piles of pamphlets, magazines and books stacked on every available flat space. A poster of Che Guevera hung on the wall between his two windows. The windows themselves were covered by burgundy, heavy velvet curtains. The room smelled musty from layers of dust. Musky from the stale body odor.

There were three large gruesome crucifixes on the opposite wall, gruesome because they projected Christ's death in all it's agony with blood streaming from His nailed hands and feet, from the crown of thorns and the wound in His chest.

The crosses were souvenirs he'd picked up from Los Penitentes, the secretive brotherhood of severe Catholics in the Sangre de Cristo mountains around Mora, New Mexico. They practiced self-flagellation. Every year, during Holy Week, they re-enacted Christ's crucifixion. Live. Nails in the hands. The whole nine yards. Except for the spear in the chest. No coup de grâce for the suffering actor.

Andrew got involved with the Penitentes when he was

attending a seminar in Taos, New Mexico, on "The Religious Justification for Violent Political Action" offered by a cadre of disaffected theologians—priests and nuns enthralled by the writings of the Latin American priests Leonardo Boff, a Franciscan, and Jon Sobrino, S.J. one of ours.

The Liberation Theologians argue that Jesus Christ preached liberation from unjust economic, political, or social evil, and that by driving the money changers from the Temple, Christ justified violence under certain conditions. Needless to say, this was not a theology popular in the Curia before Pope Francis, and the Vatican's Congregation for the Doctrine of the Faith still condemns liberation ideas as Marxist, thus avoiding the core issue about whether Christian values do demand humane and just conditions for the world's poor and needy. For all, really, as Francis would say. Justice for all.

Because he was so skeptical about the mysterious side of the Church, Andrew often ridiculed the Penitentes extreme religious practices, but he was paradoxically drawn to their art—to their bloody crucifixes, devil masks and stark oils depicting horrific flagellation. Then again, perhaps there was no paradox. Just an obsession with violence.

I lifted a pile of outdated copies of *Struggle* off of a black, Hercules hinged metal folding chair, dumped them on the floor and sat down next to him. "To protect Ignatius from whom, Andrew?"

"They got to Thomas. They want Ignatius."

"Who got to Thomas? Who wants Ignatius?"

"We were sitting in the living room while you were at the police station. Thomas was reading a book. The house was quiet."

"What book?"

"I don't know. A very thick book with a gray cover. The damn thing must have weighed four or five pounds. He stooped over as he carried it from his room."

"Okay. And…"

"Suddenly, he jumped up from his chair, began waving his hands in the air and muttering nonsense about devils and birds and, and…"

"Thomas did? Feeble old Father Thomas jumped out of his chair with a five-pound book in his hands?"

"Yes…well, he actually dropped the book, and he…he…"

"What Andrew?"

"They made me do it." Andrew started to weep. Tears streamed down his face and glistened on the surface of his thick black beard, his shoulders shook with grief. He held his face in his hands. "I want the seal of the confessional," he moaned. "Please, Peter, hear my confession."

"Of course, Andrew, but here, at this moment…I don't understand. What do you want to confess?"

"I am confessing right now, don't you understand?" Deep sobs racked his body.

"Yes, okay."

"And you won't tell anybody, no matter what?"

"I won't tell anyone, Andrew."

"They used me to kill Father Thomas."

"They…you…what? What are you talking about?"

He didn't answer me for a long while. He sat there with his head bowed, running his fingers through his hair. Finally he raised his anguished face toward mine. "He was shouting that 'it was all in the book…the book proved…' I don't know, something about devils…he acted possessed, I mean, I don't believe in possession, but that's how he acted, like one possessed."

"Go on."

"I tried to grab hold of him. He pushed me away. Much, much stronger than I would have thought. I held onto him. He shouted at me. He said I was unclean. Said I was tainted… said I…" Andrew began crying again.

"You were what, Andrew?"

"Not a real priest. He said I was a fraud. 'Violence begets violence,' the old man proclaimed. He said I should never go near Ignatius. That I would contaminate the child's soul. Me, who has done everything to protect little Iggy."

"And so…?"

"Seriously, Peter. He believes all that stuff…or believed, I should say. He really thought that devils and Heaven and Hell are a valid part of the Catholic Church. He even accepts that fat, old, drunken pedophile Charles-David…"

I rebuked him. "Don't say that. Charles-David is not a pedophile, Andrew. He's not."

Andrew stopped crying. He faced me. "The point is, Peter, that Thomas allowed Charles-David to be Iggy's Godmother, but he rejected me? Why? Because I believe Christ cared more about the poor and the meek and the helpless than casting out devils? Because I believe Christ was a real revolutionary?"

I had no answer for him.

"Old Thomas was an asshole, Peter. A stupid doddering fart. He and his version of the Church deserve to die."

"So you killed him."

"Yes. Okay, perhaps a sin of omission not commission, but I'm responsible. I stopped holding onto him and in my anger, I pushed him backwards toward his reading chair. But…but he fell sideways instead, and then slammed his head against the table."

Andrew stopped shaking and sighed deeply. "When I heard how loud the sound of that impact was, I knew he was finished, and for a moment, I didn't care. It's disgusting, I know, but I didn't care." He breathed deeply. His head dropped onto his chest. He was running his fingers through his hair again. "And outside. That noise. That infernal noise."

"What noise?" Although I suspected what he was going to tell me.

"Those birds. Whistling. Whistling in the trees." He raised his head, his eyes searching my face. "There's no such thing as the devil, is there Peter? I mean, Thomas' death was my fault, wasn't it? I'm to blame, aren't I?"

"No, I don't think so." I placed a hand on his shoulder. "I don't think anyone was to blame. I think he was having a stroke. Nothing you've told me changes my mind."

"I feel terrible."

"I believe you, Andrew. You look terrible." I took his left hand in mine. "But are you sorry for your feelings about Thomas? You know I can't offer absolution unless you're truly sorry and asking for God's mercy and forgiveness."

"I have confessed to you, Peter. I ask for God's mercy. To say I'm really, truly sorry would add mendaciousness to my sins."

"Then I can only offer you conditional absolution, Andrew. If you change your mind and make a perfect Act of Contrition and pray for God's mercy because you are truly sorry, because you have banished evil from your emotions, then…well…maybe then you will find true absolution."

I held my right hand out in front of him and made the sign of the cross, "May the almighty and merciful Lord grant you pardon, conditional absolution, and remission of your sins. May our Lord Jesus Christ conditionally absolve you, and by his authority I do conditionally absolve you from every bond of excommunication, suspension, and interdict, to the extent of my power and your need. Finally, I conditionally absolve you from your sins, in the name of the Father, and of the Son, and of the Holy Ghost. Amen."

I don't believe there really is such a thing as conditional absolution, but I wanted to ease Andrew's pain. He wasn't a murderer, or at least, he was not the murderer that really mattered.

I left Father Andrew to contemplate his soul and went to my own room. The light was still good, so I mounted the cooper's hawks painting on my easel. I immediately noticed that my Van Dyke brown alteration to the hawk's eye was turning redder. Not Venetian red as before, but redder, sort of an Indian red. I broke out in a cold sweat. I shook my head to clear my thoughts.

I don't really believe in ghosts and devils and malevolent beings. Not in the literal sense. I believe these concepts are useful allegories for understanding the presence of evil in the world. For pondering the depths of the human spirit. For presenting an antithesis to a loving God. But to consider them real?

As I fought for calm, I clicked on the day's Vespers and recited aloud from Mark, 10, 49-51: "And Jesus stood, and commanded the blind man to be brought unto him, and asked him, saying: What wilt thou that I should do unto thee? And he made answer: Lord, that I may receive my sight. And Jesus said unto him: Receive thy sight; thy faith hath saved thee. And immediately he received his sight, and followed Him, glorifying God." And I realized that, yes, I must see clearly as well.

Comforted, I then reasoned that it was, in fact, logical for a mix of still wet Venetian red mixed with fresh Van Dyke brown, *alla prima*, to develop into Indian red. Nothing strange about that. No reason to dread the red. I laughed to myself. Nothing to worry about. Dread the red. Funny.

So I worked on the hawks for a couple of hours until I lost natural light. I understood why my painting had failed. Out of fear, out of lack of faith in my own strength, I was holding back from depicting the hawk's strength, their fierceness, their determination, their power over life and death.

Denying them those qualities made them look like fat robins or very large sparrows. Which they weren't. They were raptors, natural birds of prey. Killers.

When I finished, when the light failed, I had succeeded. They finally looked like hawks.

Emboldened, I went downstairs to see Iggy. He was sleeping when I walked into the kitchen where Angela was cleaning up after dinner. She asked if I was hungry. I was, but I told her I wasn't. She worked hard enough without catering to me.

Angela watched me fussing over Ignatius. She said, "We need you now more than ever, Peter."

"You have me, Angela. I'm here for Ignatius. I will care for him. I will not let any harm come to him. Trust me." I stood over our beautiful baby, sleeping so peacefully in his wicker Moses basket.

He stirred in his sleep. His tiny arms and legs stuttered back and forth. He yawned. He opened his eyes, looked at me and smiled. Then closed his eyes and went back to sleep.

"Look, he smiled at me."

"Probably a gas bubble," she said with slight smirk. I realized she was standing very close to me. "He does look like you. He really does."

"He looks like every newborn baby," I said, although I had to admit he resembled pictures my mother showed me from my birth, but instead I added, "All newborns look pretty much alike don't they?"

"Yes, I guess so. Still…"

She put her arms around my waist. I tensed, but didn't push her away. In fact I placed my arm across her shoulder and pressed her closer. "He'll be alright," I said, trying to comfort her, trying to comfort myself.

"Yes, if you are with us," she said. "Please, Peter, I want us to be a family. Forget Holy Mother Church. She abandoned you. More than once. Think of him. Think of Ignatius, Peter, of what he really needs. Think of me. Let's build a new life. With whatever life we have left."

I wasn't prepared for her to say those things. I was moved. I was frightened. I was tempted.

I found myself wrapping my arms around her. I kissed her desperately. Longingly. Angela was the love Little Iggy needed. Angela was the love I needed. She was the love I wanted. And then we kissed passionately while little Iggy gurgled in the background.

Could we be the Holy Family after all.

The Seven Holy Fathers of the Order of the Servants of Mary, Fresco

Chapter Nine

False witnesses did rise up: / they laid to my charge things that I knew not. / They rewarded me evil for good, / to the great discomfort of my soul. / Nevertheless, when they were troublesome to me, / I put on sackcloth. / I humbled my soul with fasting; / and my prayer shall turn into mine own bosom.

Matins , Shrove Tuesday coinciding with the Feast of the Seven Holy Fathers of the Order of the Servants of Mary

Father Thomas was honored with three funeral services. The first was a simple funeral mass, a celebration of him and the completion of his life-long journey to be forever with the Holy Spirit.

Charles-David and Andrew, Angela and Ignatius and I met on Shrove Tuesday morning in St. James Church.

The church building itself is, from the outside, nondescript, simple, unbroken angles, cream white brick facing, attached rectory and offices, also in white brick.

The buildings look like they could house doctors, dentists, insurance brokers except for the small cut-out crosses that decorate the trim. The campanile is very tall, but again, not distinctive. I would not recognize the building as a church if it were not for the large, elongated crosses that sit on the apex of the roof at the front of the building and atop the tower.

The interior of the church leaves an entirely different impression only hinted at by the crosses outside. The architecture is simple, stark, austere, clean in basic concept, totally unlike a traditional American mock Gothic or baroque church, but the overall spirit is, much like a European cathedral, designed to overwhelm: the enormous 15 foot crucifix over the main altar, the oversized statuary above the side altars, the soaring stained glass windows that glow with deep luminous, vivid hues of red, blue, yellow, green and pearl white.

And one's eyes are always drawn upwards by the sheer height, 40 feet or so, to the ceiling—uncarved, unadorned, rich deep brown wood, infused over the years with the sweet smell of incense, a vision of heaven as comfort food—a nut-flaked, milk chocolate Hershey bar as a reward for a faithful life.

Charles-David decided to celebrate Thomas's funeral mass at the side altar of St. Joseph. At first, he wanted us to be at the altar of the Blessed Virgin Mary, but we decided the symbolism adorning Joseph's altar was much more appropriate for Father Thomas.

Joseph, the "stepfather" of Jesus, is represented rising above the side altar in 12-foot natural stone as a kindly, bearded man ready and willing, a hammer in one hand, an adze in the other, to teach us the rudiments of carpentry. Above St. Joseph's head is an 8-foot tall lapidarian tablet inscribed with St. Paul's words from Romans, 12-21: "Be not conquered by evil, but conquer evil with good." Very Thomas.

To honor Thomas, Charles-David said the Mass in traditional Latin, beginning with the sign of the cross, *"In nomine Patris, et Filii, et Spiritus Sancti..."* and then, *"Introibo ad altare Dei."* (I will go unto the altar of God) to which we responded, *"Ad Deum qui laetificat juventutem meam."* (To God who giveth joy to my youth.) And so we continued through the ancient call and response ritual, each of us absorbed in our own memories of the old man who brought Ignatius back to life.

Charles-David approached the Sanctus and read the Preface for the Dead, *"In quo nobis spes beatae resurrectionis effulsit...*so that those who are afflicted by the certainty of dying, may be consoled by the promise of future immortality. For Thy Faithful, Lord, life is changed, not taken away; and when the abode of this earthly sojourn is destroyed, an eternal dwelling is prepared in Heaven. And therefore with Angels and Archangels, with the Thrones and Dominions..."

Footsteps echoed on the stone floor of the nave, originating from below the choir, gradually becoming louder. A woman in high heels walked toward the main altar. As the Sanctus bell rang three times, I turned and saw her, tall, elegant, mostly gray-haired, but still strawberry blonde as well, wearing a St. Johns Knits dark navy Milano double-breasted blazer with a matching Alexa Milano skirt. Christian Louboutin alligator pumps.

She couldn't be looking for us. But she was. She did not genuflect her shapely right knee before the large cross above the high altar. Instead she turned abruptly and approached our tiny group. She proceeded to stand next to me, and whispered, "Is this the funeral service for Father Thomas Groenbach?" I nodded that it was, and so she stood close by my side drawing a wicked glance or two from Angela.

When Charles-David said the prayers in preparation for Holy Communion, I heard the mystery woman recite in a trembling whisper, three times, along with Charles-David, *"Domine, non sum dingus...*(O Lord, I am not worthy)... *Domine, non sum dingus...Domine, non sum dingus..."* I glanced sideways. Her eyes were tightly closed, but moist under her false lashes.

Her hands quivered. Her body buckled slightly. I placed an arm under her elbow to steady her. Her eyes flashed open and she stared at me, both bewildered and angry. "Please, do not touch me, Priest," she hissed. "I may not be touched."

She did not receive the Holy Eucharist at Communion.

Minutes later, Charles-David ended the service, *"Absolve, quaesumus, Domine, nimam famuli tui, Pater Thomas Groenbach, ab omni vinculo delictorum…*(We pray, O Lord, deliver the soul of Thy servant, Father Thomas Groenbach, from every bond of guilt, that in the glory of the resurrection, he may live again, raised up to the fellowship of Thy saints and the elect. Through Our Lord Jesus Christ, Thy Son…)". Those of us from the Jesuit home hugged each other. The newcomer stepped back to one side, but she joined us as we exited the church.

Outside the church, I approached the unknown woman, but before I could reach her, Angela stepped in front of me, Ignatius wrapped in her arms, and aggressively confronted the stranger, "Who are you?"

The woman remained calm, but Angela was not to be deterred. "I want to know why you are here."

The woman said, simply, "He saved my life."

"Who saved you life? Peter? How do you know Peter?"

The woman appeared confused.

"Angela," I said, "I don't know this woman. I've never seen her before."

I turned to the stranger. Because of what she'd said in church, I did not extend my hand. "Welcome." I tried a smile. She smiled as well. "I'm Father Peter Paderewski."

"Yes," she said. "Thomas told me about you." She settled her intense gaze on each of us. "He told me about all of you."

"He did?"

"He was concerned."

"Concerned?"

"About the infant."

"Ignatius?" I felt like a monosyllabic idiot, but I had no idea where this conversation was heading.

"May I see him?"

"Of course. Why not," I said although I sensed Angela was not at all pleased by my answer.

As the women fussed and cooed over the awakening Ignatius, I headed for our pathetic Astro minivan where I met up with Andrew and Charles-David who were waiting impatiently. That's when I saw Stan Milosz in his Crown Vic parked across the street. He signaled for me to come over to him. He smiled. Friendly. Cordial. "Hi, Pete, saying farewell to that old priest?"

"His name was Father Thomas."

"Yes. Thomas. Doubting Thomas. The apostle who refused to believe Jesus really rose from the dead."

"Actually, Sergeant, Thomas the apostle was called Thomas Didymus, not Doubting Thomas. *Didymus* means 'twin' in Greek. And Thomas, *Tau'ma*, means 'twin' in Aramaic."

"Geeze, you can be a pretentious know-it-all, Pete. I was trying to be friendly. Sharing a little religious repartee."

"What do you want, Sergeant?"

"Nothing. Just driving by. Remember the station's just over there behind the library." He pointed toward City Hall. "By the way, I see your niece is still in town."

"Yes."

"How's the baby doing?"

"Her baby is fine. Look, Stan, we're driving down to Long Beach to pick-up Thomas' ashes, and I…"

"Ashes? I thought Catholics couldn't be cremated?

"They can now."

"'The mills of God grind slowly…'"

"Now you're misquoting 19th Century Longfellow, by way of Fredrich von Logau in the 17th Century by way of the Greek skeptic philosopher Sextus Empiricus from the 3rd Century who was quoting some unknown poet. Anyway, your lines refer to retribution, not to how slowly the church moves."

"I'm sure you're right, Pete. Gees, you can be a pain in the ass, but I'm sure you're right. On the other hand, how do you know I wasn't referring to retribution?" He laughed. "Early this morning when you knocked upon my door, I said, Hello, Satan, I believe it's time to go…" Then the Milosz stare.

"That was blues musician Robert Johnson, 20th Century. See you around, Pete."

He waved as he gunned his 250hp V8 police engine and took off down the block.

I returned to the mini-van and to our group including Angela and the elegantly dressed woman. The chemistry between the two had changed completely. The woman was warm and friendly. Angela was relaxed, even chatty. She said to me, "Ms. Van Kirk, Lilith, is coming with us."

I stared at the woman in St. Johns Knits who I now knew as Lilith Van Kirk, then at the filthy wreck of our mini-van, then back to Lilith. Was she really going to get into our heap?

"Well, okay. Let's go then," and we all squeezed into the decrepit gray Astro with the plastic bag taped over one window.

I drove our mismatched crew south on the Pacific Coast Highway, past where I had exited the #232 bus to try and find Antonia, under the 110 Freeway, into the industrial/ port towns of Wilmington and San Pedro which together with Long Beach constitute, by far, the largest port in the United States. Once we passed the 110, all the billboards and discount store signs and fast food joints and used car lots and liquor stores catered to Hispanics in Spanish.

We continued, past dozens of enormous 45,000 gallon oil storage tanks and 100 foot tall cracking towers, the Shell refinery, past more oil storage tanks and cracking towers in the Conoco-Phillips refinery, past the Tesoro refinery, then up over the Terminal Island Freeway jammed with 18-wheelers continuously belching black diesel fuel as they were going and coming from the port which we could see through our one good window. To the West, hundreds of massive unloading cranes—a herd of steel behemoths emerging from the sea and gathering along the misty horizon.

Then we dropped down from the 710 overpass into the violent neighborhoods of West Long Beach, past five different Long Beach Police black and whites flashing their red and blue lights, screeching their sirens, past homeless ghosts dragging overloaded shopping carts, past derelict, abandoned buildings and the hand-painted signs slapped on the sides of storefront churches begging us, luring us, warning us, to seek salvation in Jesus.

At Cherry Avenue I made a left turn and headed East over Signal Hill, then under the 405 freeway past the metal clad beige institutional offices of the Boeing Company, past the concrete landing strips of Long Beach airport to the green, green grass and red tile roofs and modernized mission style architecture of All Souls Cemetery and Mortuary. Death reduced to 19,000 square feet of shopping mall commercialism, order and efficiency.

Inside, Father Thomas had been reduced to gray and white grit, wrapped in plastic inside a heavy-duty cardboard box the size of two shoe boxes. He was heavier than he first appeared.

Has everything been satisfactory? Would you like to speak to your Memorial Specialist? Would you need the services of Family Service Counselor? Then sign here.

Thank you for using All Souls Cemetery and Mortuary. We are gratified you have chosen us to help during this difficult time. Have you seen our brochure displaying the many different bronze, ceramic, glass, porcelain, and wood urns? Well then, if you need us at any time in the future, we're here for the Catholic community. We're here for you.

Back in the van. Turn north onto Cherry Avenue up to Del Amo. Turn west at the Arco Station and Spires family-style restaurant. Cruising through suburban-tract-house North Long Beach. Our Astro van burning heavy blue oil disgracing the broad, beautiful Del Amo Boulevard—six lanes, three lanes each direction, a tasteful terra cotta tiled center medium planted with drought-resistant trees and shrubs.

Then over the concrete lined, garbage strewn, barely flowing Los Angeles River up onto the entrance to the 710 freeway heading north toward Thomas' final resting place.

I kept the van as steady as I could as monstrous container-laden trucks rumbled past us, the wake of their passing pushing against the slab side of our little Astro barely chugging along at 50 miles per hour.

Charles-David brought with him an antique Chinese

Cloisonne urn, brass polished to a rust-hued patina on the inside and Sapphire blue enamel on the outside etched in gold with the outlines of exotic plumed birds, fierce tigers and somber Mandarin priests. A beautiful vase. A unique piece.

He and Andrew were in the back cargo area using a silver soup spoon we brought from home to scoop Thomas' ashes from the cardboard box into the large decorative urn and into a smaller carved cedar box we wanted to keep at the house as well as a tiny gold locket Angela intended to place around Ignatius' neck.

All of a sudden, without any warning, the plastic bag covering the missing left window ripped open and a fierce blast of foul air blew through the van.

Angela screamed and bent down to protect Ignatius. Charles-David and Andrew were yelling for me to pull over as they struggled to cover the cardboard box. Lilith was chanting incantations in an ancient unknown language.

My problem was that our Astro was trapped between a fire engine red Peterbilt 579 hauling shiny new Hyundais and a bright green Kenworth T680 hauling a flatbed with two Maersk containers locked in and strapped down.

To make matters worse, just ahead was a large rubber casing torn from a recapped truck tire. I couldn't swerve left. Couldn't swerve right. Couldn't stop. So I hit the casing full on and gripped the wheel as tightly as I could.

The Astro bounced off the roadbed, and skidded as we landed.

Angela screamed again. Lilith was still chanting. Charles-David moaned, "Oh no, oh no," and I heard Andrew banging his fist on the van's floor in fear, anger and frustration.

Meanwhile, fine white ashes swirled throughout the interior of the van, coating each of us with Father Thomas's soot. But we were upright and we'd escaped, by inches, collision with another vehicle.

By the time I was able to pull onto the shoulder, the chaos inside the Astro had devolved into a stunned silence. As we exited the van, each of us retreated into our own personal contemplation of the horror at what had just happened.

Then little Iggy broke the silence. He cooed and gurgled and blew tiny air bubbles. Angela and Lilith hovered over him, and then as they looked at each other covered in ashes, they both began to laugh uncontrollably. Charles-David started to giggle as well. Andrew broke into a subdued cackle and I finally let out a hoot myself.

There we were: three men in clerical garb, two women and a baby standing on the side of the 710 freeway covered in death dust laughing hysterically. The lookie lous created a traffic jam that must have backed up all the way into downtown Long Beach.

Eventually we dusted ourselves off. Charles David and Andrew were able to collect enough of Father Thomas to fill most of the urn, the box, and all of the locket. When the containers were sealed and stored, we re-entered the van and pulled back onto the 710.

North through Compton, under the 105, then through Downey, Bell Gardens and the City of Commerce where we transitioned onto the 5 through East LA, transitioned again onto the 101, exited at Hill Street, made a right at Temple and finally arrived at the magnificent Cathedral of Our Lady of the Angels.

"So this is the Taj Mahoney," quipped Andrew referring to

the $200 million cost of the cathedral built while Cardinal Roger Mahoney was Bishop of Los Angeles. The same Mahoney who was later disgraced for protecting pedophile priests from criminal prosecution.

But Andrew was actually awestruck by Robert Graham's art as we passed through the 20-foot tall, 25-ton Great Bronze doors, and Andrew nodded with approval at Graham's very modern 8-foot figure of Our Lady mounted above the doors, illuminated by natural light, her bare arms outstretched, a thick braid down her back and facial features that were decidedly non-Caucasian.

And he was further captivated by the Inner Bronze Doors which depict so many non-Christian and pre-Christian images: an eagle, griffin, goose, Southwest Indian Flying Serpent, bee, hand, ostrich, dove, Chinese turtle, Samoan kava bowl, the Native American Chumash man, the dolphin, the Tree of Jesse, Tai Chi. And there were more. "This shows a church that would embrace me," Andrew mumbled, "somebody had some progressive ideas about world culture." Yes, he did. The same Mahoney. A complex man.

Andrew's cynicism vanished completely when we entered the interior of the church. José Rafael Moneo, the Spanish architect, was clearly in love with light. Rather than stained glass, he designed 27,000 square feet of alabaster windows creating the most delicate, soft, warm glow that illuminates and enhances the natural elements in the John Nava tapestries, the cedar pews and the sand-colored Spanish limestone floors.

If Andrew's jaw dropped, Charles-David simply managed to have a huge, appreciative, beatific grin on his face.

Angela sat down in a pew and studied the tapestries while Ignatius' eyes roamed here and there to find the source of the beautiful light.

Lilith donned reflective Ray-Ban sunglasses.

I knelt and prayed, from the day's None, from the *Ave, Regina Cælorum*, for this was truly a house of God: "Hail, O Queen, on high enthroned, / Hail, O Lady, by Angels owned: / Jesse's rod; yea, heaven's portal / Whence hath shone earth's Light immortal: / Hail, O Virgin, most renowned, / For thy grace and beauty crowned: / Hail, O truly worthy Maiden: / Pray Christ for us so burden-laden."

Then we carried our urn to the mausoleum that was beneath the Cathedral church. Although there were two Judson Studios etchings of Guardian Angels at the entrance, and the mausoleum's floors and walls were also clad in earth-tone limestone, the mausoleum possessed a much more traditional feeling, mainly because the windows were stained glass, rescued and refurbished from the old cathedral, St. Vibiana's that was badly damaged by the 1994 Northridge earthquake. Beautiful, but more in the classic cathedral tradition.

We were met by Monsignor Father Christopher Maiz-Mier, a tall, dark-complexioned man with silver hair, a sharply curved nose, Hugo Boss rimless glasses, bleached white teeth and a CM Almy black Roman cassock with purple piping and silk fascia. Smooth. Impressive. Church marketing.

Maiz-Mier had arranged for Father Thomas' urn to placed in one of the least expensive niches. Only $45,000.00. More church marketing. Obviously he treated us well, although he did look somewhat askance at our odd group and our dusty clothes. He seemed to scrutinize Lilith with particular concern, but then he shook his head as if to cast off any doubts.

There were numerous legal documents to sign. The urn was then placed in its 12" by 12" compartment. Locked. We were given two keys. And that was it.

As we left the church, Andrew finally let go with his anger, reignited by the smooth-talking Monsignor. "$45,000.00 dollars! The Society paid $45,000.00 dollars for Father Thomas' 12" by 12" niche in this ridiculous mausoleum?"

"The Society didn't pay for it," said Charles-David.

"Who did then?" demanded Andrew. He looked at me.

"I have no idea," I said. "We were simply notified the internment had been paid for."

"I think the Cathedral is appropriate for a man of his stature," offered Lilith.

"What stature?" Andrew was still fuming. "He was a bumbling, nutty old man."

"He was a well-known exorcist in his day, Andrew," said Lilith calmly, but firmly contradicting Andrew's disrespect.

"Father Thomas Groenbach was an exorcist?" I was surprised and not surprised.

"One of the very best. A most worthy opponent…" She added quickly. "…for the Evil One, I mean."

"More Devils," mumbled Andrew.

"He was chosen to cast out my demon," said Lilith.

"Oh good Lord," said Andrew. "What nonsense."

"Not in my case, Father Andrew. I was possessed by the Whore of Babylon. Father Thomas banished her back to the Darkness from which she had emerged."

No one had much to say about that.

We did invite Lilith to our house to hear more of her story, but she said she needed to catch a flight back to Philadelphia. There was a black Lincoln Town Car waiting in the parking lot.

I leaned inside the car as she settled herself into the back seat. "It was you," I said. "You paid for the niche."

She ignored my assertion. She said, "May God and the Holy Angels protect you. You are in grave danger, Peter."

"Protect me?"

"And take care of Ignatius. He is precious. More precious than you know."

"What?"

She only smiled.

I was annoyed. "What do you mean by that?"

But she told the driver to leave and she turned away from me.

So with Thomas dead and interred, I became Ignatius' primary protector. I knew I would miss Thomas' diligence, but at least we honored the old man's passing by placing most of his remains in the Cathedral crypt. And a good measure of him was also embedded forever into the 710 Long Beach Freeway. I hoped he would approve because I might need his intercession with God in Heaven above.

While I tried to ensure Iggy's future.

Ash Wednesday, Illustration

Chapter Ten

...We pray thee, to send Thy holy Angel from heaven to bless and sanctify these ashes, that they may be a wholesome medicine to all them that humbly call upon Thy holy Name, who in their consciences by sin are accused, who in the sight of Thy heavenly mercy bewail their sins, and earnestly and meekly implore Thy gracious loving-kindness.
Holy Mass, Blessing of the Ashes, Ash Wednesday

Ash Wednesday is a Day of Reckoning.

Just one week earlier, we were celebrating Jesus' triumphant, joyful entrance into Jerusalem astride a donkey, greeted by his followers shouting hosannas and waving palm branches.

One week later, we were burning the palm branches and using the residue to mark crosses on our foreheads with the words, "Remember that thou art dust, and to dust thou shalt return." After the previous day's events, I didn't need a reminder, but I went to Mass at St. James and had my head anointed anyway. The way events were unfolding, it didn't hurt to be doubly aware.

After church, I was sorting Thomas's effects into three piles: junk for disposal in the garbage, usable articles for dispersal to Catholic Charities, and a third pile, books and writings that I wanted to investigate before I passed them on to Province headquarters.

I realized how Spartan Thomas's life was. There was almost no random junk. Catholic Charities might possibly use the ancient cast iron bed, a nicked and scared roll top desk with one missing slat, three simple Shaker ladder back chairs and two fake brass, single-bulb plastic floor lamps, but I doubted they would want them.

In his closet I found three threadbare cheap cotton blend cassocks, four JC Penny white t-shirts, one Sears white dress shirt, three pair of K Mart black polyester pants, five pair of Walmart white boxer shorts going gray, one pair of spit-shined Florsheim black oxfords and one pair of very dirty, worn down at the heels black huarache sandals. I threw away the clothes except for the Florsheims.

Then I saw a Ghurka Chestnut leather garment bag pushed all the way to the back of his closet. I opened it, and it contained the exquisite stole Thomas wore for Iggy's baptism, a tailored Super 120 black wool suit, a High Church linen clerical collar and a heavy necklace—a 4" platinum crucifix studded with rubies and emeralds hanging on a golden chain. These last items surprised me because they were all very un-Father Thomas. At least the Thomas I knew. I gave them to Charles-David.

I gathered up Thomas's books and his writings and packed them into boxes and moved the boxes into my room. I settled into my Baxton chair, and first chose what I assumed to be the "very thick book with a gray cover" Andrew described Thomas was reading when he died.

The book was a dog-eared copy of the DDD, *The Dictionary of Deities and Demons in the Bible*, edited by Karel van der Toorn, Bob Becking and Pieter W. van der Horst. There were numerous scraps of paper lodged between certain pages to act as bookmarks. Some of the scraps of paper were old and yellowed, others looked fairly recent. Among the most recent was a bookmark for an entry that referenced a depiction of a female demon on the Babylonian Burney Relief, also known as the Queen of the Night, from 1800 BCE.

The nude female clearly has talons for feet. She stands astride a pair of reclining lions, flanked by two fierce birds of prey. This deity was long thought to represent Lilith, a female demon, referred to in Isaiah 34:14, "Wildcats shall meet with hyenas, goat-demons shall call to each other; there too Lilith shall repose, and find a place to rest." Scribbled next to the entry was a handwritten notation in Latin, which included the Hebrew, תיליל, underlined three times in bold slashing strokes.

I then looked up Lilith, already bookmarked with a newer scrap of paper, and found that the name refers to the ancient female demon mentioned in the "Babylonian Talmud"— *Līlītu*. She is the same Lilith cited in the previous passage from Isaiah, in the Dead Sea Scrolls on a list of monsters and in the "Alphabet of Ben Sira" from the 8th-10th centuries.

Lilith is variously described as the wife of Satan and/or the wife of Adam, created at the same time and from the same earth as Adam, but before Eve who was created from one of Adam's ribs. In the 13th Century writings of Rabbi Isaac ben Jacob ha-Cohen, for example, Lilith left Adam after she refused to become subservient to him and then would not return to the Garden of Eden after she mated with the archangel Samael, sometimes known as Malkira, King of the Wicked, and also the Angel of Death.

These revelations made *me* feel like jumping out of my chair, raising my hands in the air and shouting about birds and devils in a reenactment of Andrew's description of Father Thomas on the day he died.

Instead, I leafed through Thomas's Clairefontaine spiral bound notebooks that turned out to be narrative documentations of his exorcisms. In the third notebook, dated, November 2, 1982, All Souls' Day or the Commemoration of All Faithful Departed, he wrote in Latin the "Story of Caroline Van Kirk":

Quinque mensis abhinc...Five months ago, John Joseph Krol, Bishop of the Diocese of Philadelphia, contacted me and asked if I would come to Philadelphia and perform an exorcism requested by the parents of a 15-year-old girl, Caroline Van Kirk, daughter of the mainline Philadelphia Van Kirks, a family whose inherited money dated back to the mid-19th Century. The Van Kirks were generous contributors to the Diocese of Philadelphia and to the Jesuit-affiliated St. Joseph's University on Philadelphia's West Side. The Van Kirks needed the church's help.

Cardinal Krol arranged for me to meet with Caroline Van Kirk's father, Herbert Van Kirk, a tall, thin, pale man with curly blond hair and a blond pencil moustache, as well as Madeleine Van Kirk, also tall, thin and blonde with dark blue eyes and high cheekbones. American aristocrats. Caroline, the child (I use the term loosely) was not present at that first meeting.

The Van Kirks described to me a very extreme but still fairly typical parent-child relationship gone bad— the daughter locking herself in her room and using filthy, abusive language toward her parents when they tried to lure her out. She refused to attend classes at Nazareth Academy High School, ate very little and ran away from home to be with equally delinquent friends whenever possible.

She burned through her annual allowance from her trust fund, was given additional funds, then spent the additional money as well. She demanded more. Her parents refused. She forged checks on her mother's account. The parents threatened to cut her off completely. She became more abusive, occasionally punching her father and slapping her mother. At some point, she was arrested for soliciting on the street in downtown Philadelphia.

The parents had taken her to a number of therapists all of whom were unsuccessful in altering or even explaining the girl's behavior. The Van Kirks attempted to have the Juvenile Court send her to rehab, but there was no evidence of drug addiction or alcohol use. And both parents swore, honestly in my opinion, they were not abusing her either physically or psychologically.

A week later, I met with Caroline herself in the Van Kirk's home. She was a beautiful young girl, blessed with her parent's genes, dressed in her school uniform, sitting very prim and proper on a couch in the Van Kirk's library.

Once her parents left the room, she sat facing me, spread her legs, patted the couch next to her thighs and asked if I wanted to "do her." I told her, no. She called me "another faggot priest." Then she masturbated. I said nothing. I did nothing. After she climaxed, we both sat there for over an hour. In silence. Then I left.

We met again three days later. This time, she appeared tired, worn, pale. Her parents said she had been ill. She was wearing a soft pink dressing gown. When we were alone, she threw off the robe and, totally naked, walked over to me and tried to sit on my lap. When I stopped her, she again called me a faggot, again she masturbated, again I said nothing, did nothing; and for the rest of our meeting we sat in silence.

These meetings, every three days, continued in more or less the same fashion for six weeks. Attempted seduction. Masturbation. Silence. Finally, at the beginning of our 14th meeting, she said, "You are a worthy opponent, Thomas Groenbach." The tone and timber of her voice had not changed. Her appearance had not changed. But I knew I was speaking with her Demon.

The Demon, being a pure spirit of high intelligence, negotiated cleverly and persistently with me not to perform an exorcism. She tempted my ego, telling me how smart and wise she found me, much too smart and wise to be wasting my time as a priest.

She tempted my id, whispering endearments about how handsome I was, how desirable a lover I could be and how fortunate I would be to have her as my young, beautiful wife if I wanted her.

She tempted my soul, conjuring poetic visions of a life everlasting spent in adventure, artistic accomplishment and political intrigue. Through all her temptations, I prayed furiously and desperately in my faith that God's love would allow me to prevail.

At the 33rd meeting, I sensed the Demon's exhaustion and frustration with my enduring strength and my unbroken faith. As she faltered in her arguments, I gathered myself for the assault and initiated the exorcism with the traditional blessing while making the sign of the cross over her with my golden crucifix: *In nómine Pátris, et Fílii, et Spirítus Sancti. Amen.*

I could see fear in Caroline's eyes, but her body neither flinched nor recoiled as I continued on with invocations to the Virgin Mary and the Litany of the Saints. A shadow of a smile crossed her lips almost as if she were recalling past battles as I recited the prayer to St. Michael the Archangel: *"Prínceps gloriosíssime coeléstis milítia...* O most glorious Prince of the Heavenly Armies, St. Michael the Archangel, defend us in the battle and in our wrestling against the principalities and powers, against the rulers of the world of this darkness, against the spirits of wickedness in the high places..."

As I recited the liturgy, a peaceful spirit came over the room, and Caroline relaxed totally, closed her eyes folded her hands on her lap and bowed her head as if she were in deep prayer.

Then I again made the sign of the cross with my crucifix, and spoke the actual words of exorcism: *"Exorcizámos te, ómnis immúnde spíritus...* We cast you out, every unclean spirit, every satanic power, every onslaught of the infernal adversary, every legion, every diabolical group and sect, in the name and by the power of our Lord Jesus Christ. We command you, begone..." And at that very moment, her eyes flickered open, very briefly, and as I looked into those eyes, those deep blue, beautiful eyes, I knew with complete certainty that the Demon wasn't going anywhere.

I finished the liturgy, and when I was finished, Caroline and I both, for our own reasons, pretended the exorcism had been a success. She thanked me profusely, as did her parents, as did Cardinal Krol. But it was all a sham. Despite her apparent return to normalcy and her seeming obedience to her family and her newfound affinity for the teachings of the Holy Catholic Church, the Evil Spirit had only insinuated itself deeper into the soul of this tortured young woman.

I failed, mea culpa, mea culpa, mea maxima culpa, and I only ask our generous Lord God's forgiveness in advance for whatever consequences may result from my failure and my inexcusable, unfathomable, inability to admit the truth.

(signed) Father Thomas Groenbach, S.J.

November 2, 1982

Andrew's description of Caroline Van Kirk's failed exorcism shook me badly. His account changed everything or it could be the ravings of, as Andrew called him, a nutty old man, writing about a very disturbed and also very nutty young woman. Which was it?

I returned to my computer and researched the Philadelphia Van Kirks. They were indeed a prestigious Philadelphia family with forebears in banking, architecture, law and brokerages. I scrolled until I found an entry for Herbert and Madeleine Van Kirk. The link was a Philadelphia Daily News story describing a terrible car accident, April 23, 1986, in which both parents were killed.

Herbert and Madeleine Van Kirk were returning home from a charity auction for the Barnes Museum, when Herbert, at the wheel of the family's Mercedes Benz 560, apparently lost control and slammed into a retaining wall as he was entering the Vine Street Expressway. The car flipped and exploded in a massive fireball.

The only survivor was their daughter, Caroline, who said she had been asleep in the back seat and was thrown from the vehicle before it exploded. I Googled Caroline Van Kirk. Except for her birth announcement, there were no entries except for a link to the same Daily News story about the accident. I held my breath and Googled Lilith Van Kirk. There were no entries. Nothing.

I pray. I believe that God is a mystery of faith. I am loyal to many convictions I do not understand and cannot explain. But human beings having devils take over their consciousness? Exorcism? Driving out Evil Spirits?

I am a Jesuit, an intellectual. I am a man of reason. I was not comfortable with Thomas's story. Not comfortable at all.

I had met Lilith Van Kirk. It was now clear that she was Caroline Van Kirk and that she had maintained some sort of adversarial yet respectful relationship with Thomas. She was certainly odd. I had seen her seductive influence over Angela. I had experienced her effect on me. She was inordinately interested in Ignatius.

But how was she a presence in Iggy's life?

And as for Ignatius, how did all of these complicated circumstances come to surround such a sweet blameless baby? And the birds, the hawks? The text messages? My paintings? And my Antonia now known as Tsilia? These were facts in their presentation, but utterly incomprehensible in their source. In their meaning. In their connections.

I shut down my computer, went to my closet and gathered my oils and pallet knife. I wanted to paint. I needed to paint. But then I remembered it was Ash Wednesday and I'd vowed to give up painting for Lent. The mortification of desire.

Self-denial of one's greatest need. Flagellation of the spirit. In preparation for, and in communion with, Our Lord's final suffering and ultimate re-birth. So what was I to do?

I think that was a defining moment, the moment when I felt completely overwhelmed and knew I really needed help.

I decided to more or less come clean with Sergeant Milosz. The "more" was to tell him about Ignatius, Antonia/Tsilia and Thomas's accidental death; the "less" was the weird stuff—the cooper's hawks, the text messages, Lilith, the exorcism. Milosz was, after all, a policeman, inexorably bound to reality. I didn't need to clutter up his mind and diminish his skills with the inexplicable.

It was not an easy decision. Before I walked down to the station, I read from my breviary, and recited, from Lauds, Ash Wednesday, the Capitulum, "The night is far spent, the day is at hand: let us therefore cast off the works of darkness, and let us put on the armour of light. Let us walk honestly, as in the day." Yes. It was time to walk honestly. More or less.

Stan Milosz laughed when he saw me standing forlorn in the outer reception area. When we were alone, he said, "So, you've come to confess your sins, Pete."

"The first rule of a good confession, Sergeant, is not to make the penitent feel foolish."

Milosz was actually somewhat abashed. "You're right. I apologize. So what do you want to tell me?"

The first thing was the scariest. "Ignatius is an abandoned baby. He was left on our doorstep. He…" Perhaps best not to tell that Iggy appeared dead.

"I was pretty sure that was the case, Father."

"You've never called me Father before."

"You've never acted like a priest with me."

"So why haven't you reported us to Child Protective Services?"

"Have you ever dealt with them, Pete?"

"No."

"I have. Let's just say that for now Ignatius seems well cared for, even loved. He's happy and healthy. He's in a very sheltered home. It was a judgment call. For now, he doesn't need to be moved."

"Thank you."

"That doesn't mean he might not need to be moved later."

"I know."

I then told him about my suspicions that the dead girl, Masha Bentz, was probably Iggy's mother."

"I think so, too," he said, "but I'm not sure of it. Could we take a blood sample from the baby?"

"It might be best."

"Good. So what was your relationship with Masha?"

"None, to my knowledge, but..." I hesitated. I didn't want to go there. I really didn't want to, but, 'Walk in the light.'

"What?"

"Nothing. Look, Stan, I did some research on the internet, and came up with the name Tsilia Bentz who has...had...a design studio in Lomita."

"And so?"

"Could that woman be Masha's mother?"

"She is Masha's mother."

"You know that?"

"Yes."

"You've talked to her?"

"No. We can't find her."

I was relieved.

"But we would like to find her."

"Well, I saw a photo of Tsilia Bentz on the internet, and I recognize her. But I knew her as Antonia Lucia Belladone."

"How?"

"How did I know her? Ummm, well, many years ago, she was…a friend."

"Don't start that canon lawyer stuff again, Pete."

I mumbled. "We…um…an affair."

"What?"

"Had an affair."

"Now, see, Pete, that wasn't so hard was it? I mean this is the 21st century. Who cares?"

"The church cares. I care."

"I'm no longer a practicing Catholic, Father, but I have to say, if that's the worst of your transgressions I'm sure you'll eventually find a comfortable place in heaven."

"That judgement won't be yours, Sergeant. Anyway, I don't know how to find Tsilia Bentz. I went to her old studio and…"

"You were at her studio?"

"Yes. I was able to get inside. The door wasn't locked so I went on in."

"You're just full of sinful little surprises today, Father."

"But I didn't find anything which would indicate where she went."

"What did you find?"

"Ummm, well, I emptied out her storage room, and it looked like she owned a photography studio rather than a design house. And there was this bizarre man, a simpleton, who talked about naked women."

"Red shoes, blue baseball hat, black coat, long black

beard?"

"Yes. You know about him?"

"He's dead. The Lomita cops found his body in the alley behind the studio where you, uh, by the way, were technically guilty of trespassing and breaking and entering."

"Dead. That homeless guy's dead? Why?"

"You tell me."

"I don't know." I considered. "Well, he did know Tsilia. He knew what she was doing there."

"Bingo, Pete." He shuffled a few papers around and then sighed. "Look, Paderewski, this is the fourth body connected to you. You're beginning to scare me, and I'm not sure how much longer I'm going to be able to protect you."

"Protect me? From whom?"

"From our investigation, from Child Protective Services, from…I don't know. Father, seriously, what's going on?"

I told him that Father Thomas really had fallen and hit his head on the table minus any mention of Andrew, birds or demons. But Milosz didn't appear too concerned about Thomas's death, so I returned to the subject of Tsilia Bentz and asked him if he knew any additional information about Truly Bent Fabrics.

He told me the fabric business was a front for producing pornography—films, videos and stills for magazines. Tsilia Bentz was making a very good living out of the operation, and her Russian husband, Vlad "The Count" Bentz was supplying the girls, mostly from Eastern Europe. "Just your standard blow and bang with some carpet munching. Most of those studios are in the Valley, but the Bentzes set up operation here in the South Bay."

I asked how that homeless half-wit died. "Shot. Low

caliber pistol. Like Masha."

"Like Masha?"

"Yeah, Pete, just like Masha. And another connection. His eyes were plucked out. And there were deep scratches all across his face. Does that make any sense to you, Pete?"

It did. Sort of, but I declined to comment.

'Walking in the light' did have its limits.

The First Day AfterAsh Wednesday, Mosaic

Chapter Eleven

… Take far away our load of sin, / Our soiled minds make clean within; / Thy sovereign grace, O Christ, impart / From all offence to guard our heart. / For lo! our mind is dull and cold, / Envenomed by sin's baleful hold; / Fain would we now all darkness flee, / And seek, Redeemer, unto thee.
Matins, The Hymn, Thursday of Quinquagesima

Angela was hysterical when I told her I talked to Sergeant Milosz.

"I'm not giving up our baby!" She was fierce.

Andrew rushed into the room. "What's wrong?"

"Shoot him."

"Who?"

"Apparently me," I said, laughing in an attempt to diffuse the situation. "Calm down, Angela. We don't have to give Ignatius up."

"What are you talking about?" asked Andrew.

"He spoke to that cop," said Angela. "He told the cop about Iggy."

Andrew turned to me. "You did?"

"Yes, I did. We have to trust someone."

"And I suppose you told him about me and Thomas as well?"

"No. Of course not."

Angela wasn't concerned about Andrew or Thomas. "What about the baby?"

"Sergeant Milosz doesn't like Child Protective Services. He thinks Iggy's fine where he is for now."

"For now..." mumbled Angela, but I knew she was thinking, for how long?

I retreated to my room. Before I logged onto my computer, I opened my phone and recited from Prime, that familiar reading from Psalm 22: "Yea, though I walk through the valley of the shadow of death, I will fear no evil; / for Thou art with me." I certainly hoped so. Things were not looking so good on an earthly level.

I decided to try a different tack in my investigation. Who was Vlad Bentz, Masha's father, Tsilia's husband? Googeling "Vlad Bentz" brought up nothing. Googeling "Vlad The Count" brought up almost three million hits. Of course. Vlad the Impaler. Count Dracula. I realized that was how Bentz got the nickname, but that information wasn't going to help me.

A Russian who could bring Eastern European girls into the country? On a hunch I tried "Vlad Import/Export." A couple of Romanian companies, but nothing domestic. The same for "Dracula Import/Export." Modeling? I tried "Vlad Modeling." Ah! A hit. "Boutique modeling agency in San Pedro." I had to smile. 'Boutique' in the rough and tumble port city of San Pedro? I didn't think so.

Everything was clear when I looked at the pictures of Vlad Modeling's girls. Even I, an aging priest, could pretty quickly figure out those women were available for more than product marketing. I called the number listed on the website. No one answered although I let it ring continuously for a minute or so. What to do?

San Pedro is an orphan town, legally part of Los Angeles,

but only umbilically connected to the city by a long, very narrow corridor snaking roughly along the 110 Freeway south from Watts through the flatlands past gang-ridden Compton, then Asian Gardena, the industrial side of Torrance, past suburban Lomita to the bustling Port of Los Angels which is the only reason the LA city fathers fought so hard to keep San Pedro as part of the City of Los Angeles. Show me the money.

San Pedro is also an area perpetually on the verge. There are charming white stucco Spanish cottages and craftsman bungalows surrounding Averill Park. From Lookout Point and Angel's Gate there are stunning views of the container ships passing into and out of the port on one side, and an open ocean view all the way to China on the other. And, there's a non-renovated central core which means the collection of low-rise storefronts and commercial buildings have potential charm unlike the steel and glass towers which dominate the downtown of San Pedro's sister city of Long Beach.

But what to do with those storefronts? They've tried trendy bars and restaurants. They've tried art galleries. They've tried cultural complexes, theaters, clubs. Some succeed. Most don't. Whatever concept developers experiment with, the results never come together as an organic whole; so San Pedro remains edgy, full of hope, perpetually on the verge.

I drove our old, gray Astro with a re-taped window down the coast on Palos Verdes Boulevard West which becomes Palos Verdes Boulevard South as the two boulevards coil their way around the Palos Verdes peninsula—a mass of shifting sand and loose granite jutting into the water to form the southern end of Santa Monica Bay and the northern end of the harbor area. To my left, some of the priciest homes in the South Bay perched on sloping hillsides with magnificent views of the Pacific. On my right, even pricier homes sat on beaches or seaside cliffs.

The only flaw in all of this perfection was that the land was extremely unstable. It didn't require a major earthquake to shake loose a landslide. A minor quake would do just fine. I drove along the cracked, crumpled asphalt through the Portuguese Bend area that was rebuilt and resurfaced every few months as the land bucked and shimmied on its westward march to swim in the blue waters of the great Pacific Ocean.

The houses began to shrink in both size and opulence as Palos Verdes Drive suddenly stopped being Palos Verdes Drive and became 25th Street in San Pedro. The road dropped into central San Pedro and the Astro felt more at home among the older used cars and pick-up trucks parked in front of simple two-bedroom homes handed down by Serb, Croatian and Italian families who came to America to start a new life but still made their living from the sea.

I turned north on Gaffey, a commercial street that was in effect one continuous strip mall, until I reached 8th street where I turned west into San Pedro's downtown.

If 7th Street was home to the struggling art galleries and upstart theater companies, 8th Street was the sketchy cousin who preferred to hang out with the vagrants in the Anderson Memorial Senior Citizen's Center Park. I left the van in front of the Mirabella Vineyard Company "Home of the famous Dago Red Wine and Wine Vinegar." I was reminded that Charles-David once joked that it was difficult to tell their one product from the other.

Next door to Mirabella, to the east was the A1 Grocery, an Italian grocery/delicatessen with faded and chipped green, red and blue paint on the exterior. Next to the grocery was a nondescript, beige storefront with large, plate glass windows covered on the inside by closed blinds and a glass door also closed to view by a heavy gray curtain. No signage on the windows or the door, but a call box on my left as I faced the door had above it a small computer-printed notation: "Vlad Modeling." I rand the bell, and a buzzer released the front door lock.

The long, narrow room did not appear to be a den of iniquity. To the contrary, the Office Depot standard gray partitions and generic dark wooden desks arranged on top of industrial charcoal carpet presented the image of a low-rent real estate or accounting business.

I approached the reception desk where a long-haired blond woman sat typing on a computer with her face turned away from me. I was trying to formulate what I was going to ask when the woman turned and with a smile said, "How can I…." She never finished her question.

The smile dropped off her face, and for a few seconds both of us just stood staring at each other, wishing we could disappear. But of course we couldn't. Finally, I broke the silence, "Katie?"

She followed up with, "Father Pete?"

Then we both spoke simultaneously, "What are you doing here?"

It was a moment that usually produces laughter. Neither of us laughed.

I pulled myself together. "Katie, you do, uh, work here? You work for Vlad Modeling?"

"What do you want, Father?"

Those blue eyes. That face. Get thee behind me… "Can we talk somewhere else, Katie?"

We quickly agreed to meet on her lunch break in an open-air bar/restaurant, The Dragon's Snout, over on 5th Street. I don't usually drink at lunchtime, but I ordered a draft Flat Tire, and felt the alcohol calm me down. But just a bit.

Katie working for Val Modeling? That was astonishing. And presented difficulties on the one hand, but her employment might also mean I could find out more about the business than I had expected to.

I ended up with a half hour wait so I sipped my beer and pulled out my Android and read from Sext. I was meditating on lines from Psalm 73: "Thou hast made the sea firm through Thy power; / Thou hast broken the heads of the dragons in the waters. / Thou hast broken the heads of the dragon, / and hast given him to be meat for the people of the Ethiopians. / Thou hast broken up the fountains and the torrents, / ... Thou hast fashioned the morning light and the sun..." when the sun appeared before me and sat down across the table from me, and I was speechless again.

She said, "So what's up, Father?"

"Does Kenny know you work for Val Modeling?"

"Sure. Is there a problem?"

"Uh…I don't know. Isn't the business a front for…uh…"

"Prostitution?"

"Well…yes."

"Sort of…you want something to eat?"

"Not really."

"Let's go for a walk then."

We headed east on 5th toward the water and the San Pedro marina. As we passed by the Sunset Hotel, she casually asked if I'd like to get a room.

"No!"

She laughed, giggled really. "I was just teasing you, Father. You seem so very serious about all of this."

We crossed Harbor Boulevard into John S. Gibson Junior Park in front of the Los Angeles Maritime Museum. Gibson was a powerful LA City Councilman for 30 years and its President for 16, known for his public folksy ways and behind-the-scenes ruthlessness. A religious fundamentalist he was fond of saying he never entered a council meeting without saying a prayer.

I felt like I could use a prayer at the moment, but instead I finally responded to Katie's remark. "If by 'all this' you mean prostitution, well, prostitution is serious business, isn't it?"

"Oh please, Father. No one cares anymore. Do you surf the internet?"

"Of course."

"Well, then…Anyway, I'm not a whore, Father. I just do the books. The owner pays me well, very well."

"You're such a beautiful girl. You and Kenny are such a great young couple."

"Puleeze, would you stop. Why do I have to be either a whore or perfect. Can't I just be a normal Southern California girl trying to do the best I can?"

We strolled past the flying bridge and massive anchors from the de-commissioned cruiser, USS Los Angeles that once sailed off the coast of Hungnam to Haeju during the Korean War but was then sold for scrap. She may have lost her usefulness, but flags still fluttered proudly from her mast.

Katie was insistent. "You know, Father, sometimes I hate being pretty. It just screws everything up. And by the way since you're being so 'holier than thou' what were you doing at Vlad Modeling?"

"Did you know Vlad Bentz?"

"Sure. Of course. He's there now."

"That's impossible. He's dead."

"No he's not."

"A Russian guy they call The Count?"

"No, The Count was Vlad's father, also named Vlad. He was Bulgarian actually. The father died in a fire. Just a week or so ago. But his son's very much alive."

I sat down on the concrete bench that surrounds the American Merchant Marines Memorial—a pool with a bronze sculpture depicting two merchant seamen climbing a Jacob's ladder after making a rescue at sea. I felt as if I were trying to rescue my own sanity.

"Did your Vlad…."

"He's not my Vlad. Can't you understand I'm only the bookkeeper, Father Pete?"

"You're really not involved in the…in the…"

"In the good stuff?" She laughed again. A beautiful warm laugh. "No I'm just an innocent, Father."

Alright. I decided to stick to the business at hand. "Does the younger Vlad have a sister?"

"Yes. Or at least he did. I never met her. She also died recently. The family's been going through a rough spell."

"That's for sure."

I was in the real world. I could hear flags snapping. I could see water rippling in the pool beneath the statue. I could feel cold concrete. But everything seemed topsy-turvey. Nothing seemed real.

Finally I turned toward Katie. "Have you ever met young Vlad's mother?"

"Not lately. She used to come around all the time. With

The Count. Why?"

"Was she Russian as well?"

"You mean Bulgarian? No, I don't think so. She had a Slavic name...Tesla..."

"Tsilia..."

"Yes, that's right, Tsilia. But I never heard her speak anything but English. With no accent. She didn't look Slavic. Actually, she looked Italian."

"Italian?"

"You know, thick dark hair, brown eyes. Full figure. She had great cheek bones. She was beautiful once, I imagine. Still was in a way."

"Yes."

"Why, do you know her?"

I stood. "I imagine you have to get back to work."

"I can come and go when I want as long as the work gets done."

"Why do you really work there, Katie?"

"I'm telling you the truth. Vlad pays well, double what anyone else would pay me."

"But it's not a good place. In fact you might me in danger."

"What? Me?" she laughed the laugh that melted my heart. He long hair blew across her face, the sun highlighting the blonde streaks. "Nothing will happen to me. I told you, I'm one of the innocents."

I left Katie siting in the sun on the quay and returned to Riviera Beach.

I was lying on my bed in my room. No painting. No computer. My thoughts randomly trying to make connections, but mostly they trailed off into unconnected mysteries. The more knowledge I gained, the less I understood. I started to pray for guidance, but Andrew knocked on my door and then walked into my room uninvited.

"Where's the van, Pete?"

"I parked it down the street, in the shade."

"Where are the keys?"

I forgot to put them on the ledge in the kitchen. I went over to my desk, retrieved the keys and handed them to Andrew.

"Angela and Iggy and I are leaving."

"You tried that once before, remember?"

"We have to get out of here before they come for Iggy."

"Andrew…"

"Don't try to stop us, Peter."

"Where are you going?"

"We'll go to Canada. Angela says the nuns will protect us if we can get to Quebec."

"That's a long way, Andrew. The Astro will never make it."

"You better pray it will. You're good at that. Praying. Not doing anything. Just praying."

My heart was pounding. I couldn't imagine life without Iggy. Without Angela. Why was God allowing this to happen? "Andrew, I …"

"There's nothing you can say, Peter. This is your fault. Why did you have to talk to the cop? Ask yourself. If Iggy means so much to you, why?"

"I needed help. I don't understand what's happening."

"Nothing's going on. Nothing. It's all in your head. It's all that devil nonsense affecting your brain, Peter. Waste of time. Jesus was a man of action. He wanted to make things right. I'm going to make this thing right. This time I am."

"Andrew I…okay…look, at least, don't take the pistol

with you. I beg you not to. It will only make trouble. Leave the gun here, please."

He surprised me and gave me the little Bobcat that he had stuffed in his waistband. I had never touched a gun before. Its shape felt uncomfortable in my hand although it weighed much less than I imagined. I put his gun in my desk drawer then I walked downstairs where Angela was waiting with Ignatius. I tried to convince her that leaving was madness.

She spoke to me in French with tears in her eyes. "*Au contraire*, staying here is madness, Peter. You had your chance. We could have been a family, but you're in love with your cold, uncaring God. You love Him more than you love me. You love Him more than you love Ignatius."

She turned to leave. "My God, a loving God, a kind generous God that cares about people. My God will protect us. He will. I am sure of it."

I was too stunned to answer her. Any words I might want to offer died in my throat. I went outside and helped them load up the old Astro. I heard the hawks whistling in the trees. I heard the old wreck of a van cough to life and pull away.

I was terrified. I was loosing everything. I realized how much I did love them, but I turned away from them. I couldn't bear to say good-bye. I bowed my head and prayed for their safety.

As I walked back to the house, my phone rang. I expected some weird voice chattering nonsense, but it was Kenny. He was crying and I could barely understand him.

"Father Pete…Father Pete… you have…to come to…" he had trouble breathing, "come to the hospital right away."

"What happened, Kenny?"

"Katie…"

"Something happened to her?"

"She's unconscious…O God, Father. They don't…please come…"

"Where, where are you?"

"Little Company of Mary. Hurry…" The connection was broken.

The hawks' whistling stopped, and they began their haunting, screeching calls to each other. In frustration and anger I threw my phone into the tree, but I didn't come close to hitting anything. My phone landed on the ground and fell apart.

Shattered.

Healing the Blind, Illustration

Chapter Twelve

O God, the heathen are come into Thine inheritance, / Thy holy temple have they defiled, / and made Jerusalem a place to store fruit. / The dead bodies of thy servants have they given to be meat unto the fowls of the air .
Matins, Psalm 78, Friday of Quinquagesima

Katie was dying, the doctors were reluctant to say it was so, but I could hear their hopelessness between the lines they threw out to try and comfort us. Dr. Oliver Brandon, an overweight, prematurely white-haired, emergency room specialist was gentle but direct. "If things do not turn around soon," he said as he reviewed Katie's chart, "I will be honest, she will not make it."

I turned toward Kenny. "What happened to her?"

He shrugged his shoulders. Shook his head.

I asked Dr. Brandon.

"We do not know," he said.

Back to Kenny. "Where did they find her?"

"I found her. When I came home from the beach. She was lying in the back yard on a lounger. I called to her. She didn't respond. I approached her and realized she was barely breathing. I called 911 and started artificial respiration…my God, what could have happened?"

"But…" I stopped myself.

"But what?"

"I…" For some reason I didn't want to tell him I'd spoken

to her not five hours earlier and she was fine. "She was just lying there in your back yard?"

"Yes. She often sits outside in the evening under the trees."

"Trees? Were there birds in the trees?"

"Birds? What do you mean?" He thought for a second. "No, I don't think so. Why? What would birds have to do with anything?"

I realized my question sounded ridiculous. I changed the subject. "A healthy young woman doesn't just collapse for no reason," I said to the doctor.

Dr. Brandon sighed. "And that is why we are confused. The blood tests show nothing unusual. The MRI shows nothing amiss. The EKG shows nothing wrong. But her vitals keep crashing. Very low pulse. Very low blood pressure. Little response to stimuli. I believe she had some sort of shock to her brain, but there is no sign of head trauma."

Kenny was trembling. He spoke softly. "You have to try something. Anything." His eyes were red. Snot dripped down from his nostrils onto his upper lip. "Anything."

Brandon faced me. "Therapeutic hypothermia. We could put her into an induced coma. Give her brain a rest. Her organs a rest. We could see what happens."

"What are you talking about?" demanded Kenny. "You want to put her into a coma? What if she never comes out? No!"

"Katie's brain is still using a lot of energy responding to sense impressions, thoughts and muscle movements even though that does not appear to be the case," said Dr. Brandon. "We need to slow everything to the absolute minimum to allow healing."

Kenny was adamant. "You're shutting her down

completely? No."

I said: "He's not going to shut her down. He's only going to cool her."

Brandon continued, "We will anesthetize her and put her on a respirator. Then we administer a very cold, 3.9 degrees centigrade, saltwater drip to cool her from within. We cover her with cooling blankets also at 3.9 degrees, and place ice bags on the exposed parts of her body."

Kenny was horrified. "But she hates being cold."

"She will not feel it. She will not shiver for example. That is why we anesthetize her. We will keep her body between 32.8 and 33.9 degrees, that's 91.04 to 93.02 to you. We will monitor her constantly, all her vital signs, all the time."

"For how long?"

"Ten, twelve hours."

"Half a day. No, no. She'll die."

That's when I had a crazy thought. I was embarrassed to speak it, but I somehow sensed, knew, felt, whatever, that if he were with us, Thomas would be mumbling, "Freeze the Evil One. Freeze Him out! The cold will force Him back into the fires of Hell."

But I could only say, "Kenny, you just said we should try anything. Let's go to the chapel and pray."

The Little Company of Mary is a Catholic hospital and so the chapel was a comfortable place to rest before the cross of our Lord and Savior. I put my arm around Kenny's shoulder, and said, "Just as Jesus suffered, died and was reborn, so too, we pray, shall Katie be reborn and returned to the arms of her loving husband."

Kenny, exhausted, let his head slump against me. Soon, he fell asleep. I gathered up a pillow and two blankets from the nurse's station, returned to the chapel and settled him down on one of the chapel pews where he fell into a restless sleep.

But I could not sleep. Since I didn't have my phone to say my breviary, I sat there with my hands folded in my lap and talked to God the way I used to when I was young and perplexed by life and needed Him to be my friend.

Well, here we are. You are here, aren't you? Not the You over there in the stained glass performing miracles. And not the You up there on that cross suffering. Sure okay, I know You suffered for Kenny, for Katie, for Angela and Andrew and yes, for Ignatius, lovely little Ignatius.

You suffered for me as well, but look, I'm the one who's suffering now and I don't need to see You in pain, I need to see You as wise and all knowing, generous and forgiving…forgiving…oh, God, do forgive me.

Did I do this to Katie? To Thomas? To Masha Bentz? To her father? To the halfwit who simply liked seeing naked women? Am I the cause of this killing? I really, honestly can't figure out what's happening.

And I've had it, God. I'm getting too old for this. I'm worn out and frustrated and not getting anywhere at all. And Sergeant Milosz is right, isn't he? I've become a toxic priest. A harbinger of death and desolation.

Okay, You're right, God, I shouldn't go on like this, a maudlin hysteric. We were always taught in the novitiate that despair is the one sin You can't forgive, right? Because You are hope. Because You can only offer salvation if we believe. Okay. Okay. I believe.

So…let's get down to the Big Issue, right? Is there an Evil One behind all this? Are their devils? Do You really have some sort of ongoing grudge match with Satan and his boys? And his girls for that matter. What is Lilith all about? And Antonia? Where is she? If she exists that is. What the hell was she doing making pornography? Yeah, what the hell…

You know, God, we Jesuits, at least we post-Inquisition, post-Enlightenment Jesuits, aren't into this devil stuff. We leave that side of Catholicism pretty much to the Dominicans. But sure, we go along with it. Why not? The devil, Satan, Beelzebub, the Antichrist, Lucifer, Angel of Darkness, Evil Spirit, King of Hell, Mephistopheles, Prince of Darkness are all powerful metaphors for the presence of bad karma in the world.

Karma? I don't know, God, does the concept of karma still work in this conversation? Why not. Oh well, You know what I mean. Shit happens. I know, I know, You don't make it happen. Can't make it happen.

So let's get back to the devils. You see, if I'm really struggling against a…well, let's call it, a supernatural force of evil, then, I really don't know what to do. Okay, Father Thomas seemed comfortable in that world of the spirits. Well, not comfortable. Let's say he knew how to operate within it. But then he was an exorcist, the last of a dwindling breed. I'm a university professor, canon law. How could I be more logically oriented?

Okay, so I've done some very illogical things. Screwed up my life in completely irrational ways. But you know my weakness, God. You know my weakness. If only we priests could marry. I know you wouldn't care. I know you never said one word about married priests one way or another. But then, since I'm being honest with you, I have to admit, even if I had been married, I might have strayed. Something about a pretty face, a nicely shaped breast, a cute behind, long legs…see what I mean? Even sitting here in a chapel talking to you. I'm embarrassing. I really am.

So, even though I've screwed up my life, I've never felt until now that I screwed up the lives of others. And oh, dear, dear God, if this mess is all my fault, please protect Little Iggy from me. I love him so much. I…I will do anything to save him. But what is the right thing? What will save him?

Why didn't I fight for him when they took him away? Because I do love him and I want him to be safe. I do love him and I can't stand the thought that being near me might destroy him. When he smiles, I smile. When he coos, my heart coos. When he is afraid… Oh, God when the hawks swooped down toward us…I was terrified. Terrified.

I can't let him go. But I have to let him go. I can't keep him. I can't keep him. Me, a priest. A bad priest, but a priest. With work to do.

But I miss him already. Please protect my Iggy and my Angela and crazy Andrew. Please don't let Andrew do anything stupid. Please protect them on their journey. Did I say, my Iggy? My Angela? What's happening to me, God? What's happening to me?

Hmmm, well, we haven't gotten very far about the devils, now have we? What do You really think? Should I ask You for a sign, for dipping Your finger into the temporal world? A Sistine ceiling moment?

Milosz seems a good guy at heart? But he sure is angry at You. A lot of bitterness in that man. Maybe he has problems with good and evil as well. He surely must be overwhelmed by disgusting memories of the terrible things he's seen.

But has he seen devils? I doubt it. What would happen to a policeman who believes in devils? That would sort of load the dice in favor of the bad guys wouldn't it? It would make his job more or less useless. He'd be like a priest who believes in devils. He'd be like Father Thomas.

Did Thomas's life become useless? Sitting in our home, not talking to anyone, reading his newspaper, spilling coffee as his hands shook and trembled. Did he give up after Lilith Van Kirk defeated him? No. I don't think so. He battled to the end. He truly gave up his life for Iggy. Ignatius Loyola was his last stand. And it killed him.

Will it kill me?

I went on like that for most of the night while Kenny tossed and turned on the church pew. It felt good to pray like that. I decided that even after I picked out my new phone, I would pray more often without my breviary. Meditation on scripture has its limits. Sometimes it's good to go directly to the source.

As the new dawn lit up the faux stained glass of the chapel windows, Dr. Brandon entered and walked over to us. He looked terrible. His face was haggard. He hadn't shaved. His white hair hung in his face. His scrubs were wrinkled and his belly jiggled beneath his lab coat. A very tired medical Santa Claus. I hoped he had a present for us.

"We're going to restore Katie's body heat now," he said quietly. "I thought the two of you might want to be there." We did.

Bringing Katie out of her hypothermia was mostly a process of slowly warming her body back to its normal 98.6 degrees Fahrenheit. At first, the worry lines and taut neck muscles around Dr. Brandon's face seemed to relax. He nodded as he watched the Welch Allyn monitors. He almost chuckled. "She seems to be coming around nicely," he said.

Kenny managed a brief smile as he rocked back and forth in anticipation. He was certain her eyes would open, she would stare at him in joyful recognition and he would kiss her like in the movies. I just watched and kept my emotions under control although I desperately wanted Kenny's wish to come true.

As time passed, Katie's body completely recovered from the induced hypothermia, but she did not raise her head and open her eyes to recognize Kenny. Dr. Brandon grew gloomy. Kenny fidgeted and his eyes darted around the room from Katie, to the monitors, to the nurse, to Dr. Brandon, to the wall, to the floor, to the DRE Versailles P100 operating table where Katie was breathing peacefully, regularly. Her face was pink, healthy, her lips red, her cheeks even rosy, but there was no expression to her features. She wasn't coming back to us the way we knew her.

By that point, Dr. Brandon had a furrowed brow and clenched teeth as he again studied the monitors and Katie's charts. "What the hell's going on," whispered Kenny.

"On the positive side," said Brandon, "her vitals are all back to normal, strong and healthy. But…"

"But what?" said Kenny.

"Why don't we talk outside," said Brandon as he turned to leave the room. The automatic door whispered open, and then shut behind us when we were in the hallway.

Sergeant Milosz was waiting. I should have expected him. I didn't, so I wasn't ready to spar with him. "Father Paderewski, why am I not surprised?"

"Who's he?" asked Kenny.

Sergeant Milosz turned to Brandon. "Can I talk to her yet?"

Now Kenny was angry. "Who is this guy?"

Dr. Brandon answered, "Sergeant Milosz, Riviera Beach police." He turned to the Sergeant, "No, you can't talk to her now. She's still resting."

Kenny exploded. "Resting! She's not resting. She's still in a coma, doc. And a real coma this time. I told you. I told you." His anger faded quickly toward despair. He moaned and his shoulders slumped. "I knew it. She hates the cold."

"But she's no longer dying," said Dr. Brandon softly. "Now there's hope she will fully recover." He hesitated and rubbed his chin. "I mean that. There's no medical reason she can't fully recover."

"To?" I asked.

"To her normal self."

Milosz smirked. "And we all want that, don't we, Father Pete? Especially you."

Kenny jerked out of his lethargy. "What's that supposed to mean?"

Milosz still had that smirk on his lips and an intense stare in his eyes. "I've been talking to an old friend, Lieutenant Jeremiah Wilson, LAPD, working out of San Pedro. He says there are numerous witnesses who saw your wife, first in a bar and then in Gibson Park with a man who, by their descriptions, looked a lot like our Father Pete here."

He turned to me. "Were you with this man's wife yesterday down in San Pedro?"

I was trapped. "Yes, but…"

Suddenly Kenny screamed, "You son-of-bitch. I trusted you." He lunged toward me. His hands wrapped around my throat as he threw me backwards. I was able to stay on my feet for a moment, but Kenny's strength and my lack of oxygen sent me crashing to the floor rather quickly. I remember hearing a loud smack as my head hit the linoleum. Then my ears were ringing. Stars floating across my fading vision. Everything went black.

Very black.

Renouncing Satan, Altarpiecee

Chapter Thirteen

Then the devil taketh Him up into the holy city, and setteth Him on a pinnacle of the temple, and saith unto Him: If Thou be the Son of God, cast Thyself down.
Terce, Ant., Being the First Sunday of Lent

In my unconscious state I saw…

Lucifer's forces arrayed along the bluffs that rose from the ocean south of Malaga Cove in Palos Verdes. I caught a glimpse of Lucifer himself, his chest protected by a pewter breastplate, his head covered with a black leather helmet. Massive brown spotted wings spread out from his collar bones and his talons held a finely honed iron blade. His face had Sergeant Milosz's forehead and eyes; his nose mouth and chin were those of Andrew including a course black beard.

Below, on the beach, along the surf line were the Forces of Light led by Archangel Michael who actually resembled the Roman Neptune, the Greek Poseidon, with a three-pronged spear, long white beard and a crown of olive green kelp. His wings were shimmering aquamarine and his eyes were fathomless blue. Sometimes he was Father Thomas, but as the battle began, he looked a lot like…a lot like…me.

The sky darkened, filled with thick, black, mountainous clouds rolling in on rising winds from the west over Catalina Island. There was a clap of ear-splitting thunder and bright yellow veins of intense light flashed across the skin of the clouds. The earth began to quake violently. Massive landslides broke loose from the bluffs and rolled toward the sea. The voice of God rumbled across the Beach of Armageddon saying, "It is done."

As God spoke, a comet with the face of little Ignatius Loyola shot across the sky, and the Forces of Darkness atop the bluff began their march to the sea, and the Forces of Light along the shore advanced toward the bluff. Lucifer's talons reached out and placed a death grip around my neck, in the background...

...the clamor and clatter, steel striking steel, and metal trays bouncing off the tile floor...

I opened my eyes and there was Charles-David, a sheepish grin on his pink, embarrassed face. "Sorry," he said, "Didn't mean to wake you. Knocked over the tray there on your... well, anyway, nice to have you back, Peter."

Charles-David was sitting next to my Hill-Rom 1150 hospital bed. Of course, I didn't know it had been three days since I last opened my eyes until he told me. I did know I had a terrible headache and my neck was sore and aching. Then I remembered why.

"What happened to Kenny?"

Charles-David smiled. "Nothing. Milosz wanted to arrest him, but I told him you wouldn't want that."

My throat was killing me. I massaged my neck. "Right now, I'm not so sure. How's Katie?"

"The same."

I croaked, "Good Lord, what's happening to us?"

"Indeed," said Charles-David. Then he said, "I did hear from Andrew."

"And...?"

"They're in Vegas?"

"Vegas? Las Vegas? Nevada?"

"None other." He must have seen the look on my face. "The

Astro blew out something called a head gasket on Highway 15 near the Nevada state line. Near a town called Primm. They were forced to stay the night at a gambling house called Whiskey Pete's.

"The van needs a new engine and they've no money to fix it, so they boarded a bus on into Vegas where they're staying at a cheap hotel in the old downtown near Fremont Street.

"What now?"

"They don't know. Andrew told me they might just stay in Vegas."

"Really?"

"Apparently."

"Why?"

"I don't know."

I was irritated. It was getting hard for me to talk. "I think I should go there."

"I'll go with you. We'll rent a car."

"How?"

"I'll sell the Swarovski cruets and my set of eight Thomas Forester & Sons tea saucers."

The next day, Charles-David phoned Andrew to tell him we were coming, and then we picked up our Chevy Aveo ($138.50 for the week with 700 free miles from 699 RentACar) and headed out on the road from Riviera Beach, California to Las Vegas, Nevada, through the Mojave Desert on US Highway 15.

That highway is as straight and boring as you can possibly imagine, so I asked Charles-David what he thought about devils. I hoped that my liven things up.

"You mean the kind I see after consuming a bottle of Mont LaSalle Chateau Des Freres or the ones I confront teaching the little monsters at St. Aloysius Country Day?"

"I'm serious. The ones…the specters… I feel strange even talking about this, but, you know, the…beings who tempt us to evil. Satan, Lucifer, you know what I mean."

"Yes, of course."

"What do you think?"

"Well, I don't know, Peter. For someone like me, it would be easy to blame my drinking on the devil. It would be easy to blame my affection for men on the devil. But that wouldn't be true. I drink because I'm afraid, and I like men because God made me that way."

"Well, yes, but you're talking about individual weaknesses or desires. I'm asking, do you believe in devils, or angels for that matter, who are actual, real spiritual beings that bring grace or sin into the lives of human beings?"

He didn't answer right away. A massive 600 HP shimmering black Western Star 18-wheeler passed us on the left, its slipstream pushing our poor Aveo toward the shoulder. I struggled with the wheel to keep us on the highway.

"As a priest…"

"I don't mean as a priest, Charles-David, I mean as a person. In your daily life. Do you make accommodations, allowances, whatever for interventions by spirits, angels, devils?"

"Why are you asking me these questions?"

For the first time I told someone about all that had happened since that morning when Ignatius came into our lives. There was plenty of time. Hours and hours of nothing much to see. Unless you're into sand. And scrub. Barren rock. Blazing sun. Visions of Hell on earth able to strike a permanent fear of mortal sin inside your heart.

Of course Charles-David knew some of the information I was sharing with him. He was the one struck by the rock that announced little Iggy's arrival, but he didn't really know about the cooper's hawks, the Venetian red in my painting, the mutilated bodies, how Thomas died, Antonia/Tsilia, Truly Bent Fabrics, my talk with Katie, Vlad Bentz. By the time I finished, we were skirting the southern edge of Death Valley heading toward the state line and Primm.

"So," I asked, "what do you think?"

"What do you think?" Charles-David had experienced a great deal of therapy and had acquired the skills.

"I think that as a lawyer, a logical thinker and as a Jesuit, that all these happenings I have described to you have a rational explanation, and I believe that in the end, a rational explanation will turn out to be the case. But as a person in the middle of this whirling dervish of a story, I cannot deny what my eyes have seen. And in my soul, I'm scared."

"I must say, your stories have managed to upset me a great deal as well, Peter Paderewski. Frankly, I could use a drink."

There'll be plenty of that in Las Vegas, I thought as we approached the city, rising like a shimmering mirage as evening settled over the beige and pastel desert.

Las Vegas. An adult Candyland, bright lights and dancing water, circuses and naked bodies, avarice and gluttony all plunked down amid air-conditioned high desert desolation where despair will haunt you at 3:00 AM after a night of depressing debauchery.

Charles-David quoted Dante during our descent from the Las Vegas Expressway onto South Las Vegas Avenue: "Through me you pass into the city of woe. Through me you pass into eternal pain. Through me among the people lost for aye…. Before me things create were none, save things Eternal, and eternal I endure. All hope abandon ye who enter here."

Just for fun, I asked him to repeat the words in Italian. He did. Sounded more poetic. Less ominous.

Three blocks south of the expressway, Las Vegas Boulevard crosses Fremont Street. To the right is the renovated "Freemont Street Experience" celebrating Old Las Vegas. We turned left into the Fremont Street you might not want to experience, drove 10 blocks and pulled up in front of 20-foot orange pole with a plaster yellow ball on top. Atop the ball was a sign, Desert Moon, then below that sign, attached vertically to the pole, an orange neon sign that read, Motel and below that yet another orange sign advertising XXX Movies. We entered the long narrow parking lot and pulled into a slot in front of Room 17.

"This is a gay hotel," Charles-David murmured.

"Come on, how would you know that?"

"Fabulous landscaping for such an out-of-the-way place."

I trusted his assessment. We knocked on the door. There was no response. We knocked again. We heard Angela ask, "Who is it?" I told her it was Charles-David and me. She opened the door just a crack with the security chain still attached.

When she saw that it really was us, tough, unbreakable Angela broke down and started weeping. I heard her repeat, through her tears "Thank God, you're here. Thank God, you're here." Then she collapsed into my arms and I held her close.

I raised my eyebrows and tilted my head as I looked toward Charles-David as if to imply, what else can I do? He smiled knowingly.

Ignatius Loyola was sound asleep on one of the two double beds. Andrew was nowhere to be seen. I asked Angela where he was.

"I don't know," she said. "He's been gone since last night."

She started weeping again. "*Je suis très peur*, Peter. Really scared. Poor Iggy. *Je suis le protéger*. But he is safe. Our baby is safe."

That drew a perplexed, confused look from Charles-David, but I signaled for him to check on the baby instead of studying Angela and me.

I did my best to calm Angela and find out whatever I could about Andrew. She told me he became increasingly certain that someone was following them. He insisted they all three must stay locked in their room until Charles-David and I arrived.

Then late the previous night, they ran out of food, so after peeking through the front window for an hour while he studied the parking lot, Andrew told her he was going to the small market he across the street. He slipped out through the bathroom window and said he would be back within fifteen minutes. He never came back.

I consulted with Charles-David about what he thought we should do. He felt strongly that we should put Ignatius and Angela in the Aero and head back to Riviera Beach as quickly as possible. I saw the wisdom in that, but I was reluctant to abandon Andrew.

We argued back and forth for awhile. Then we agreed to stay the night, and if nothing new turned up concerning Andrew, we would leave early in the morning.

It was not yet dark, so Charles-David and I decided to visit the tiny market across the street to discover if Andrew ever made it there. Angela refused to be left alone in the room again, so she swaddled Iggy in blankets and we all made our way across Fremont Street to what turned out to be called Sisters Oriental Market with a Thai Food restaurant attached next door.

While Charles-David and Angela ordered spring rolls, rice and mild green curry, I questioned the clerk behind the counter at the market. He was a short man, not much over five feet, stocky, mid-twenties, with spiked, gelled black hair and a wispy shock of chin whiskers.

He spoke very little English, so the interview wasn't going well until I mimed a running man with a dark full beard entering the store at which point he smiled and nodded. "Ye, ye. He here las' ni?"

"Yes! Did he buy anything?" I mimed walking through the store and putting purchases on the counter.

Again he smiled, nodding. "Ye, ye…den he lef. Quick, quick."

So he had been there. I knew I wouldn't get much more from the clerk, so I joined Angela and Charles-David for another dash back across Freemont to the Desert Moon. Once inside we adults ate greedily while Ignatius nursed with equal vigor at Angela's breast.

After eating we didn't talk much. I'm not sure any of us knew what to talk about that wouldn't simply make us more anxious. Instead we prayed.

Three frightened adults and one peaceful baby. Huddled together in cheap motel room with lilac purple bedspreads and a badly executed trompe-l'oeil of exotic desert landscapes decorating the walls. The gold polyester curtains tightly drawn. One weak night light burning on a black enamel side table.

I still didn't have a new phone, so Charles-David pulled out a dog-eared, hard copy breviary from his overnight bag and read from Vespers, Psalm 113: "The idols of the heathen are silver and gold, / even the work of men's hands. / They have mouths, and speak not; / eyes have they, and see not. / They have ears, and hear not; / noses have they, and smell not. / They have hands, and handle not; / feet have they, and walk not; / neither speak they through their throat...." He continued reading until exhaustion overcame us all.

Since there were two double beds, Angela and Iggy curled up on one while Charles-David and I stretched out on the other. Charles-David rolled onto his side and faced the wall. I was facing the other bed.

Sometime during the night, I was awakened by squealing tires, slamming doors and a creaking gate. I crept out of bed, went to the window and peeked out from behind the curtains.

Whatever it was that awakened me was gone. Only moonlight. Reflected neon. An occasional car or truck out on Freemont. No movement. No odd sounds.

I crawled back into bed. I was falling asleep when I heard Ignatius stir, whine a little and then begin rooting for a middle-of-the-night snack. I opened my eyes. Angela's eyes were also open. Staring at me. Her shirt was undone. One naked breast was exposed. Iggy was sucking on the other one and massaging Angela's blue-veined flesh with his chubby fingers.

Angela offered a tentative smile. I continued to stare at her. She puckered her lips and blew me an air kiss. I became aroused. I groaned and turned over. Facing Charles-David's back. Trapped between Scylla and Charybdis. Eventually I drifted back to sleep.

I managed to release Lucifer's talons from around my neck, but the Forces of Darkness were relentlessly pushing us backward into the ocean's riptide. I could feel, first my heels, then my calves and then my knees sloshing in the cold salt-water sea.

The sky grew even darker. I could barely see the shapes around me. I was drowning. Suddenly there were a series of hammering thunderclaps and the Voice of the Lord in the Heavens roaring…

"Open up! Open up!"

I leapt out of bed. Terror-stricken. My head foggy. Pounding on the door. Igantius crying. Angela screaming. Charles-David cowering on the bed. I pulled back a curtain.

The parking lot was filled with red and blue flashing lights. Three men in uniform. Guns drawn. One policeman had a fist raised to pound on our door again. I shouted as loudly as I could, "There's a baby in here! There's a baby in here!" I unlocked the door. I started to turn the knob. The door exploded in my face. I was knocked backwards onto a bed.

Angela shrieked. Iggy was howling. A gun went off. Policeman ordering, "On the floor. On the floor. Everybody face down, on the floor."

I was screaming, "There's a baby. There's a baby," but the police only responded with another command that we all lie face down on the floor, hands behind our backs.

As I felt the plastic zip ties being placed around my wrists and ankles, I asked the officer handling me what was going on.

"Shut up," was his answer.

I heard Charles-David whimpering, "But we're clergy; we're clergy. Catholic priests. *Sacerdotes Católicos*."

A gruff voice responded. "We speak English, *pendejo*

maricón.

"But it's true," I said. "We are priests."

Another younger voice. "Then maybe you'd like to say a prayer over the body of your buddy."

"What body?"

The gruff voice. "The headless body. In the dumpster."

Angela shrieked again, but I wasn't so worried about her. Ignatius had stopped howling.

I dreaded the sound of his silence.

St. Peter Damian, Fresco

Chapter Fourteen

They humbled his feet in fetters, the iron entered into his soul; / until the coming of His word. / The word of the Lord inflamed him: / the king sent, and delivered him; / the prince of the people, and he set him at liberty.

Matins, Psalm 104, Feast of Saint Peter Damian, Bishop, Confessor and Doctor of the Church

By the time I was dumped into the rear of a black and white Chevy Tahoe and brought to the detention center, I had been told that the bullet fired inside the room went through the roof. It did not cause any physical damage to either Angela or Ignatius.

But Iggy had been oddly quiet while the police were questioning us. True, he was always a peaceful baby, but I was worried. The officers did let Angela cradle him in her arms and she managed to control her own weeping, but I was worried. I had reason to be worried. I was responsible for him. And Angela as well.

I was comforted when the police used a pleasant young woman to help Angela and Ignatius into an unmarked gray sedan. Our poor little guy had already suffered enough in his brief, traumatic life.

It only took ten minutes for the Las Vegas police to deliver Charles-David and me from the Desert Moon to the Clark County Detention Center at 330 South Casino Boulevard, but it took almost the entire week before we would be able to return to the relative safety of our house on Dolorita Avenue in Riviera Beach.

Charles-David and I spent the remainder of the day we were arrested as well as the following night in a holding area of the center. At first I was scared when I saw our fellow detainees. One very large man, 6'3" and at least 350 pounds, from Torreón, Mexico, nicknamed ironically *El Enano*, the Dwarf, approached Charles-David who was shaking on a bench in the corner, partly from fear but mostly from the DTs.

El Enano towered over Charles-David and I was trying figure out what I could do to intervene when *El Enano* suddenly dropped to his knees and asked Charles-David to hear his confession.

After that episode, both Charles-David and I spent the morning hearing confessions and counseling the distraught. Perhaps God wanted us to be there. Perhaps we did something good in the midst of all that squalor and despair.

I was uncertain and confused about Andrew's grisly murder. Beheaded? Ridiculous. Who beheads people in America? Andrew's death was an entirely new level of violence that was simply incomprehensible to me. And that's what I told the Las Vegas police.

That's also what I told the judge at our arraignment hearing, and that's what I told Sergeant Milosz when he appeared in the holding area of the courthouse with a Las Vegas detective, Max Wiggins, a young guy with close-cropped light brown hair, black jeans, black t-shirt and a nonchalant air.

Milosz was angry. "I warned you I wouldn't be able to protect you any longer, Pete."

"I know."

"Now there's another dead body."

"I know."

"The next dead body might be yours. Or that baby you say you care so much about."

Wiggins added: "We almost killed you in your motel room, Father." I recognized his voice as the younger cop from the raid. "We didn't know who or what we were going to find."

"Maybe you could have simply knocked politely and asked?"

"Your friend was beheaded, for Chissakes. You wanna' see his body?"

"Have you found his head?"

"Not yet, but we will."

"I'll see him when you find it." Then sarcastically, "I think that will help with the identification."

Wiggins turned to Milosz. "Kind of a wise ass isn't he?"

"You don't know the half of it," Milosz responded with an aggressive chuckle.

They finally found Andrew's head placed in a Ziploc Big Bag Double Zipper bag, wrapped inside of a white Hefty Cinch Sak with Odor Block tall kitchen bag behind the Sister's Oriental Market on Freemont. The young clerk I'd talked to made the grisly discovery when he was sorting through the garbage for pick-up. According to Wiggins, the severed head shook the clerk pretty badly.

I would imagine so. Seeing Andrew's head and body unattached lying next to each other on the Clark County Coroner's morgue tray disturbed me as well. I prayed through the night for his soul. I also prayed that should we meet in Heaven, that he would forgive me for assuming he was paranoid. And for taking away his pistol.

After they found Andrew's head, Charles-David and I were released from the detention center, but Wiggins demanded we stay in town for a few more days while the Las Vegas police checked out the details of our story.

During that time I managed to have three conversations with Milosz. He stayed in Vegas so we could go back to California together. I guess he appointed himself our unofficial bodyguard. Fine by me. Andrew's body convinced me I was in way far over my head so to speak. Way, way far over my head.

Milosz and I painstaking reviewed all of the incidences that had occurred since Iggy showed up on the doorstep of our house. However, no matter how many times we went over the facts of the various events, no one insight emerged to make things any clearer.

We both agreed that we needed to find and interview Antonia/Tsilia Bentz. She was the key, but she was the lost key. The Riviera Beach police working with the considerable resources of the California State police and then the Las Vegas police, the Nevada state police and even an official liaison from the FBI, were not able to come up with any information whatsoever about where Tsilia Bentz was living. Or if she was living. Or where she was hiding. If she was hiding. Nothing.

I suggested Milosz interview the younger Vlad Bentz, the dead Count's son, and Katie Johansson's employer.

"We already talked to him after Ms. Johansson was found comatose. He's a cool customer. Very smooth. No record. Vlad Modeling is obviously an escort service, but no one has ever filed a complaint against them."

"What about taxes," I said. "Don't the bad guys always trip up over taxes?"

"He pays his taxes. Pays quite a bit in taxes. Your Ms. Johansson does his books, doesn't she?"

"She's not my Ms. Johansson."

"We have no legitimate reason to bring Bentz in for a serious interrogation, Pete. Even if we did, he'd have his lawyer with him, and I'm sure the lawyer would be a good one. A very good one."

"I could talk to Bentz."

"No."

"You forget, I am a lawyer."

"Canon law."

Pay back. I chuckled. "Seriously, I do know how to question people."

"Look, Pete…Father…Paderewski, whatever, this Val Bentz…He's a dangerous man. Evil. Smart. A true ally of the devil himself."

"What do you know about devils?"

"More than you might think." He shook his head, his eyes downcast. "More than you might think."

I wanted to pursue the topic of devils. "We're the good guys, Stan. God is on our side, not the side of Vlad Bentz."

"That's what I used to believe. I don't anymore."

That was the second time he'd made a remark like that. "Why are you so bitter about God, Sergeant?"

"Doesn't matter."

"I am a priest. You can talk to me."

"Doesn't matter."

I didn't push him any further. About devils. Or God.

When I returned to Riviera Beach, I purchased a new phone. Another Samsung Android. There was a new model, the Samsung Galaxy S III 4G. Even more features and functions I would never use. I bought it anyway. Stretched the limits of my vow of poverty.

Oh well. All my vows were stretched to the limit at that point. In debt to the Jesuits. In debt to God.

I called Vlad Modeling. A woman answered. I asked to speak to Vlad Bentz. The woman said: "Concerning?"

"Katie Johansson."

"And you are?"

"A friend."

"Of Mr. Bentz?"

"Of Katie."

"Your name?"

"Peter Paderewski. Father Peter Paderewski. S.J."

"Just a moment, please."

I was put on hold. The background music was the exotic chanting of Bulgarian throat singers. Very Medieval. The woman came back on the phone. "Mr. Bentz says he would prefer to meet you in person?"

"Sure. Why not?"

"Can you be here this evening around 7:30?"

"Yes."

"Do you know where we're located?"

"Yes."

"7:30 this evening then, Mr. Paderewski."

"Father."

"What?"

"Father Paderewski."

"Excuse me. Yes. Father Paderewski."

7:30. It would be dark. Not certain I liked that part. What was I getting myself into? Meeting Vlad on a sketchy street at night. In San Pedro.

But Vlad Bentz wasn't a reincarnation of Vlad the Impaler. Not Dracula. Not a vampire. He wasn't even Romanian. He was Russian. No, Bulgarian. No...actually, he was... American. The dead Masha Bentz's brother if my information was right. If.

I took the 232 Metro Bus south on the Pacific Coast Highway to the Wilmington Transit Center then transferred to the Metro 246 into downtown San Pedro. I left the bus at Pacific and Ninth. I noticed the San Pedro branch of Hope Chapel on the far side of the street as I crossed Pacific. Turned left. Walked over to Eighth Street and turned right just as the day's last light was disappearing behind the shipping cranes and cargo ships in the harbor.

Vlad met me at the door. Alone. If he was a vampire, he didn't look the part. If he was a devil, he didn't look the part either. But then, what would a devil or a vampire look like?

Bentz was small, just over five feet tall. He had dark hair cut close on the sides. Left long on top for lift. Soft brown eyebrows. Penetrating gray eyes. Clean shaven. Two-button Ermenegildo Zegna charcoal gray tropical wool suit. Brioni cotton-linen open necked shirt. Bruno Magli navy suede Pilson loafers. He wore an 18-karat gold necklace with a cross that I didn't recognize.

I was wearing my best blue jeans. The pair without paint stains. And my J.C. Penny ultra-white cotton t-shirt with the slightly frayed collar. My open-toed huarache sandals.

Bentz started by asking how I knew Katie. I answered that I was a friend of her husband. Didn't mention that her husband tried to kill me.

"How is she?" Bentz asked.

"Alive," I said.

He nodded.

I scanned the office. Simple. Modern. Framed, oversized photographs of beautiful women decorated the walls. Three Eames management chairs. Two in front of Vlad's aluminum Shaker Base Table. One behind. Two Steeman lamps providing soft, ambient light. Not very San Pedro. Not at all.

"It's good she's alive," said Bentz.

"Good? Yes, of course." I stared at one of the photographs. I was surprised. "Isn't that her," I asked.

"Who?"

"Katie."

"Yes."

"So she *is* one of your models?"

"Oh no, no. I just like looking at her." He stared directly into my eyes. "She is beautiful, no?"

"Yes…yes she is.

"So what's your interest in her? In Katie. I mean…after all, you're a priest, right?"

This conversation wasn't going in the direction I wanted. "I'm not actually here to talk about Katie."

"Really. I was under the impression…you told my assistant…"

"I'd like to ask about your mother, Tsilia Bentz."

"Ah! And what possible interest could you have in Tsilia?"

"I need to find her."

"There are many people looking to find Tsilia Bentz." He walked over to the wall next to me. Pushed a button. A panel opened in the wall. A wet bar appeared. "A drink, Father?"

"No." I tried again, "About Tsilia Bentz…"

Vlad would not be hurried. He poured himself two fingers of Bunnahabhain 18 Year Old single malt. I could smell the peat. Charles-David would go nuts.

"About Tsilia…" I asked yet again.

"Yes. Dear Tsilia. What exactly do you want to know about Tsilia?"

"Where is she?"

"Why should I tell you?" When I didn't answer, he walked over to another of the photographs hanging behind his desk. Another blonde. "She looks remarkably like Katie, don't you think?"

I hadn't really noticed.

"I suppose, yes."

"I'm told you have a…hmm, weakness for pretty women. Would you like to meet her?"

This was ridiculous. "Are you pimping me, Bentz?"

"Of course." He finished his scotch. Poured himself another. "She's not my mother, you know."

I knew he wasn't referring to the blonde. "Tsilia?"

"Yes. Tsilia. She's not my mother. And, honestly, I don't know where she is. Do you?"

"Why would I be asking you if I knew where she was?"

"I'm told you and Tsilia were once…ummm…very close. If she were my mother, perhaps you could be my father?" He laughed at his little joke.

"The Count was your father."

"Yes. He was my father."

"Who killed him?"

His face darkened. The air in the office grew chill. "No one killed him. He died accidently…in a fire."

"And Masha, your sister, who killed her, Bentz?"

He whirled around and approached me. He stopped less than a foot away. I could see that the pendant on his gold necklace wasn't a true cross at all, but a double dragon wound into the shape of a cross.

For a moment, I thought Vlad would strike me. Just for a moment. Then he relaxed. He placed his hand just below his neck. "I see you like the dragons." He unhooked the necklace. "Here, you can have it." He handed it to me, then gazed directly into my eyes. "Women. Gold. Everything is yours, Father Peter Paderewski, S.J. Everything. Just give me what I want."

"And what do you want, Bentz?"

"I think you know."

"Katie?"

"Katie?" He was truly perplexed for a moment. Then he laughed. "Katie…poor Katie. How did pretty little Katie get mixed up in all this?" He moved away. He stood before her photograph. "You can have Katie back as well."

"It's not me who wants her. Her husband…"

He shrugged as if to say, who cares. No answer. I threw the necklace on his desk. He kept his back to me. I wanted to know more, but the conversation was clearly over. I left him standing there staring at Katie's picture.

But it felt like I was being followed as I made my way back to the 246 bus stop on 9th Street. I turned around. Looked around. Didn't see anyone. I stood near the concrete bench next to the Hope Chapel parking lot.

Suddenly I heard a crack. The back railing on the far end of the bench was shattered. Shards of concrete exploded into the air and broke apart on the sidewalk. A bullet? I ducked behind the bench. No more shots. Obviously a warning.

I stood up. Looked around. Still didn't see anything. I went to investigate the damaged bench, but just then the 246 approached. Any further investigation could wait. I made the wiser decision. I hopped up the steps onto the bus.

My ride back to Riviera Beach was uneventful. My arrival was equally so. Charles-David was in the kitchen talking to Angela. He was drinking. Water.

Angela was sitting with Ignatius on her lap. The baby was sleeping. Angela and Charles-David wanted to talk. I didn't. I needed to think. I made excuses. Went up to my room. The Galaxy chimed a bell tone. It was Sergeant Milosz.

"Thought you might want to know."

"Know what."

"The hospital called. Katie Johansson's come out of her coma."

"When?"

"When? Oh, about an hour ago."

I could barely get the words out. "An hour ago?"

"Yes. What's wrong, Pete?"

"I was talking to Vlad Bentz an hour ago…. He said we could have Katie back. He…"

"What are you talking about?"

"I…" I disconnected.

My phone immediately chimed again. I didn't answer it. It chimed again. I turned off the ringer.

I sat in my Baxton. I tried to think. What in the hell? I startled myself with my choice of words. Maybe hell was the right word and not a curse.

To review: The Count was the younger Vlad's father but Antonia/Tsilia was not his mother. Despite the answer he gave me, he obviously knew his father was murdered. His sister Masha was murdered. Was Antonia/Tsilia Masha's mother? Was the Count her father? How did young Vlad know about my past? How did he know Katie was going to be alright? How did…

I quit asking myself questions. Questions I couldn't answer. Instead I went to the MacBook and loaded my breviary onto my new Galaxy phone. I opened Compline, Psalm 87: "O Lord God of my salvation, / I have cried in the day, and in the night before Thee. / O let my prayer enter into Thy presence, / incline Thine ear unto my calling; / For my soul is full of evils, / and my life draweth nigh unto hell. / I am counted as one of them that go down into the pit, / and I am even as a man that hath no strength, cast off among the dead. / Like unto them that are slain, and lie sleeping in the grave…"

Like Andrew. Like Thomas. Like Masha.

But not Ignatius. Not Angela. Not Charles-David. So I prayed for them. For the living. As fervently as I have ever prayed. I prayed for their souls. I prayed for their lives. Then I prayed for myself. I prayed for my soul.

Trembling. In fear. I prayed for my life.

St. Mathew, Fresco

Chapter Fifteen

O God, Thou art my God; / to Thee do I watch at break of day. / My soul hath thirsted for Thee, / my flesh also in many different ways. / In a barren and dry land where no water is: / so in the sanctuary have I come before Thee, that I might behold Thy power and Thy glory. / For Thy mercy is better than the life itself: / my lips shall praise Thee....

Lauds, Psalm 62, Feast of Saint Mathew, Apostle

The new day rose sunny. Offshore weather. A warm wind blew in from the desert. Rustling the magnolias. Bending the palms. Bringing some warmth to my heart. Until I checked my phone.

There were a dozen or so unanswered calls. Most from Milosz. One from Las Vegas. One from Kenny. I really didn't want to answer any of them, so I walked down to the ocean and sat in the soft sand. I looked out across the sea. Pelicans flew in formation. A pod of dolphins. A whale spout. Gulls drifted on thermals.

We were all glad just to be. And I, part of it.

By late morning, I had two more voice messages and three text messages from Milosz. I had to face him. But first I wanted to stop by Kenny's lifeguard hut. I approached from the side. He was there. Staring out at the ocean with his field glasses. I called up to him, "How's Katie?"

He lowered his Fujinons. Turned toward me. "She's home. Sleeping."

I walked up the ramp and stood in the doorway.

"Look, Father," he said, "I'm…"

"Ego te absolvo."

He grinned. That big wide Kenny smile. "Thanks. Doctor Brandon told me she's going to be okay. She doesn't remember much. Doesn't know what happened."

"Maybe that's best."

"Maybe so."

"Look, Kenny," I said, "Do you remember when Katie first went to work for Vlad Modeling?"

"Sure. I wasn't very happy about it."

"Why?"

"Well, you know…" he blushed, "but the money was fantastic. After the Bentzes moved here from Philadelphia, they were looking to hire people who had local contacts. Katie knows everyone. And she's very good with the books. You wouldn't think so. But she is. And she had nothing to do with the uh…the uh…modeling."

"From Philadelphia…?"

"The Bentzes? Yeah." He looked at me. "Hey, what's wrong, Father Pete?"

My chest seized up. I was dizzy. I grabbed the door frame and held tightly. Kenny rose from his chair and walked toward me. "Are you going to be sick, Father?"

I waved him off. "You did say…uhm, uh, you did say the Bentzes moved here from Philadelphia?"

"Yeah, so what?"

"Pennsylvania."

Kenny flashed a grin. "Unless there's another one." He studied my face again. "Why? What's the difference?"

Big difference. But I didn't care to explain that to Kenny.

"Is Katie going back to work?"

"Vlad fired her."

"He fired her?"

"Said he couldn't take the chance. Said she might have a relapse."

"A relapse?"

"Gave her a great severance package. A bundle of money and free health care for a year." He pulled down the neck of his red t-shirt. "And this necklace. A present for me." The gold double dragons.

"Don't wear that, Kenny!"

"Why not?"

"It's…it's evil."

"What are you talking about?"

"Don't wear it." I turned to leave.

"In the end, we're very lucky."

"Lucky? I don't think so."

"Are you alright?"

"No, I'm not alright."

I left him.

I had recovered from Kenny's revelations about the Bentzes sufficiently enough to make my way up the bluff by way of the sloping concrete ramp. Slowly. Stopping every few steps to hold on to the railing and catch my breath. I shuffled north along Esplanade toward city hall. I felt like a very sick senior citizen. Looked like one too. Bent over. Muttering to myself.

Sergeant Milosz was shocked when he saw me. I sat in his office and did my best to calm my nerves. The hockey sticks were gone. The baseball gloves and bats were back. Milosz leaned back in his chair and waited for me to speak.

I mumbled: "Did you know that the Bentzes…" I took

another deep breath to steady myself, "the Bentzes came here from Philadelphia."

"Of course I know that. But they had no criminal record there. No arrests. Not even a traffic ticket."

"Philadelphia, Stan."

"Yes. I know. So what, Pete?"

"Father Thomas was an exorcist in Philadelphia. Lilith lives in Philadelphia."

"You're not making any sense, Paderewski. Who's Lilith?"

I continued my deep breathing. I collected my thoughts. I took my chances. "Stan. You once said you believe in devils. In evil."

He nodded.

"Well, Father Thomas was an exorcist in the Philadelphia diocese some thirty-five years ago. At that time, Cardinal Krol asked Father Thomas to exorcise a powerful devil who had taken over the soul of a young woman named Caroline Van Kirk, the daughter of a prominent Philadelphia family. Father Thomas agreed to perform the exorcism.

"After a long and arduous series of confrontations, the devil was supposedly cast out from the young woman who was then able to resume a normal life. The Cardinal believed it. Her parents believed it. Father Thomas did not believe it.

"He believed a devil had not really been cast out. He was convinced that an evil spirit burrowed deeper into the poor girl's soul in order to wreck future havoc. A few months later her parents were killed in a fiery car crash. Caroline survived."

"But what's this have to do with us?"

"Bear with me. Father Thomas petitioned his province to live out his retirement in Southern California. For some reason, perhaps guilt over his failure, perhaps because he was in a perpetual, personal dual with this particular devil, Thomas stayed in contact with Caroline who eventually called herself Lilith. One of the ancient names for the wife of Satan.

"At some point the elder Vlad Bentz split with Lilith and he also moved with his son, the young Vlad, to California. I believe they went into business with Antonia Lucia Belladone, who then apparently gave birth to a child, Masha Bentz. If true, then the Count was her father. At some point Antonia Lucia marries him and changes her name to Tsilia Bentz. You with me?"

"I think so."

"Twenty years later, a baby shows up on our house's doorstep. The Count's daughter, Masha Bentz, is murdered. Is Masha Iggy's birth mother? Do you have DNA results yet?"

"The lab says it will be at least another two weeks. Around Easter."

"Well, I'm sure the DNA will show Ignatius is Masha's son, therefore the grandson of Count Vlad Bentz."

"Then maybe this Lilith woman is his grandmother?"

"Maybe…Yes. That's possible. Likely, actually. Now that I know about Philadelphia, that makes sense.

"Anyway, Father Thomas dies. Lilith shows up at his funeral. She says she wants to honor Father Thomas. She pays for his internment in the cathedral. But she seems most interested in Ignatius…and me.

"Then Andrew and Angela try to escape to Canada with Ignatius. Their van breaks down in Vegas and Andrew is murdered. Brutally. Gangland style. Russian Mafia style."

"Where do the devils come in?"

"Maybe not at all. Maybe this is just the story about a

twisted family inundated with criminal intrigue and mental illness."

"What do you think?"

"My rational mind, my legal training, my Jesuitical prejudices all lean toward the twisted family theory. But there are other…uh…hmmm…details I've not told you."

That's when I finally shared with Sergeant Milosz details about the cooper's hawks, the weird phone messages, alterations in my painting, my dreams, my conversation with Katie before she mysteriously collapsed. When I finished, Milosz was visibly shaken.

"So," I said, "what do you think about my stories?"

"They could just be products of your imagination under terrible stress."

"Yes. Of course. No question."

"Or…" Sergeant Milosz slumped back in his chair. He became uncharacteristically pensive. "Now I'm going to tell you a story. You've asked me why I'm bitter about God. The boy I told you about. The boy who was molested. The boy I coached, that beautiful child…" his lips quivered. He fought against it. He began to cry.

"That angel was my first son. The priest…the monster who molested him…who violently, heartlessly, molested him, expressed no remorse. He was cold. He was calculating. He was evil. Evil through and through. A devil? Possessed by the devil? A twisted, sick monster mind? What's the difference, Father? Really, what's the difference?

"I arrested him. I reported his abuses to Cardinal Mahoney's office." His tears dried up. His voice was dry, flat. "The diocese took his case 'under advisement.' I spoke to numerous canon lawyers and one civil attorney. They all assured me that the offending priest was being dealt with. I talked to the DA. I pressed for a criminal indictment. I threatened to go to the Times. But...all this happened before the highly publicized scandals changed how these cases are handled.

"The allegations were covered up. The priest was sent out of the country. One month later, my angel..." his tears were again flowing down his cheeks, "was hit in the head by a carelessly thrown baseball bat. A terrible accident. One in a million chance the doctors said. Hit him in exactly the right spot. A tragedy. A tragedy..." His voice broke. Then he pulled himself together. "It was no accident. Somehow that devil priest made the 'accident' happen. I am sure of it.

"Anyway, I waited six months. Then I took a trip. To Mexico. To the small village where this priest was molesting more young boys." Milosz looked me directly in the eye. "I found him. He will never molest another child, Paderewski. Never. Except in hell."

We were both silent for a few minutes. I was shocked, but did my best to hide it. Milosz didn't need my censure. He needed closure. Finally I said: "I will assume I've heard your confession, Stan. I can offer absolution if you make a serious statement of contrition."

"Fuck your absolution, Pete! Fuck contrition. I enjoyed watching him suffer. I enjoyed the startled look on his face. I don't give a shit about God anymore. I don't give a shit about the Church. God doesn't care about us. God doesn't protect us. It's all bullshit."

I was helpless before his onslaught. Helpless. I couldn't think of anything to say. Dealing with my own pain. Dealing with my own fear. I was even tempted to meld with his despair. Instead, I left him in his office. Alone.

I acted, again, like a bad priest. While I do believe only love can save us from our darkness, as I walked home, I did not feel God's love. I could not talk to Him. He was not there. Not in my heart. Desperate, I took out my phone and tried to read from my breviary. I could not say the words. I could not pray.

It was only when I entered our house on Dolorita that love pulled me back from the abyss. Charles-David was cooking. Still not drinking. He was entertaining Angela with stories about the boys at St. Aloysius Country Day. In French. Laughing. Not angry. Not feeling sorry for himself.

Angela was sitting at the old Formica-topped, rusted chrome kitchen table. She was also laughing. Smiling. Chatting. Happy. Perfect.

Ignatius was asleep. Swaddled in his Moses basket. Peaceful. Content. Protected by a man and a woman who cared for him. And in their caring, they loved him. He was loved. And I loved him, but I couldn't care for him. I was afraid. Afraid I wasn't protecting him.

I was the outsider. In my black mood. I was the intruder. I slumped down on a chair near Angela. She looked at me. "What happened?"

"I'm very tired."

"You're more than tired."

I didn't answer her. The room was silent. I was draining away all their good feelings. Then Angela lifted Ignatius out of his basket and placed him in my arms. I shook my head. But she left him on my lap and walked back to her chair.

I stared at Ignatius. He opened his eyes and stared back at me. I smiled. He smiled. I felt the tears welling up in my eyes. I didn't want him to see me crying. I tried to laugh instead, but the tears came anyway.

I lifted him onto my shoulder. He fit inside my hand spread across his back. I pressed him against my body. Gently. I slowly rocked back and forth on my chair. Weeping. Snot ran from my nose. I needed to do something.

Suddenly, through my tears, I started humming. A song from long ago. Brahms. The lullaby my mother sang to me. My tears stopped. I could breath. From a distant memory, the words came:

> Lullaby and good night, thy mother's delight.
>
> Bright angels beside my darling abide.
>
> They will guard thee at rest,
>
> thou shalt wake on my breast
>
> They will guard thee at rest,
>
> thou shalt wake on my breast.

I felt much better, but then I looked at Angela, and she was crying. Charles-David turned away from the stove and there were tears in his eyes as well. But I realized all of our tears were tears of joy. Tears of hope. Tears of love.

I continued to rock Iggy until I could feel his regular measured breathing on my neck. Then I laid him down in his basket. And went upstairs to my room.

When I saw my empty easel, the urge to paint was overwhelming. I even removed a canvas and my box of oils from the closet. Then I remembered my Lenten vow. No painting. Could further deprivation actually enrich an already deprived soul? Whatever. It was my vow. I would keep it.

I went to my MacBook instead. Tried to find new clues to where Antonia/Tsilia could possibly be.

I remembered she used to tell me about a family vacation cabin in the mountains. When she was a little girl. Running through the woods. With her dog. But where? Which mountains? I couldn't remember. I Googled maps of the areas surrounding the Los Angeles basin. No towns or villages or areas triggered any memories in me.

I tried a different idea. I had read that it's very easy to get birth records on-line. I tried doing so, and it was easy. In no time, I had records for Masha Bentz and the younger Vlad Bentz.

I discovered that, just as I suspected, young Vlad was born in Philadelphia. His full name was Vladimir Abaddon Bentz. His parents were listed as Vladimir Apollyon Bentz and Caroline Lilith Van Kirk. Suddenly I remembered why I treasure the internet. One mystery was easily solved.

Wow. So, Lilith *was* Val's mother.

Finding the murdered Masha Bentz's records was a little trickier. Just in case my hunches were incorrect, I searched Pennsylvania birth records, but I didn't find any match.

I searched California. Still no match. For the moment, I was stymied. Could Masha have also had another name? I Googled Masha and found that Masha is a diminutive for Maria. Quickly checked Pennsylvania. Pennsylvania had no Maria Bentz. But California did.

I found out that Maria Hecate Bentz, Masha, was born in Idyllwild, California. Her mother was listed as Tsilia Lucia Bentz. Not Lilith.

I was right. Lilith was not Masha's mother.

Lilith was one of Iggy's grandmothers, but Antonia/Tsilia was also Iggy's grandmother. Masha's father was listed as Vladimir Abaddon Bentz. So, although my head was spinning, the relationships were clear.

The younger Val and Masha were half brother and sister.

Same father. Different mothers.

I decided I'd done enough work for the evening. I was very tired, but just as I was getting ready to shut down my computer, another thought occurred to me. Masha Bentz was born in Idyllwild, California. Where was Idyllwild?

I Googled Idyllwild. A hamlet in the San Jacinto Mountains in Riverside County. Well, I wasn't so tired anymore. I searched the property records for Riverside County. There it was. A property in the mountains. Owned by Antonia Lucia Belladone. That's where she was. I was certain of it.

After that discovery, I finally went to bed. Restless. Tossed and turned. Around 2:00, I heard a soft knock on my door. Then the handle turned, and the door opened. Very, very slowly. To be honest, given recent events, I was terrified.

Then I saw, in the silver light shining through my bay windows, Angela. She was carrying the Moses basket. She placed the basket on the floor next to my bed. I looked inside the basket, and there was Little Iggy. On his back. Swaddled in his soft blue blanket decorated with smiling yellow teddy bears.

I could barely hear his gentle breathing. I rested my hand on his blanket. I could hardly feel his chest moving. In the darkness I could scarcely see his handsome little face relaxed in sweet, silent sleep.

Then I heard a rustling sound. It wasn't Ignatius. I looked up from the basket toward Angela.

She removed her nightgown and stood naked in the moonlight. She knew I was watching her. She wanted me to watch her. She ran her fingers through her thick dark curls. She cupped her milk-swollen breasts. She ran her palms down across her taut tummy. Her fingernails down her long powerful thighs. She raised herself up onto her tiptoes and spread her arms in a greeting to the moon.

Then she crawled into bed next to me. She touched me, but I was already hard. She knelt over me and spread her legs. She pulled me up inside her. She rocked gently at first. Then she felt my excitement. She was nourished by my passion. We were sustained by our rhythm. And then we both came in a shuddering, climactic orgasm.

Angela slept like a baby, and the baby slept in his basket next to us. But I could not sleep. I did not need my phone to recall the lines from Solomon's Song of Songs:

> You have stolen my heart, my sister, my bride;
> you have stolen my heart
> with one glance of your eyes,
> with one jewel of your necklace.

> How delightful is your love, my sister, my bride!
> How much more pleasing is your love than wine,
> and the fragrance of your perfume
> more than any spice!

> Your lips drop sweetness
> as the honeycomb, my bride;
> milk and honey are under your tongue.
> The fragrance of your garments is like
> the fragrance of Lebanon.

> You are a garden locked up, my sister, my bride;
> you are a spring enclosed, a sealed fountain…

I remained sleepless. From the ecstasy. From the torture.

Forbidden love.

St. Gabriel of the Sorrowful Virgin, Fresco

Chapter Sixteen

He hath sent from heaven, and delivered me: / He hath made them a reproach that trod upon me. / God hath sent forth his mercy and truth: / and He hath delivered my soul from the midst of the young lions; / in confusion did I sleep.
Sext, Psalm 56, Feast of Saint Gabriel of the Sorrowful Virgin, Confessor

For three days, 72 brief hours, Angela, Ignatius and I pantomimed a post-modern vision of the Holy Family. During the day, I was the older, gray haired, protective Joseph. Angela the devoted, loving virgin mother. Ignatius the preternaturally calm, spiritual and wise baby. Our nights were filled with the quiet, intense passion Angela and I had denied ourselves for a very long time.

Meanwhile, I met with Milosz and shared my internet investigations about the Bentz family and where I thought Antonia/Tsilia was hiding.

"Why does she need to hide?" he asked.

"I don't really know," I answered. "She must be afraid. She must have some information. She might know about the murders."

"Could she be the killer?"

"No."

"What makes you so sure, Pete?"

"I told you. We were once very close, Sergeant."

"And because you had an affair with her, you know she's not a killer?"

"Yes."

"Do you know how many spouses of murderers swear they had no idea their lover could possible have killed another human being?"

"Antonia Belladone is seductress. She loves everyone, men and women. She is not a killer."

"She's not Antonia anymore. She's Tsilia now. What about Tsilia Bentz?"

I started to repeat my assertion of Antonia's innocence, then I stopped myself. "I have to admit, I don't know. I don't believe someone could change that much."

"You should have spent more time in the confessional, Father. You obviously know very little about the depths of the human soul."

"There's one way we can find out. I can go out to Idyllwild and talk to her."

"That might be dangerous, Paderewski. I'll call the Riverside County police. Let's have them check out the property. Bring her in for questioning."

"She won't talk to the police. She was a runaway for many years. Back when she was a teenager. She doesn't trust cops."

"But she trusts you?"

"Yes. She'll talk to me. I'm sure she will."

"Then why do you seem so nervous?"

I became aware my foot was tapping the floor and I was gnawing on my right thumbnail. "I'm not sure I want to talk to her."

He laughed. "You still got the itch?"

"No. She destroyed my life."

Milosz hesitated. "Okay. I'll go with you."

"I told you she won't talk to cops."

"I'll stay in the car," he said somewhat facetiously.

We decided to leave early the next morning. I didn't tell Angela where I was going. Or why. I did tell Charles-David, but I made him swear not to share that information with Angela. I also asked him to keep a close watch on Ignatius. Against my better judgment, I even told him about Andrew's pistol in my desk. He was horrified by my suggestion he might need it.

When I walked out the door to meet Milosz, the cooper's hawks were gliding back and forth from the towering eucalyptus tree in the back of the house to the magnolia in front. The two young males were rousting about, nipping at each other's tail feathers.

I opened the door to Milosz's Crown Vic. Just then a large older male in the magnolia started whistling. A warning?

I asked Milosz to roll down his window and listen to the birds. He did, but he didn't think there was anything unusual about their behavior. "They're roosting all over the city. Chasing away the crows. Doing battle with the gulls. Pushing out the starlings. They leave the songbirds alone. I like hawks. They manage the riff-raff."

"Sort of like cops?"

"You might say that."

Milosz drove out the 91 Freeway through endless suburban sprawl toward Corona, but then, instead of taking the 15 toward Las Vegas, we stayed on the 91 until it became the 60 as we entered the Moreno Valley—a surprisingly green, agricultural area irrigated by water stolen from somewhere.

The Moreno is a valley of giants. Giant SUVs. Giant pick-up trucks. We stopped for gas at a 76 station near Lake Perris. Giant blond, blue-eyed men and women all over 6 feet, all over 200 pounds, trailing giant blond, blue-eyed children through shuffling groups of tiny, brown skinned agricultural workers milling about looking for a chance to work.

The 60 begat the 79, the Ramona Expressway, which then begat the 74, the Idyllwild National Forest Highway which rose from the valley floor into the San Jacinto Mountains.

The 74 was a tortuous, twisting mountain highway difficult for the Crown Vic—a street automobile, an expressway ride unsuited for the mountains. Milosz kept the car on the road although I was certain we were going over the edge and down the mountain at least three separate times.

As we climbed above 5,000 feet, we arrived in the village of Idyllwild, nestled in the forest between Tahquitz Peak and Suicide Rock. The property I found on Google was another 1,000 feet up from the village, near the end of dusty, unpaved Grinding Slab Road, tucked in among the ancient ponderosa pines and dry hills shadowed by the 10,000 foot San Jacinto Peak.

We parked the Crown Vic as far off the dirt and gravel as possible. Milosz exited the car with me.

"No," I said. "She won't talk to you."

"Don't be stupid, Pete. You might need protection."

"You can't protect me from her power over me."

"I'm coming with you, Pete."

I shrugged. "Suite yourself."

We carefully climbed a switch back stairway that clearly suffered from years of neglect and dry rot.

At the top of the stairs, the property flattened out into a natural basin eroded away from the steep hillside hundreds, maybe thousands of years earlier. There was a wood frame house and several outbuildings.

All the buildings had seen better days. Two of the smaller outbuildings had caved in roofs and broken windows. The main house was weatherbeaten, the cedar siding turned slate gray or even black in those areas where the elements created the greatest damage. The front porch railing was falling away and the floorboards were dangerously cracked and broken.

"Doesn't look like anyone lives here," said Milosz.

I let his voice fade away into the eerie, overwhelming silence. We truly were in the middle of nowhere. "She's here," I said.

"Don't think so," he said but he was wrong.

As I spoke, the front door opened. There she was. "Peter," she said.

"Antonia."

She looked miserable. Nothing like the Antonia I remembered. Dangerously thin. Her thick black hair gone white. Eyes sunken deep into her sockets. Her sockets surrounded by black, sagging bags. Dry skin. Open sores on her lower arms. She was wearing a dirty, thin K Mart, faded yellow cotton shift. Barefoot. Leaning against the door jam. A Dorothea Lange photo from the Depression era.

I couldn't hide my shock. She noticed and started to laugh hysterically. She quickly wiped away her tears with the back of her hand.

"Hey, who's the cop, Peter?"

Milosz joined me at the door and introduced himself. "Sergeant Stanley Milosz, Riviera Beach police." He extended his hand. She didn't take it.

"I don't talk to cops."

"I told him you wouldn't."

She sighed. "Oh well, what's the difference now." Never

entirely predictable.

She turned and walked back into the house. We followed her.

The interior was sparsely furnished. Two Belden Idyllwild Pinecraft chairs and a picnic table. The stone facing above the large old fireplace was blackened with soot. The worn white café curtains were torn and turning beige from the dust. Dirty dishes were piled in the sink. There was a sleeping bag and a light blue striped pillow with no pillowcase on the bare floor near the fireplace.

Antonia told Milosz and I to sit in the chairs. She leaned her back against the table. "I knew someone would find me. Eventually. I didn't think it would be you."

"I remembered you telling me stories about the mountains," I said.

"You remembered me?"

"Of course."

We were all silent for a while. I kept staring at her. Searching her cabin with my eyes. Then staring at her again. "What happened, Antonia?"

"I fell into the bottomless pit, and God was not by my side to rescue me."

"Oh, Antonia…"

She held up her right hand and waved it, palm out, in front of me. "Don't…don't, Peter. Don't declare how much you care. Above all, don't pity me. You had your chance. You left me alone. To the devils. To the demons."

"I…"

"Yeah, sure. You were a priest. You had vows. You made a mistake. A big mistake. Blah, blah, blah."

"I also paid a price. A high price."

"Good."

Before our bitterness could develop any further, Milosz spoke to her. "Was Masha Bentz your daughter?"

"Yes."

"You know she's dead?"

"Yes."

"Do you know she was murdered?"

"Yes."

"You didn't want to contact us? You didn't want to claim her body? You didn't want to bury her?"

"No. No. And no." She stopped leaning against the table and began pacing back and forth. "She was dead to me two years ago. I tried to hold on to her. I tried to protect her. It didn't work. She wanted to be like me. She wanted Satan. And all his works."

I shook my head. What was Antonia talking about?

Milosz asked, "Masha wanted Satan?"

"Yes. And she got what she wanted."

"Don't you want to know who killed your daughter?"

"I know who killed my daughter."

"Who?"

"Satan."

"Angela," I said, "you're talking nonsense."

She whirled around. "Oh…really? Am I, Peter?"

Milosz spoke softly, but clearly. "Ms. Bentz, what do you mean when you tell us that Satan killed your daughter?"

She raised an eyebrow. A crooked smile. "You're the policeman, you figure it out."

"Help me to do that. For your daughter's sake. Please, Ms. Bentz."

"Don't call me that."

Milosz was patient. "Antonia?"

"Lucia. I am neither Antonia nor Tsilia. I am Lucia."

"After St. Lucia, Virgin Martyr?" I offered facetiously.

She produced a mischievous smile. "Hardly." She returned to leaning against the old picnic table. "No. Lucia. The Light Bearer. Concubine of He who was the original Light Bearer.

I was angry with myself. Disappointed. How could I have once given up so much for an affair with this demented woman? It hardly seemed possible. Even if it was a long time ago. Even if I was…

"Much younger?"

Could she read my thoughts?

"I know what you're thinking, Peter. We were much younger then."

"You've changed."

"You haven't. Still uptight. Boring. A believer." She snorted. "God is dead, Peter. Didn't you get the message?"

Milosz wanted one more chance. "Who killed Masha, Lucia? Was it you?"

"We might all be better off if I had. But I didn't."

"Did you know she was pregnant?" asked Milosz.

His question shook Antonia. "Pregnant?"

"Yes."

"Pregnant…oh, my God, no." She slumped down onto her knees. Her voice rose in pitch and volume. "So they killed the baby? They killed my grandchild?"

"No," I said. "The baby's alive."

She stopped. "But how…"

Milosz said, "She had the baby before she died. Then she abandoned him on Father Paderewski's doorstep."

She stared at the backs of her hands. "Him. A boy?" She

started to cry. "A little boy. Imagine." She looked directly into my eyes. "Left on your doorstep? Is it true, Peter?"

"Yes, Antonia. It's true."

Her voice lowered. Her speech grew slower, slurred, dreamy. "Yes, of course. That's what they wanted. A boy. They wanted a baby boy." She began to stare at her hands again. Rotating them. Wiggling her fingers.

"Who are they?" urged Milosz, "Who wanted a baby boy?"

But Antonia ignored him. "And I will never get to see him." The pain in her voice was real.

"You can see him," I said. "You can come with us. Back to Riviera Beach."

"No…no I can't, Peter." She curled up on the floor into the fetal position. "I made…arrangements. For when I was found. Now I've been found. This is the end." She was whimpering. "You found me. You lost me. Now you've found me again and you will lose me again."

I stood up and then knelt next to her. I touched her on the shoulder. She shrank away from my touch and screamed, "Get away from me, Priest! Get away!" I looked toward Milosz. He shrugged his shoulders as if to say, what can we do?

I stayed on the floor next to her and prayed for her. In my own words. I prayed for Him to forgive me for what I had done. I prayed for Him to forgive her for everything she had ever done. Her whimpering turned into inconsolable weeping. As I made the sign of the cross, in the air, in Latin, *"In nomine Patris et Filii et Spiritus Sancti…"* She looked at me from a very dark, dark place deep inside her, a place so lost I could not fathom her fear. She whispered, "I'm sorry, Peter. I'm really sorry. I loved her." She stared at me with pleading eyes. "I loved you."

I couldn't deal with that. I muttered without really thinking, *"Ego te absolve…"*

"It's too late," she wept. "It's too late."

I felt Milosz' hand on my shoulder. "It's time to go, Peter."

I stood up. "We can't just leave her like this."

"I'll radio the Riverside County police from my car."

"But…"

"There's nothing more we can do for her right now. She needs to be in a hospital."

"I need…"

"You need to get out of here. Questions will be asked."

We slowly made our way back down the stairway and sat in his car. Milosz tried his radio, but he couldn't get a clear signal. He backed out onto Grinding Slab Road, barely avoiding a steep drop off and two ancient towering pines.

Just as we moved forward, there was an enormous earthquake. Except it wasn't an earthquake. A jagged flaming beam fell from the sky right next to the Crown Vic. Smaller smoldering shingles landed on our roof and the windshield. Thick black smoke rose from the hillside above us. I tried to open my door, but Milosz set the locks before I could lift the handle. He spun the rear tires as he roared down the mountain toward the village.

"I have to go to her," I shouted.

"She's dead, Pete. Don't you get it? She's dead. Now let's get the firemen up here before the whole area bursts into flames and even more people die."

Luckily, the forest was not so dry that early in the spring. The Idyllwild Fire Department and the Pine Cove Volunteer Fire Department with help from the Riverside County Fire Department's Bell 205 water dumping helicopters were able to stop the flames before they spread more than a couple hundred yards beyond Antonia's property.

We hung around Idyllwild while Milosz explained to the locals that he had just finished questioning Tsilia Bentz in connection with a murder in Riviera Beach when her house exploded.

They weren't very happy that he hadn't checked in with them beforehand, but their hands were full dealing with the fire emergency.

Near dusk they brought Antonia's charred and mangled body, collected in a First Call, black, medium-duty human remains bag, into the parking lot behind the police station where I saw her, or parts of her, for the last time. For what it was worth, I recited a silent prayer over the bag. Her remains were then transferred to a Riverside County Mortuary van for delivery to the Coroner's Office.

I didn't talk much on the way back to Riviera Beach. I was devastated. My mind was focused on Antonia's accusations that I had thrown her to the devils. That I had an affair with her and then abandoned her. That I was responsible for what happened to her.

Was that why, many years later and out of the blue, she sent her incriminating letter to the provost at Edmund Campion? Was that why she tried to destroy me? Did I deserve to be destroyed?

I was already in my mid-forties when we first met. Years spent in the novitiate, then as a scholastic, then ordination and eventually my PhD. She was an executive assistant in the Dean's office. We talked occasionally. One day we ate lunch together. Then lunch another day. She knew I painted. She asked me about impressionism, expressionism, cubism, Monet, Chagall, Picasso. She asked me to take her to the LA County Museum of Art. She made me feel smart. Accomplished. Then she told me she was given tickets to the LA Opera's production of Faust. Would I go with her?

After the opera: What did I think of the Dr. Faust character? The devil, Méphistophélès? The beautiful young Marguerite? Did I believe in devils? Would Faust really abandon a life of scholarship for a young woman? Why was Méphistophélès so intent on Faust's soul? On destroying Marguerite? Would I like to come upstairs to her place to have coffee and talk some more?

Our affair lasted only three weeks. I was in love with her, but I wanted to stay a priest. What had she wanted? I was ashamed to admit I never really thought about what she wanted. Or needed. Not only a bad priest, but a bad man.

Of course, those memories also made me think about what was happening with Angela. Was I repeating the same pattern? Was I a serial molester? A serial idiot? A serial loser? Or simply the bad priest I knew myself to be. A shameful priest.

Milosz interrupted my thoughts. "So, what are we going to do now, Pete?"

I smiled, "We?"

"I'd say we've become a team, like it or not."

"Thanks." I was at a loss, so I threw the question back at him, "What do you think we should do?"

"I guess we need to go after the last man standing."

"Young Vlad."

"We've no one else." A beat, then he added, "Unless you want to go after the devils."

"They may be one and the same."

"Perhaps, but the problem is, we don't have evidence against Vlad. I can't pressure him." He thought for a moment. "What about Katie Johansson? Would she talk about Vlad Modeling?"

"That's not fair to her."

"No. It's not. But we can ask her anyway. Tell her what's going on. Let her decide."

"I don't like it."

It was late when Milosz dropped me off on Dolorita in front of our house. The place was dark. Everyone was asleep. I crawled into bed. I prayed for the strength to stop with Angela if she came to my room that night. She didn't.

For once my prayers were answered.

Sts. Perpetua and Felicity, Fresco

Chapter Seventeen

God is our hope and strength, / a very present help in trouble, which hath found us exceedingly. / Therefore will we not fear, though the earth be moved, / and though the hills be carried into the midst of the sea; / the waters thereof rage and swell, / and though the mountains shake at the strength of the same.

Matins, Psalm 45, Feast of Saints Perpetua and Felicity, Martyrs

Over the next few days, Milosz and I set out to build a case against Vlad Bentz. Milosz spoke with the DA and checked the FBI database again. No luck. I searched the internet for any links that might reveal other connections to Vlad Modeling. No luck. Worse. Bentz had removed the website and scrubbed any references to Vlad Modeling in San Pedro.

There was a link to a site for a young Romanian guy who was trying to create a modeling career in London. And a link to a site called the "Dark Tube" which featured underage girls, but the site was registered and hosted in Russia. Even if that filth was connected to Vlad Bentz, there was no hope of making a legal case. Bentz knew how to cover his tracks. Or intimidate anyone who would try to hurt him. If we were to find Bentz's weakness, it would have to be through Katie.

But I didn't want to use Katie to get Bentz. She might point us to irregularities that would at least get Milosz a warrant, but she'd already suffered enough. She didn't deserve any more pain.

Actually, she didn't deserve what she suffered the first time.

She was a good kid. Not altogether innocent, true. But not guilty of any evil either. Who would condemn an American girl for trying to earn the most money possible? No one. Making money was our national pastime. Even God was all about money. TV preachers. Mega-churches. The diocese of Los Angeles for that matter. Maybe the Jesuits, despite our vow of poverty. Life in these times is all about money everywhere.

So, yes, it had to be Katie. There was no other way.

Milosz and I went to see her at her house she shared with Kenny. Their place sat on a hill overlooking El Reclusión Park in Riviera Beach. Kenny remodeled their dated, post-war, two-bedroom bungalow into a charming contemporary. Light Charcoal paint. Plantation shutters. Natural Black Slate fieldstone. We sat on the weathered teak chairs around the teak table on her back patio.

We watched the children playing on the blue and yellow Miracle Playground in the park. A tree house. Two slides. Rock climbing wall. Monkey bars. Children running and screaming and laughing. Shrieks of delight. We could not have arranged a better background for our argument that any help she could give us might save a baby boy's life.

After we told her what we needed, she said, "I'd like to help, but I can't."

"I understand," I said. She was such a beautiful, sweet girl. Kenny was a good guy. They didn't need more trouble.

Milosz was not so agreeable. "Of course you can, Ms. Johansson. Bentz doesn't have to know where the information came from."

"No," she said, "you both don't understand."

"What's not to understand?" asked Milosz.

"Accounting wise, tax wise, from the bookkeeping, I can't think of anything Vlad did that wasn't totally above board. He insisted on it. His records are totally clear and legal. Totally."

"But you knew what was going on with the 'models'," I said.

She blushed. "Well, sometimes, yes. What the models may have negotiated individually was not Val's concern. All company business was recorded as 'modeling sessions.' And the actual amounts were entered into the logs. And taxes were paid. Even Social Security and Workmen's Compensation. There was no cheating."

"An unfortunate phrase," I remarked.

Katie blushed again. "You know what I mean."

Milosz hesitated a moment. He looked at me. Raised his eyebrows. I shrugged. I didn't know where he wanted to go. "Ms. Johansson, did you ever see anything, or observe anything that hinted at Satanism?"

The question actually made Katie laugh. "You're kidding?"

"Devil worship, animal sacrifice, blood rituals, the supernatural."

Still in a jocular mood, Katie said, "I know what Satanism is, Sergeant. I just can't think of a man less Satanic than Vlad Bentz."

I didn't agree with her assessment. I felt I needed to tell her. "I went to see Bentz while you were still in a coma, Katie. He told me we could 'have you back' and he predicted your recovery before you were recovering."

"That's creepy."

"Yes," I said, "it was."

"I mean that you went to talk to him while I was…while I was sick."

205

Embarrassed, I ignored her concern. I tried to focus on Ignatius. "There's a beautiful little baby that may be in danger from Vlad Bentz. We need something to stop him. Anything that may occur to you."

She sat silently. She watched the children playing in the park. She frowned. "There was one thing. Not illegal but odd. We would occasionally receive large wire transfers from something called Van Kirk Enterprises, a business in Philadelphia.

"I asked Val about the company. He indicated that Van Kirk Enterprises was a major investor in Val Modeling, and I should treat the money as an investment. Which I did."

"How large?" asked Milosz.

"Six figures. Sometimes close to a million."

"Hmmm," muttered Milosz. "Money laundering?"

"I really don't know. But not from our end."

"Did Val Modeling make that kind of money?"

"From the modeling itself, no. But we owned a huge website business, Val Digital. Very lucrative."

"Let me see if I can work something from that angle," Milosz said.

"The website wasn't illegal."

"Probably not. But at least it's a shot."

We left Katie on her patio. Back in the car, Milosz asked me what I made of "…this Van Kirk business?"

I reminded him about why Lilith Van Kirk knew Father Thomas in the first place.

"Looks like we may have a devil problem after all, Pete?" That wasn't news I wanted to hear.

Meanwhile, back home, I was trying to sort things out with Angela.

I was still in shock over Antonia's suicide. I felt guilty. I was guilty. Then I lied to Angela. I told her I didn't want us to sleep together. I didn't tell her why. I was a coward. I said, "For awhile. Until we are sure Ignatius is safe." She was petulant, suspicious.

"Won't he be safer if he's with both of us?"

"I'm still close by."

"You don't want to be with me."

"That's not true. Maybe I want it too much."

"There you go, Peter. That's just such bullshit. Why do men think women will believe a line like 'I love you too much to be with you.' Bullshit. Bullshit."

"Okay, Angela. Okay."

"It's the scar isn't it? My scar. 'Marked for life,' my mother said. 'No man would ever love me,' my mother warned me."

"Your mother was wrong."

"Women have told me all my life. When I entered the convent, Mother Superior even told me the scar was a gift from God. That my disfigurement would ward off evil and keep me safe. 'The devil doesn't want damaged goods,' she told me. 'He only sets out to destroy what is beautiful.'"

"That was a horrible thing for her to say."

"She was a horrible woman."

"Angela, it's not about you, it's…"

"…all about you? All about your problems. *Criss de tabarnak*, don't speak that second biggest bullshit line."

"What do you want me to say?"

"That I'm ugly. That you don't want me."

"That's not true."

"*Merde*! You're so full of it, Peter Paderewski." We could hear Ignatius crying out from his basket in the kitchen. "Why can't you just be a man and take responsibility for the things you do?" She stormed out of the room, and went off to care for Iggy.

I might as well have told her the truth.

I headed for the stairs and ran into Charles-David on the landing. He shook his head when he saw me. "Why don't you admit you're in love with her?"

I was taken aback.

"Yes. Remember, I have antennae for matters of the heart."

"I remember."

"You two have been circling each other long before Ignatius came into our lives."

"No. That's not true."

"It is true."

"I never even considered…"

"I don't know why you insist on being a priest, Peter."

"That's perverse coming from you, Charles-David."

"You love her. She loves you."

I was angry. "What does someone like you know about love?"

I meant to hurt him. I did. His eyes misted up. His chin quivered, but he stiffened his upper lip. *"Et tu, Brute?"*

I started up the stairs, then realized I didn't want to leave my cruelty hanging like that. I turned around to apologize, but he was gone.

In my room, I was shaking with guilt, remorse and anger. I needed to paint. Why adhere so strictly to Lenten vows when my life was falling apart? I had to put my feelings down on canvas. I had to do it. So I did. Another broken vow.

Madonna and Child. I needed to paint Angela and Ignatius.

From the very first time I saw Angela hold Iggy upright next to her face, I thought of the Murillo that hangs in Florence. The Pitti Palace. Not so much about the Christ child. Too old to be Ignatius, although even the newborn Iggy was squirming and twisting, grasping at life. It was the face of Murillo's Madonna. Round forehead and cheekbones tapering to a narrow chin. Cupid bow lips. Long neck. Sensuous.

But the Madonna's eyes made the portrait. Loving yet pained. Hopeful yet resigned. Intensely human. Tired. Sad. Proud. Angela.

I already had one canvas stretched. Gesso painted. I pulled it from the back of my closet. I did some triangulation sketching with a pig bristle brush. Burnt Sienna paint.

Start with Angela's face. Not looking toward Ignatius. No. Looking directly at me. I positioned Iggy below her chin at a roughly 60 degree angle, resting against her left breast. Asleep. Cradled by her left arm into her shoulder. Just roughed him in.

I couldn't decide what I wanted for Angela's body. I considered nude. I did. I sketched the familiar curves of her breasts and shoulders. Her waist. Her thighs when sitting. But then I left her body in vague outlines. Just to get the feel of her. Next to the feel of him.

I stepped back. The proportions felt right. The contours flowed gently, peacefully. I was impatient to work on her face. The other details didn't matter. Even Ignatius. I understood this was a painting about Angela's soul.

Of course, the problem was how to capture her beauty, her sensuousness, her intensity without focusing on her scar. Imperfections are difficult. They make a person accessible and yet they can become the focal point if painted with too much force. So I worked on her eyes.

Her eyes should draw the viewer's attention. They should tell her story. Dark Brown. Large pupils. Heavy lids. Periorbital puffiness. Step back. No. Too much.

Scrape with the pallet knife. Rub out with linseed oil. Try again. Not so heavy. Not so puffy. No. No. Now too flat. No character.

One more time. Remember how she looked the first time she held Ignatius in her arms. How she looked the first time she climbed into my bed and stared into my face. Remember. I stepped back. Yes. Those were the eyes I wanted. Yes.

The rest of her face came easily. I fleshed in the details with relaxed, practiced strokes. Conserving my energy for the test to come. I decided to drape her body with classical vestments. Details later. I worked briefly on Ignatius. Details later. Hours passed. I stepped back. Paced the room. I was loosing the light.

The scar. I needed to deal with the scar. I tried Cadmium red. Way too much orange. Only that color when she was angry. Mix in a touch of yellow ochre. No, that's not right either. I spent another half hour just trying to get the color. Couldn't do it. Then my natural light was gone. I failed. I needed to know more about the scar. I needed to understand what happened and what that experience did to Angela.

I opened all my windows to release the toxic fumes from the oils, the thinners. Cleaned my brushes. Slumped exhausted into my Baxton chair. Took out my Galaxy and tried to recite Vespers, Psalm 127: "Thy wife shall be as the fruitful vine / upon the walls of thine house; / Thy children like the olive-branches / round about thy table. / Lo, thus shall the man be blessed / that feareth the Lord."

I didn't read any further. I didn't need to meditate on those words. Their meaning was obvious. I made a decision. I rose from my chair, determined to go downstairs and tell Angela I loved Ignatius, I loved her and that we would all be together.

I started looking in the kitchen. Angela and Iggy weren't there. They weren't in the living room. Nor the dining room. Angela's room? No, they weren't there either. I was somewhat alarmed. They must be in with Charles-David. I knocked. No answer. I opened his door. No one there.

Alarm was turning to dread. Where? Out in back? No. It was fully dark. The small study in front? Probably not. Check anyway. And there they were. Completely quiet. And not alone.

Lilith. Couldn't be. It was.

I looked toward Angela. She was sitting on our discolored, faded gray corduroy sofa. She had silver duct tape across her mouth. Her eyes were frantic, but her head moved slowly left to right signaling I shouldn't be impulsive.

Ignatius was lying in his Moses basket next to her. He appeared to be okay. I next shifted to Charles-David whose mouth was also taped. He was struggling to release himself from plastic cable ties binding his wrists and ankles.

Lilith sat by herself in our tired Moroccan leather easy chair next to the Ikea Aröd reading lamp. "You might tell him to stop," she said indicating the shifting and squirming Charles-David. "It won't do any good and he might hurt himself."

"Lilith? Why?" was all I could think to say. She was wearing knee-high, soft black leather Valentino Ascot riding boots, denim hipster jodhpurs, a diamond white Armani silk blouse and Ray Ban Aviator mirror-lensed sunglasses. Indoors. At night. The absurdity almost outweighed the reality. The reality that we were clearly in big trouble.

"What the hell?" I said.

"Exactly," she said.

"What do you want?"

"You still don't know, Peter?" She gave a short laugh and shook her head in feigned amazement. "What a shame. And you, a Jesuit."

"Why don't you just tell me."

"It's so much more fun to see you confused. Overwhelmed. Impotent."

"This is ridiculous," I said as I moved toward Angela.

"Don't, Peter."

"What are you going to do? Hit me with your riding crop?" I reached down to remove the tape from Angela's mouth.

"Please step back, Father Paderewski." A male voice. I turned around. Val stepped out from the shadows. Gun in hand. He held a Seecamp LWS .32, California edition. Very small pistol. Very big impact. I raised my hands palms out. I stepped back.

"Okay," said Lilith. "We're going for a ride."

"Horseback?" I said, more bravely than I felt.

Lilith just stared at me. "How droll. I underestimated your sense of humor, Peter."

Val was growing impatient with our banter. "Get up, Angela. And bring Ignatius. Not in your arms. In his basket. Paderewski, turn around and leave the room slowly, very slowly." As I started to turn, Charles-David tried to stand upright. Val pushed him back onto his chair. "You stay put, you fat sloppy faggot."

Lilith gently reprimanded him. "Now, now darling."

Val stood next to Charles-David and placed the barrel of his weapon against the quaking priest's temple. "We have no use for this one, *Матушка*." He chambered a round and released the safety. I saw urine run down Charles-David's pant leg and a terrible stench filled the small room. Charles-David shat himself.

Val laughed heartily and pinched his nose to mock Charles-David. "Peee-uuu. Phew."

Lilith actually giggled like a little girl. Then she turned back toward us. "Come on you three." Three. Not Charles-David.

Val didn't kill Charles-David after all. He merely warned him not to talk to the police or terrible things would happen to Ignatius. Left Charles-David humiliated. Weeping softly.

The rest of us climbed into a black Chevy Suburban parked in the driveway. There was a baby car seat already in place. Facing backwards. Next to the window.

Lilith didn't blindfold Angela nor did she bind Angela's wrists. She told Angela she wanted her to be free to take care of the baby. She did tie Angela's ankles.

Then she cable tied my wrists and ankles, placed a black bag over my head and made me lie down on the third row seat. Then she jumped in front with Val. We backed out onto Dolorita, and then turned onto the Pacific Coast Highway.

Heading south. I tried to keep track of where we might be going. Sounds. Turns. Vehicles. But after ten, fifteen minutes all the stimuli were one big blur.

As it turned out, I needn't have worked so hard. We unloaded in the driveway behind a warehouse. It was Antonia's old warehouse in Lomita. I recognized it immediately when they removed my hood.

They put Angela and Ignatius in the office area where they had added a bed, two straight-backed chairs and a collapsible card table.

They put me in the garage from which they had removed all the studio equipment and added nothing. I spent the night trussed up. Still in ties. Alone on the cold cement floor.

In the morning, Lilith cut the ties. I was in terrible pain. I was free but I couldn't move. Small stretches. Gradual stretching. Eventually I could stand up. They let me go to the bathroom. Then I was allowed to join Angela and Ignatius in the office where we were served Trader Joe's Instant Oatmeal and Starbuck's coffee. It could have been worse.

Lilith was finally forthcoming. "We want the baby. We want the boy you've misnamed Ignatius."

Angela lifted Iggy out of his basket and held him tightly to her chest. He woke up. I thought he would cry, but he was his normal cheerful self. He didn't know he was in any danger. As long as Mommy was there.

I worked to stay calm. "Misnamed?"

"A Christian saint. Really, Peter, what were you thinking?"

"I don't understand."

"His heritage. Not Christian. He's ours, not yours."

"Then why haven't you just taken him?"

Angela looked at me as if I'd lost my mind.

Lilith was calm, collected, precise. "We want him legally. Without trouble. Free and clear. He is the heir to…to my dreams. My victory. He will also get my money. He will be raised a Van Kirk."

"Van Kirk means…of the church."

"But not your church, Peter. The Dark church. My

church."

"He's an innocent, beautiful little baby, Lilith. Don't do this to him."

"But, Peter, you don't understand. I will do everything for him. I am his grandmother. He is a Van Kirk; he is of our essence…"

I interrupted. "So you are his grandmother?"

"One of his grandmothers anyway." She tilted her head mischievously. "The only living one."

"But…?"

"More importantly, young Val is Ignatius' father."

For a moment, I was speechless. "Masha got pregnant from her brother?"

"Val and Masha weren't related by blood, Peter. Val is my son conceived with his father Count Vlad. He is also Van Kirk blood. Masha, on the other hand, unfortunate, sad Masha, Ignatius' birth mother, was that whore Tsilia's daughter…"

"But she was also conceived with Count Vlad."

"No. The Count was not Masha's father. He gave her his last name, but he was not her father."

"Then who was?"

Lilith snorted and shook her head, baffled by my obtuseness. "You, Peter. You are, excuse me, you were…" The head tilt again. The mischievous smile. "…Masha's father."

The horror overwhelmed me. Then I realized, "But…but that means…"

"Brilliant, Peter. Yes. Congratulations. You are Ignatius' grandfather. Also the only living one, and we need your cooperation."

I was stunned into silence. I was Iggy's grandfather. Poor murdered Masha was my daughter. Then, as I remembered

Masha—dead, disfigured, abandoned in the park beneath the Moreton Bay Fig—my stomach churned violently. I ran to the bathroom and vomited up my breakfast. I took a deep breath, then emptied out everything else in my stomach. I tried to stand, teetered, then collapsed onto the linoleum. Unconscious.

The only safe place to be.

St. Thomas Aquinas, Fresco

Chapter Eighteen

Yea, they said in their hearts, the whole kindred of them together: / Let us abolish all the feast days of God from the land. / ...O God, how long shall the enemy reproach? / shall the adversary blaspheme thy Name for ever? / Why dost thou turn away thy hand, even thy right hand? / out of the midst of thy bosom for ever?
Sext, Psalm 73, Feast of St. Thomas Aquinas, Confessor and Doctor of the Church

In my unconscious state I was...

...sitting on a flat rock outcropping atop a craggy hillside looking down upon two angels. The younger one is dressed in many layers of rich colorful fabrics despite the heat. The older one is dressed in a flimsy golden gossamer drape that does little to hide the full curves of her breasts and buttocks.

They are wandering through their garden that surrounds an adobe house. All around their house the land is dusty, brown and barren, but their garden is a lush collection of lemon and orange trees, bougainvillea and date palms. Scattered throughout the garden are lesser angels, naked, watering the plants, raking the pebbles into decorative patterns, plucking fruit from the trees, keeping watch over the mother and daughter.

I watch the mother kiss her daughter on the cheek and walk into their house. Suddenly the dessert trembles from the force of a colossal turbulence. All around me huge boulders tumble down the hillside, but my perch remains solid, secure. A jagged cleft opens in the earth, and Beelzebub emerges dressed in Armani carrying a small pistol. A crooked smile on his lips.

I cup my hands around my mouth and howl a warning, but no one pays any attention to me.

The devil approaches the daughter, and none of the lesser angels move to protect her. I stand and wave my arms, but no one sees me. The devil drags her through the garden back toward the cleft in the earth. He wraps his arms around her and leaps. The turbulence ends. The cleft disappears.

The mother comes running from the house. She searches for her daughter. Her search becomes more frantic. She questions the lesser angels. No one has seen anything.

I find myself floating down the hillside. Not touching the ground. As I approach the mother I realize she has Antonia's face. Antonia's body. As I remembered her. Before she became Tsilia.

I tell Antonia what happened to her daughter. She flies into a rage and chases the lesser angels from the garden. When they enter the desert, they are no longer naked. They are covered in filthy rags. Their hair is tangled and greasy. Antonia turns her rage on me. Why had I not protected her daughter? Why was I weak, afraid, cold, distant? Didn't I realize the girl was my daughter as well?

While she is haranguing me, the earth behind her reopens and we both fall into Hell. We wander in the sulfurous smoke through dark caves, around pools of burning oil, over pits of glowing charcoal.

We enter a large hall. The ceiling is encrusted with pulsating, glowing blue crystals. In the middle of the hall, surrounded by slithering, slimy, scaly creatures, Beelzebub sits on a black iron throne. Next to him, but on the ground, her arms wrapped around his hairy calves our daughter lies spooned by a hideous, red horned toad.

The devil sees us. He howls our names. Our daughter turns her head in our direction. She cannot see! Her eyes are bloody sockets. Antonia screams in horror, in terror, in desperation, "PETER...

"…Peter, wake up! Wake up, please, Peter."

I awoke and slowly the fog inside my brain faded as I oriented myself. I was in the warehouse. In the office. On a bed. Angela was kneeling next to me. Iggy was…where was Iggy? Ah, he was in his basket.

"Angela, where's Lilith? Where's Val?"

"They left, but I'm sure they'll be back."

"Yes, they will."

"What are we going to do?"

"I don't know."

"Wonderful. *Merci beaucoup*." Sarcastic.

"Don't, Angela. I need to think."

"Can they really take Ignatius?"

"Yes and no." I tried to sort out the logic of their plan. "If Val really is his father…and Masha was his mother…and I cooperated…"

"I'm his mother."

"Angela, please."

"I really am, Peter. In every important way. I am. I am."

"Not in one important way. Not before the law."

Masha. My daughter. God help me. God have mercy. On her. On me. She must have known I was her father. She wanted me to protect her baby. She left him on my doorstep. What madness haunted her? She was afraid. Of her mother? No. I think Antonia actually did love her. Of Lilith? Did she know about Lilith? She was afraid of someone.

Concentrate. She was killed by a .32 caliber pistol. Val has a .32 caliber pistol. Would he have killed her? The mother of his child? He was capable of it. But why? Oh, of course. At that point, he, like me, like Milosz, thought Masha had thrown their child into the ocean.

Did he kill his father, The Count? Probably. I had no idea why. Maybe as a favor for Lilith, for his mother. Because the Count had abandoned Lilith and taken up with Antonia/Tsilia? Possibly.

And the homeless guy? Of course. Val was trying to find Antonia. Looking for information about Iggy.

Why Andrew? Andrew who was trying to run away with Ignatius. Surely Val killed Andrew. By then he knew his baby was alive and Andrew was taking Iggy out of the country.

How did he know the baby was alive? Ah, Father Thomas. Still in touch with his great failure, Lilith, Val's mother. Thomas still battling demons. The old fool.

In the end, Andrew was right. Thomas was an old fool. But he also saved Iggy's life. And he fought to protect Iggy. He did.

So why didn't Val kill me? I guess they really did think they could get Ignatius peacefully, legally. Since I was weak. They could buy me off.

But Angela? Why did Val and Lilith want Angela alive?

Just then, Iggy woke up. Angela gently lifted him from his basket and placed him on her breast. Oh my! This beautiful baby was my grandson.

For a moment all the bad feelings and the terrible realities went away. I saw the wonder of him. He was me. My flesh. My blood. My communion. I would never let Val and Lilith have him. Never.

And Angela. She was right. She had become Iggy's mother. I wanted her to raise him. To love him. To care for him. I would not let them kill Iggy's mother. A second time.

Were the Van Kirks devils? Was Lilith simply insane? What difference did it make? Either way they were evil. Either way this was madness. I needed to stop them. I needed to escape. I prayed, please, dear God, show me the way. And He did.

It was amazingly stupid and simple. Stupid on their part. Simple for me. Like many people who have automatic garage doors, especially well-made, steel, tight fitting garage doors like a Hörmann up-and-over, they assume that when the door is closed, it can't be opened. Except by a properly tuned, radio controlled, remote garage door opener. Or a doorbell type switch on the inside wired directly to the door's motor.

Val did take the remote control. Worse, I could not find any direct doorbell type line switch. However, I knew if I could reach the motor and unplug it, then release the pin attached to the motor arm, I could lift the door manually. If it was properly balanced. If I could figure out how to reach the motor and the pin.

Angela and I brought the table and chairs from the office. We placed the table beneath the motor. I told Angela to climb onto the table. I handed her one of the chairs. Then I joined her on the table and held tightly to the chair as she climbed onto it.

She tried to reach the motor but she wasn't tall enough. She raised her eyebrows and looked at me. Okay, I was taller, but I could see I wasn't going to be able to reach the mechanism either. We considered stacking the other chair on top of the first one, but that seemed suicidally precarious.

I was sweating profusely. There were tears of frustration forming in Angela's eyes. Time was short. We needed to act fast. There was only one solution. I had to stand on the chair. She would have to climb up next to me. Then I would lift her high enough so she could unplug the motor and pull the pin. If the chair could not support both of us, or if I dropped her… I put that scenario out of my mind.

So, I made sure she saw where the plug was inserted in the socket, and that she knew where the release pin was. I braced myself, legs spread as far as the seat of the chair would allow. I wrapped my arms around her buttocks and carefully lifted her until her knees were near my shoulders, her crotch in my face. Ridiculous. But neither of us could laugh at the humor of it.

Then she started to sway. I tensed my thighs as much as I could, but I was loosing her. Just as we started to fall, she was able to grab onto the motor with her left hand and stabilize us. "Quickly," I begged her, "quickly. I can't hold you any longer."

Angela pulled the plug and released the pin. She slid down my body. Crotch. Breasts. Lips. I was so proud of her I kissed her. Then I kissed her again before we jumped off the table. She went to get Ignatius. I leaned against the door to try and push it open.

As it turned out, the door was not so well balanced. I placed my back against a steel brace and pushed with both of my legs. That move allowed me to create a three-foot high gap between the bottom of the door and the floor. Angela slid Ignatius in his basket through the opening. She looked at me. Fear in her eyes. "How are you going to get out?"

"The chairs," I gasped. "Get the chairs."

She ran to the chairs, grabbed them both and placed them on their sides in the opening.

"Go," I said, "Go, go." She scooted under and joined Ignatius on the other side. I slowly lowered the door until it rested on the chairs. The door was very heavy. The chairs not so strong. I could hear the wood stressing. Now or never.

I fell to the ground and slipped through the opening just as the chairs gave way with a loud, CRACK. Splintered wood flew across the pavement and the door slammed back into place. I missed being guillotined by about two seconds.

No time to reflect on that. We needed to negotiate the fence. I'd done it before. But not with a baby and a basket. Was God really on my side? Before we attempted the perilous climb, I tried to slide the gate open.

The Lord is my shepherd; I shall not want! Our three guardian angels were working overtime. Val hadn't bothered to lock the gate. Once the gate was open, we took off running down the alley. Side-by-side. Iggy in the middle. Each of us with a firm grip on his basket. Like refugees crossing the border near Tijuana.

We made our way to the Pacific Coast Highway and the bus stop at Vermont Avenue. Within minutes a 232 bus going north to the airport appeared. The doors opened. We climbed on board. No money. We begged the driver. He was adamant. I told him we were being followed by bad people who wanted our baby. No reaction.

Angela cursed him up and down with the most vulgar epithets. Thankfully in French, because a tiny old lady, permed white hair, wrap-around dark glasses, sitting in the front of the bus, holding onto her purple cane, opened her purse and handed me a ten dollar bill. I handed it to the driver. He pointed to a sign, "Exact change required."

"Get serious," I said. He kept pointing to the sign. The doors remained open. The bus didn't move. Lilith and Val must have returned at the warehouse by then.

I turned back to the lady. Gave her back her ten dollar bill. Shrugged. Did she have exact change? She rummaged through her purse. The doors remained open. The bus still didn't move. The other passengers were beginning to grumble. Angela was shaking.

Finally the woman handed me the proper two one dollar bills and two quarters. Angela and I entered the bus and sat down, totally exhausted, next to our sweet benefactor. But she wasn't interested in Angela or me. She took off her dark glasses. She wanted to play goo-goo eyes with Ignatius.

Charles-David was in the kitchen when we arrived back home. There was a full glass sitting next to him. A glazed look in his eyes. I was certain he was drunk, but he smiled at me. "Diet Coke," he said. Still sober. Good.

I gave him a quick account of what happened. Then I borrowed his phone to call Milosz. I was half-way into my story, when Milosz put me on hold and called the Lomita police. When he came back to me I said, "They'll be gone by now."

"Sure, but we need to see what they left behind."

"Can you offer us some protection here at the house?"

"Some. Budgets are tight. I will make sure someone drives by every couple of hours. But look, Pete, they're on the run, and I don't think they'll come back to your place."

"I do. They want the baby." I remembered something Kenny once told me about a phone's GPS. "Sergeant, they have my phone."

"That's seems the least of your problems…"

"Cell phones send out a constant signal that can be traced."

"You're right. Okay. We'll put a trace on the signal. We'll get them for sure."

I disconnected and turned back to Charles-David.

"We don't need extra protection from the police," he said.

"What?"

He reached into his pocket, removed his hand and dumped a pile of bullets on the table. "Hornady, .22 caliber, 60 gram hollow points."

"For?"

"The Bobcat. I've still got it."

"Charles-David, I didn't mean you should…"

"He made me shit my pants, Peter. I've had it. Never again."

I didn't approve. Didn't approve at all. But what could I say? I'd not been humiliated throughout my life.

Twenty minutes later, Milosz called back. He was excited. He said they found the signal from my phone.

Then he called back again two hours later and said they found my actual phone in a dumpster behind a 7/11 in Carson. No sign of Val or Lilith.

A very tiny piece of me was glad Charles-David bought the bullets. Since I was sliding down the slippery slope of immorality, I might as well have a lethal weapon along for the ride.

I went to talk with Angela. We hadn't discussed my newly revealed relationship to Ignatius. She displayed a bittersweet resignation. "I knew he looked like you," she said.

I was also sad, nervous, confused. "You were right."

"It sort of complicates things, Peter. Between you and me."

"Yes."

"I don't want to be sleeping with Ignatius' grandfather."

"No. Of course not."

She released a deep sigh. "It's always something. If it's not the scar…"

"About that scar. Where did you get it, Angela?"

An even deeper sigh. She switched to French. "*Je suis né sourd*... I was born deaf, the seventh child of eleven children, the last daughter in a very poor, very conservative, very religious Québécois family that farmed in the Beauce, a very isolated region south of Quebec City. I am told I was also a very beautiful child..."

"*Je crois que c'était vrai*...I believe that.

"*Merci*. When I was four-years-old, my mother took me to a shrine, The Basilica of Sainte-Anne-de-Beaupré, perhaps you've heard of it?

"*Bien sûr*. The North American Lourdes."

"*Exactement*. The basilica was the biggest building I had ever seen. And the most beautiful. My mother believed that after we prayed there, I would no longer be deaf.

Because she believed, I also believed I would hear just like all the other little girls in our village. We even climbed the *Scala Santa* on our knees in commemoration of Our Lord's Passion and to insure that our request for a miracle would receive special attention.

"Then, we entered the Basilica itself. I remember the moment very clearly. There were two pillars covered with crutches and canes and braces left by the faithful who were healed by a visit to the shrine.

"I stood there in awe, hypnotized by the hundreds and hundreds of prosthetics hanging like oversized ornaments on a giant stone Christmas tree. At that moment, the basilica's nine heavy bells began peeling. Of course, I could not hear the bells, but I felt their vibrations, more powerful than any I had ever experienced. In my excitement, I tripped and fell against the edge of the pillar.

"The fall opened up a gash which caused this scar." She

ran her finger down her disfigured flesh from her right eye to her chin.

"Why didn't she take you to a doctor?"

"Because I could hear! It was a miracle. My mother decided my transformation was our pact with God. I gave Him my beauty. He gave me my hearing. When I was 15, she sent me to the Ursuline sisters in Quebec City. My placement was considered a great honor. Our convent was founded in 1639, and I was living in a National Historic Monument." She heaved a sigh. "A great honor. I was 15. I only knew I was ugly."

"No one ever suggested plastic surgery?"

"Why? I was blessed. My scar was given to me by God. I was protected from the devil. I was inoculated from evil. I told you what Mother Superior said to me."

"Yes. I remember."

"*Alors maintenant vous savez*. So now you know."

"*Tu es très courageux*. You're very brave.

"*J'aurais mieux aimé resté sourd*. I would rather have stayed deaf."

I held her in my arms, but she was stiff, distant.

After a moment she said, "I need to be with Ignatius."

She didn't kiss me when she left.

There were a few hours of daylight remaining, so I returned to my room and stood before my Madonna and Child. I finally understood her scar. I wanted her to know I understood.

Linseed oil and my pallet knife cleared away the residue of cadmium red and yellow ochre. I mixed Alizarin crimson with titanium white and added small measure of cerulean blue. All the wrong colors. You would think.

But I blended them into the flesh tones on her face. They worked perfectly. I stood before my easel and closed my eyes. Then I opened them.

I saw my Madonna's soul.

St. John of God, Mosaic

Chapter Nineteen

The eyes of the Lord are upon them that love Him. He is their mighty protection, and strong stay, a defence from heat, and cover from the sun at noon, a preservation from stumbling, and a help from falling. He raiseth up the soul, and lighteneth the eyes; He giveth healing, life, and blessing.

Matins, Lesson iii, from the Book of Ecclesiasticus, Feast of Saint John of God, Confessor

Late that evening, violent weather rolled in off the Pacific. The old Mamas and Papas song was right, "It never rains in California, but girl, don't they warn ya'? It pours, man, it pours."

It certainly poured that night. Unusually so. I pushed my Braxton over by my window and sat there watching for any sign of trouble. I saw our old house's drain gutters clogged with eucalyptus leaves send Niagras spilling over the edge of the roof crashing into the yard below.

The city's storm sewers backed up and Dolorita flowed more like the Colorado River than a suburban street. Palm fronds were strewn across the sidewalks. White magnolias and red bottle brush blooms were stripped from the trees. Riviera Beach was under a severe storm watch. There would be no police surveillance on our house that night.

I must have fallen asleep around 2:30. Then around 3:00, there was a lightening flash. Then immediately, tremendous thunder. That got my attention. I jumped up from my chair. Sparks flew from a utility pole across the street. A transformer burst into flames.

The power lines went down. My desk light flicked off. My computer screen died. Not the most comfortable situation. Given the risks. But my room was lit by the flickering flames from the burning transformer. Almost as if I had a warm, cozy fireplace.

I heard a sound in the hallway. Then my door flew open and in came Angela with her arms wrapped around Ignatius. "What was that noise?" Terror in her eyes.

"Lightening strike on a transformer. We won't have power until they fix it."

"How long will that be?"

"Not before morning. Not in this storm. With these winds.

"Oh." She was worried.

"You and Iggy can sleep in my bed." She looked at me. Held my glance a little too long. "I'll stay in my chair," I said.

Angela climbed into bed, cuddled Ignatius next to her. I pulled a blanket over them. Within minutes they were both breathing rhythmically. Sound asleep. They trusted me. They thought they were safe and secure.

Then there was another sound in the hallway. Feet padding toward my door. I put my finger to my lips to hush Charles-David as he swung into the room. But the intruder wasn't Charles-David. It was Val Bentz.

Val focused on Angela and Ignatius in my bed. Then on me in my chair. He called out over his shoulder, "*Матушка*, come here. See this precious little scene of domestic tranquility."

Then he turned toward me, threw back his head and laughed. High pitched. A touch of hysteria in his voice. He wagged the index finger of his left hand. The Seecamp .32 was in his right. "Naughty, naughty, naughty, boy, Father Peter."

Another lightening flash. Another thunder clap. Reflections from the fire flashed across Vlad's face. Eyes wide with what I can only describe as madness.

Angela sat up in bed, saw Val and screamed at the top of her lungs. Her screams awakened Ignatius and this time he felt her fear. He began howling as well. Not that it mattered to anyone outside our house. The storm took care of that.

Then Lilith entered the room still dressed in her faux riding outfit. She calmly walked over to my bed where Angela was clinging to Ignatius. She spoke softly, totally in control. "Angela, please stop crying. You're terrifying our little boy."

Lilith leaned over and stroked Ignatius on his head and down his back. Then she pulled Ignatius away from Angela before she slapped Angela with the back of her hand. Hard. Very hard. Across Angela's scar, but Angela didn't flinch.

Lilith attempted to kiss Iggy on the forehead when she noticed the locket on a thin gold chain filled with Thomas's ashes around Iggy's neck. She fell back as if she had been violently pushed away from the child. She dropped Ignatius back into Angela's arms. She turned away and walked toward me.

I was frozen in my chair. Any bravado I might have displayed was shattered. The raging storm. The fire. Val and his nasty little gun. Lilith's raging anger. I felt weak, incapable of action.

Lilith positioned herself next to the window, next to my chair. She stood erect, shoulders back, proud of her strength, of her power. Her face was illuminated by the flames as she stared into the howling winds and sheets of rain. As if in a trance. She was truly a vision from the eternal inferno of hell itself. What could I say that would change the mind of this monster?

Lilith spoke in a different voice, lower and gravely. "You are such a fool, such a damned stupid fool, Peter Paderewski. You could have enjoyed everything. Money. Power. Any concubine you might desire. You could have watched your grandson grow to manhood and assume his powerful, rightful, chosen place in this world."

She glared down at me. I was shaking, recoiling into my chair. She looked disgusted. Her words were heavy with scorn. "You choose instead the bleak promise of an afterlife devoid of pleasure or feeling. I can assure you, Peter, the Almighty is boring, Peter. Boring, boring, boring."

I searched for a response to her insane pronouncements. None was forthcoming. It was actually Angela who spoke. "Stop! I am marked by God, Lilith. You cannot harm me. And while I hold Ignatius, he is also protected. By me. By his locket. By Thomas."

"Oh really?" Lilith chuckled. "Your pathetic, disgusting scar? You think your disfigurement will protect you? How childish, how foolish." She tittered nervously. "And that quaint antique? We'll soon be rid of that, my dear."

"You will never get this baby."

Lilith was annoyed. "Oh, but I will. He will be the first Van Kirk with our new blood. Our dark blood. Our powerful blood. Conceived in lust. Descended from a priest. He is our savior! And you! You are only his temporary mother. He needs you. You will be rewarded for your guardianship," she smirked, "not because you have a deformity."

I could hear the words of their exchange, but they were speaking to each other on a plane beyond my comprehension. It was the realm where Father Thomas dwelled. It was the world of spirits and magic. It strained credulity to believe they were both serious, but they did not interact as if they were speaking in metaphors.

Val brought us all back to a certain reality. "*Матушка*, there is so much to do. We must do it and leave this place."

"Yes," said Lilith. "Yes. You are right. We must do what must be done." She seemed genuinely sad when she knelt down next to me and looked into my eyes. "We could have grown old together, Peter. We could have experienced so much fun watching our grandchild. I think he will miss you."

Finally my anger overcame my fear. "Old? Together? With you? You're disgusting, Lilith."

"Oh, I know," she said. She laughed. "You find me disgusting, but you sleep with a witch, that enchantress who stole Val's father away. From me. Big mistake. And her stunning daughter. The gorgeous sister who seduced my son, her brother. That daughter who tried to kill our grandchild. That…"

"She did not want to kill her baby. She left him with me."

"Yes. Smart move. Look how well you've protected him. You're pathetic, priest."

"You are truly mad, Lilith."

"Oh, am I? Now you are a psychiatrist? Priest, painter, lover, lawyer, psychiatrist. A true Renaissance man." She snickered dismissively.

"*Матушка*…"

"Alright. Alright, my son. I'll take Scarface and the baby to the Suburban. You can deal with Grandpa here. And the fat one. Downstairs. On your way out." To me, "Ciao, Peter. It's been grand."

She moved toward Angela and Ignatius. "We're not going

anywhere," Angela insisted.

"Darling, please. Do you want our baby to see his grandfather's brains blown out? Do you want murder to be one of his most vivid childhood memories?"

Brave Angela anchored herself to the bed with Ignatius in her arms. "Let me see how powerful you are, Lilith, wife of Satan, against the will of Our Lord and Savior, Jesus Christ and His beloved servant Father Thomas Groenbach."

"Bitch! Look at you lying here half naked in a priest's bed. You're no child of God, no friend of Thomas…" Lilith hissed, but she seemed unable or unwilling to move against Angela.

"*Матушка*…I hear sirens. We must leave. We must silence all of them."

"Not the baby. Not your son."

I became aware that the flashing lights through my window were no longer primarily caused by flames from the utility pole, but were, in fact, reflections from emergency vehicles responding to the fire. "Lilith," I said, "the Riviera Beach police, the fire department. They're all just outside on the street. You'll never get away. Especially with the baby. Your grandson. Don't put his life in danger. End this now."

While Lilith and Val were standing at the window studying the situation, out of the corner of my eye, I saw Charles-David in my doorway. Suddenly his rotund shape moved surprisingly quickly from the door to just in back of Val. Then, without hesitation, Charles-David placed the Bobcat next to Val's skull and fired a hollow point into Val's brain. The report was an unexpectedly soft pop, but the results were extremely effective as skull fragments and brain matter splattered against the window.

Val crumpled onto the floor. Lilith shrieked, and dropped

down next to him. She cradled his head in her arms, his blood draining onto her white silk blouse and denim jodhpurs. She kissed his face and ran her fingers through his hair. Then she looked up at me, "It is finished. Now, I will kill the baby as well."

I said to her: "You will not kill the baby, Lilith." I stood and gestured toward Val dying on the floor. "Mother, behold your son, and what you have done to him."

She howled. Not to be but to spirits unknown. "Why have you forsaken me?"

I ran to Angela who had covered Ignatius with my blanket so that he was spared seeing the horror taking place so near his innocent soul. I lifted them both into my arms and carried them down the stairs to Angela's room. I left them there on her bed and locked her door.

I could hear Lilith's continued shrieks as she fled through the house out the front door. I followed her onto the street.

Lilith was running toward the fire. In the rain. I heard someone yell, "Stop. Police. Get down on the ground." It was Milosz. In a crouch. Feet spread. His pistol held in firing position. Pointed at Lilith.

Lilith whirled around. She was standing next to the utility pole. The broken wires hissed and snapped and writhed like slithering snakes. She was soaked. Her clothes clung to the outlines of her tall, angular body. Her strawberry blond/gray hair hung in ringlets below her squared shoulders. Her eyes were defiant.

She enunciated clearly and loudly in the unintelligible, ancient tongue she used when we were delivering Father Thomas's ashes to the cathedral. The firemen were transfixed. The police were stunned. I stood mesmerized She was magnificent in her way. Then she focused on the crowd gathered in front of her and spoke to us:

"This day I will be with My Maker in our paradise deep beneath this earth. But it is not the end. It is the beginning. I will always be with you. On your shoulders. Whispering in your ears. Calling you. To join us. We are the future. We are the world. In chaos. In Darkness." I trembled as she raised her arms out from her side and turned her palms toward us.

Milosz yelled, "Don't move, but before he could stop her, she grabbed the 7,000-volt lines still attached to the burning transformer. One in each hand.

Her body was immediately encircled by a blue white aura. Steam rose from her skin. Smoke shot out of her mouth and her ears. Her eyes popped out of their sockets. Then she fell, her body completely rigid, onto the grass.

I ran to her, but Milosz stopped me. "Those lines are still alive. You'll be electrocuted just like she was."

He was right. So I prayed for her from a distance away. I recited the words of exorcism rather than a prayer for the dead: "I command you, unclean spirit, whoever you are, along with all your minions now attacking, Caroline Lilith Van Kirk, this servant of God, by the mysteries of the incarnation, passion, resurrection, and ascension of our Lord Jesus Christ, by the descent of the Holy Spirit, by the coming of our Lord for judgment, that you tell me by some sign your name, and the day and hour of your departure.

"I command you, moreover, to obey me to the letter, I who am a minister of God despite my unworthiness; nor shall you be emboldened to harm in any way this creature of God, or the bystanders, or any of their possessions."

Astonishingly, Lilith sat bolt upright.

Then her body crumpled.

"Post-mortem electrical stimulation," murmured Milosz.

I preferred to think it was her demon departing. I had my sign. At that point, I felt comfortable reciting a prayer for the dead: "*Absolve, Domine*...Absolve, Oh Lord, the soul of Caroline Van Kirk, the faithful departed from every bond of sin. And by the help of Thy grace, may she be enabled to escape the judgment of punishment. And enjoy the happiness of light eternal."

Charles-David joined us on the street. He handed the Bobcat to Sergeant Milosz. "There's another body in the house. I am the killer."

"Don't say anymore," I advised Charles-David.

"But, Peter..."

"As your lawyer. No more. Not now."

Milosz nodded in agreement. He had no wish to arrest Charles-David.

The rain stopped. The storm blew over and quickly passed on to the east. The winds subsided. The first light of dawn gave shape and substance to the eerie scene around us. More police cars arrived. Crews from Southern California Edison. Two mortuary vans from the Los Angels County Department of the Coroner.

Milosz and I talked for awhile. I filled him in on the details of what happened. Most of them anyway. When we were done, he shook my hand. "I was wrong about you. You're a good man. A good priest."

"No. I'm not."

I was exhausted. I went inside the house. Linda Alvarez was finished interviewing Angela. We acknowledged each other as we passed in the hallway. Then I entered Angela's room.

"How's Ignatius?"

"See for yourself." She picked him up off the bed. He was awake. She handed him to me and I held him against my chest.

I wanted to hug him so hard that he would become part of me and never be endangered again. He was so tiny. I just held him against my heart. Precious. Then I looked down into his eyes. He smiled. A bubble formed on his pink lips.

"Just gas," said Angela.

"Yes," I said. "Just gas." But there was a twinkle in his little eyes.

"I can't stay here any longer," said Angela.

"No. Of course not."

"Do you think they'll let me keep Ignatius?"

I smiled. "Well, it appears I'm his only surviving blood relative. I will therefore, at some point, get to make the decision. My decision will be yes. After all, you are his mother."

Tears streamed down her cheeks. She sniffled, but she laughed. "Yes. Yes I am. I really am."

I wanted her to hug me. I wanted to tell her I loved her. I wanted to kiss her. I think she wanted to kiss me too. But we didn't hug or kiss or speak. I gave little Iggy back to her.

I walked outside again. There was yellow police barrier tape everywhere, but most of the city workers were gone. A few of the neighbors still in bathrobes were surveying the area where, what they would soon refer to as 'the incident,' happened. What else were they to name the bizarre events that took place so near their homes?

Three cooper's hawks were perched in our magnolia

watching the two who were pecking at the ground where Lilith died. They acted as if they were searching for something. They didn't find whatever it was they were looking for. They whistled to the birds remaining in our tree. The birds in the tree whistled back.

Then all five rose into the air, rising higher and higher, gliding on their resplendent wings away from our house. Until they were tiny specs heading northeast.

I never saw them again.

A few hours later, as I approached the beach at the bottom of Avenue C, I noticed the surf was still high. Eight-to-ten footers pounding the shoreline. After effects from the storm. The serious experienced surfers were enjoying the danger. The dumb ones were getting their boards smashed.

Dolphin fins skimmed just above the waterline 50 yards off to my right. They were having fun as well. I reached into my pocket to retrieve my phone, then realized I didn't have one. I was on my own.

"Oh my God I am heartily sorry for having offended Thee...no, that's not what I want to talk about. I'm tired of apologizing. I did the best I could, and in the end, everything turned out about as well as could be expected. More or less. Hey, I'm flawed. Human. We can't all be perfect like You.

"So, I guess what I really want to ask You is, what do I do? I thought I wanted to stop being a priest and live with Angela and Ignatius. But that doesn't feel right now.

And You know, I've sort of realized, with all that's happened. The battle between good and evil. Counseling people in trouble. Praying. Caring for others. Maybe I like being a priest. No. Not maybe. I do like being a priest. This kind of priest. I like talking to You and I like helping people. That's a start isn't it? To being a good priest?

"Still, I'm afraid, God. Not of You. Not of Satan, if he even exists. I'm afraid of…of myself. I am my own personal devil if we want to look at it that way. I know You are All-loving, All-forgiving. But there must be a limit. There must be a point at which You will say, 'Paderewski, enough is enough. Try some other line of work. I don't need you laboring for me.' You must already feel that way sometimes. After all these years.

"And Ignatius. You'll take care of him, but will he be okay without me? I know we'll still see each other, or at least I think we will. I will miss him so much. Day to day. I love him so much. He's going to have a rough road. When he finds out what happened to his birth mother. To his father. To his grandmothers. To his other grandfather. It won't be easy for him to overcome those stories. When he hears them. When he knows the truth. Can I make it alright for him?

Angela will do her best, and her best will be better than I could hope for. But he also needs to know he has good blood. Can I hold myself up as good blood? That's what it comes down to. We all need to know from whence we came. How will I help him to understand what I don't understand. I'm not sure I can. Not really.

"So I'm going to need your help, God. I'll be all alone. Except for You. If You could give a little nudge here or there. Give me some idea about what You might have in mind. What do you think, huh? Can we work something out?"

At that very moment a large brown pelican dropped straight down, diving out of the ultramarine blue sky into the roiling sea. Seconds later, he emerged on the surface, riding the waves, with a mackerel flopping around in its beak. A strange sign.

I decided it would do for the moment.

The Transfiguration, Raphael, (c.1520)

Chapter Twenty

They have sought my soul in vain, they shall go down into the nether parts of the earth: / They shall be delivered into the hands of the sword, they shall be a portion for foxes. / …for the mouth of them that speak wicked things shall be stopped.
Lauds, Psalm 62, The Octave Day of the Ascension

Our little drama was replayed over and over again on the 24-hour news channels. Especially Lilith's electrocution. As it turned out, a 70-year-old woman who lived in a renovated 1.5 million dollar Cape Cod house two doors down from our old cottage caught 'the incident' on her cell phone and uploaded it to YouTube.

Her clip went viral and received 4,376,235 hits in just five days. Fire. Attractive woman. Sparks. Steam. Smoke. Twitching. Gruesome death. Apparent Zombie revival. Throw in rumors of Satanism and Jesuits and a mysterious baby. The lookie lous were driving down Dolorita Avenue every day for three weeks before interest faded.

There was talk about a film. We had agents calling. We had screenwriters calling. We had producers sending invitations for lunch. What about a TV series? Show runners were throwing around big numbers. I was tempted because I thought we could set up a trust fund for Ignatius. But then we realized all they wanted were intimate details that could very well ruin many lives. Including Iggy's. I said no. I was a Jesuit after all.

It turned out that Iggy didn't need the money. Lilith had willed what was left of the Van Kirk fortune to Ignatius. Less than a million, but more than enough to take care of him until he was on his own. Angela was somewhat nervous about the source, but I argued if she were going to take care of him, she needed some kind of support. She shouldn't let superstition rule the rest of her life. She suggested I should take at least some of the money. I said no. I was a Jesuit after all.

Charles David decided he did want to leave the priesthood. Funny. When he was questioning me about why I wanted to remain a priest, he was really questioning himself. Fair enough. He and Angela cooked up a scheme whereby Charles-David would go to Quebec with Angela and Ignatius. They would set up a family of sorts that would allow all three to nourish each other. Maybe he was still a Jesuit after all.

When they first presented their plan to me, I thought it was the most ridiculous idea. Charles David was persistent. "I'll have no problem with the language. And Quebecois have a European respect for learning, for culture, for refinement."

"For wine as well," I said.

"I don't drink anymore," he said seriously.

"That's good. I wouldn't want a drunk taking care of Ignatius." I knew I was being a jerk. I was grumpy. Upset.

"And you," I said to Angela, "how are you going to be satisfied living with a…" I hesitated. "…I mean, with living a celibate life?" I turned on Charles-David. "Or have you changed that as well?" It felt good to be mean. I wanted to hurt them. Both of them.

A string of profanity escaped Angela's lips. Then she said, "You're a hopeless, misogynistic chauvinist, Peter Paderewski…S.J."

"What do you mean by that?"

"What the hell do you think I mean?"

I thought about what she said, and then it came to me that she was right. I was sad and angry and afraid. They were going to take Ignatius far away from me.

"He is mine more than he is yours. Either of yours."

Angela was livid. Her scar a cerulean red. A warning. She started to leap toward me.

Charles-David intervened. "Peter, why are you saying these things?"

I didn't answer him. I stewed in my own self-pity.

"Think of Ignatius," said Charles-David.

"I should think of Ignatius? If I remember correctly, you were the one who didn't want him here. You were the one who wanted to hand him over to the authorities."

"I was a drunk." He let that sink in. "Look, Peter, Ignatius needs a new life, away from all that's happened. He needs to be in place where no one really knows his history, and no one is likely to bring it up."

"Why not San Bernardino?" I said. Charles-David laughed, but my sarcasm was the last straw for Angela. She gathered up Ignatius in her arms and stormed out of the room.

"You're making this very difficult for her," Charles-David said quietly.

"Difficult for her? She has Iggy."

"That's not her difficulty." He waited for me to say something. I just sulked. Finally he said, "Don't you realize she still loves you?"

The minute he said that, I unexpectedly started to cry. He was right. She loved me. And I loved her. Of course he was right. But our love could not work. Angela and I both knew it could never be like we wanted. For Ignatius' sake. For our own sakes, for Christ sake.

"I'm sorry," I said. "I'm really sorry." And then the tears truly started to flow.

I went up to my room, and placed my Madonna and Child on the easel. I finished off the details with little or no effort. No passion. The heart and humanity of the painting was already set down on canvas and my vision, through my moist eyes, was too cloudy to see clearly. I couldn't believe what was happening. I couldn't believe I was going to have to live without my Ignatius, without my Angela.

For days, I was haunted by everything that had happened. There was still so much I didn't understand. Who sent the text messages in Latin? They stopped after Thomas died. But he was a feeble old man. He didn't even own a cell phone. Or did he? I guess I'll never know. The cooper's hawks? Were they devils? Allies of devils? Or just birds that chose that particular time to nest in our trees? I couldn't decide. How could I decide? My altered painting of the hawks? Could have been so many causes. Paint, especially oils are so tricky.

And what of the Van Kirks? They were clearly insane, but from human dysfunction or supernatural possession? Could Val have really caused Katie's coma? I would probably never know the answer to the mystery of the Van Kirks either. In life, even for Jesuits, a lot of things are simply unknowable.

That evening, realizing my questions would not find answers, I focused on my reading of None, Psalm 118, the Feast of the Ascension of Our Lord, "Rivers of water run down mine eyes, / because men keep not thy law. / Righteous art thou, O Lord; / and true are thy judgments. / …I am small and despised; / yet do I not forget thy commandments.

/ Thy righteousness is an everlasting righteousness, / and thy law is the truth." The truth I had chosen to accept. The truth I would try to live for the remainder of my life. I would try.

The next morning I got a call from the Chancery Office of the Archdiocese of Los Angeles. They said a Monsignor Francisco Montoya wanted to meet with me.

"Why?" I asked.

"Will you meet with him?"

"About?"

"He wants to talk."

"He must have something on his mind."

"Yes, he does."

"What would that be?"

"I'm certain he'll share his thoughts with you when you meet."

I was tired of the mind games so I went ahead and made an appointment. After all the publicity, I expected the worst.

In contrast to the grandeur of the Cathedral, the business offices of the Archdiocese are located on the 5th Floor of a dated, boring glass and concrete, 13-story Pereira and Luckman, late 1950s modern office building, on an unimpressive stretch of Wilshire Boulevard between Vermont Avenue and Normandie, once called the Mid-Wilshire District, now better known as the commercial heart of Koreatown.

There was a time when the area was at the very center of LA nightlife. The old Hollywood watering hole, the Coconut Grove nightclub was located in the Myron Hunt-designed luxurious Ambassador Hotel, home for the Academy Awards presentations six time in the 1930s and early 40s. Seven US presidents stayed there and the Coconut Grove itself was a performance venue for celebrities like Frank Sinatra, Barbra

Streisand, Bing Crosby and Benny Goodman. A way hip place in its day.

Then came 1968. Bobby Kennedy was assassinated in the pantry of the hotel kitchen after his victory speech when he won the California Democratic primary. By the 1980s, the hotel became a sad, empty derelict rented out, in the time-honored LA tradition, for filming and special events. Finally, at the turn of the century, in an even more honored LA tradition, the hotel with all its memories was torn down.

Monsignor Francisco Montoya's office was as bland and dated as the building. He did have a window office with a southern view of the Baldwin Hills and maybe on an especially clear day, a glimpse of the ocean. I wasn't interested in the view. I wanted to hear about how I was going to be crucified.

Montoya was around 5'9", thinning brown hair, rimless glasses, dark suit from Nordstrom's Rack instead of a cassock. He was not fat, but he was soft and fleshy in the way many church people are. He didn't make eye contact. All business, but not straightforward.

He started by telling me he watched the news coverage of our incident at the Jesuit home. Even he was already calling it 'the incident.' Then he got to the point. "I'm sure you are aware the diocese is under some pressure?"

"About?"

"Um, our handling of priests who…"

"Yes?"

"Indulge in unsavory behavior with young men…"

"Boys…"

"Yes."

"And girls."

"Sometimes. But there are other matters as well."

"Like?"

"Financial matters."

"Oh?"

"Anyway, I have discussed your background with your Provincial General's office in Los Gatos."

"And…"

"You're a lawyer…"

"Canon law."

"And you have some knowledge of evil…"

"What?"

"You have encountered earthly temptations."

"Earthly temptations?"

"But not with uh, boys…"

"No."

"Or little girls…"

"Little, no."

"And you are considered to be faithful to your vows of poverty…"

"Yes."

"…and virtually incorruptible."

"More or less. Yes."

"To the point then. The diocese could use a man like you, a priest like you. Unofficially. On, uh, special assignment. Sort of a consultant."

"A consultant?"

"Consultant, investigator, researcher. For difficult issues."

We talked some more. What the Monsignor wanted to know was whether I would be interested in working on cases "that the Church did not want to handle officially but were also cases not ready to be turned over to the police. A liaison between the diocese and the police so to speak," was how the

Monsignor put it. Acting unofficially. "Off the books so to speak."

I would be paid. A pittance, but paid. I could have a small office. But not in the Chancery. A car. Subcompact. And a place to live. Rent not to exceed $855 a month. Seriously? In the LA area? Oh well. A question from me. "And the Provincial General agrees to this?"

"They are happy to have us take you off their hands so to speak."

"But I would still be a Jesuit?"

"I suppose."

"Okay."

"Okay, you'll do it?"

"Yes. I'll do it."

I took the work because I found I enjoyed investigating. The position also meant I could be involved in helping others. Probably some who desperately needed help. On both sides of the issues. And because a salary meant I could visit Ignatius from time to time. I wanted that. I needed that.

When I told Sergeant Milosz about the job, he congratulated me. "You'll be good at it," he said.

I nodded. I appreciated his comment. I looked in the corner of his office for the usual sports equipment. Tennis racquets. Two smaller ones and one adult size. A bag of balls.

"Do they like tennis."

"Not as much as hockey. No contact. Kids like contact. Long as they don't get hurt."

I searched his eyes to see if he was implying more than he was saying. I couldn't read him. I waited a few moments. Trying to decide if I wanted to ask what I knew I really did not want to ask. Finally I said, "What do you think about the devils now?"

He went therapeutic on me. Again. "What do you think, Father?"

"Everything that happened has a perfectly rational explanation. More or less."

"More or less," he grinned.

"Maybe when people think they are devils, they become devils."

"With the power to do extraordinary things."

"Yes, but does their courage come from God or a belief in God?"

He thought about that. "You mean, if devils don't exist, does God exist?"

"Yes. But since you don't believe in God, you don't believe in devils."

"No. In the end I don't. The bad guys are merely crooks, murderers, rapists, thieves."

"How about the priest you killed?"

"I never said I killed a priest." He was upset. Angry. I crossed a line. I apologized. Dropped the subject. I became conciliatory. "Well, thank you, for all you did for us, for me, for Ignatius. Especially for Ignatius. I hope not reporting him didn't get you in trouble."

"Questions were asked. Nothing will come of it."

"So…" I stood. We actually hugged. Both of us surprised and embarrassed, but we hugged.

I walked slowly along the beach back to Dolorita. I was disturbed by my conversation with Milosz, "…if devils don't exist does God exist?" did have a certain logic. If I denied believe in one, then why not in the other?

I watched the seagulls drifting on the breeze coming in off

the water, a young blond surfer coaxing five more yards from a dying wave, mothers playing with their babies in the sand. I thought of Kenny in his lifeguard hut. And Katie. She was alive. They were in love. Maybe they'd have a kid sometime soon. Maybe that's what mattered. Life. The sheer joy of it.

I climbed the bluff and headed for the house. I was in no hurry. I knew what awaited me. An empty nest. I would be alone. Everyone gone. Gone. Gone.

We had one last night together. Charles-David stayed in his room. Angela made dinner for herself, Ignatius and me. A last supper. Candlelight. Cloth napkins. Marlborough 2012 New Zealand Sauvignon Blanc. Rosemary roast chicken. Garlic mashed potatoes. Corn on the cob. Brownies. My favorites.

She couldn't eat. I tried, but I couldn't either. We just sat at the table staring at each other. At Ignatius Loyola. Holding it together. Willing ourselves not to break down. For Iggy's sake.

He was a perfect little man. Gurgling. Cooing. Arms jerking this way and that. He let go one huge fart which made me laugh. Angela laughed as well. As usual, Iggy removed tension from the room. Replaced it with happiness. Replaced it with love. Stinky love.

An hour later he pooped. I helped clean him up, put on a clean diaper, dressed him in a tiny clean white nightshirt. I held him tightly in my arms. I inhaled his odors. His breath. His skin. I handed him to Angela, and she placed him at her breast.

I went upstairs and retrieved the portrait, the Madonna and Child, from my easel. I came back downstairs and gave it to her. She looked at me, questioning. "It's yours," I said.

"Take it with you."

"It's…" she almost lost it. Deep inhale. "…beautiful, Peter. You should keep it," she said. "To remember."

"I don't need a painting to remember," I said.

Angela let me swaddle him. The blue blanket with the little yellow teddy bears. The one he was wrapped in when…. I almost lost it. I didn't. I held it together. For Iggy's sake. I placed him in his basket.

"Well," I said.

"Well," she said.

"Take care of our baby."

"He is ours," she said. She smiled.

God, I wanted to kiss her. But I didn't.

"Yes," I said, "he is."

"Well," I said.

"Well," she said.

I smiled. Weakly. More like a grimace. Then I turned. Walked out her door. Went back to my room. I held it together. I took out my phone and recited from Compline, Psalm 4, "Know this also, that the Lord hath chosen to himself the man that is godly; / when I call upon the Lord He will hear me. / Stand in anger, and sin not; / commune with your own heart, and in your chamber, and be still."

As still as the night.

Expulsion of the Money-changers from the Temple, Giotto di Bondone (c.1305)

If you enjoyed reading **The Innocents**, then you can look forward to reading the next book in the Peter Paderewski S.J. Mystery Series, **The Root of All Evil**.

Chapter One

...Jesus went up to Jerusalem and found in the temple those who sold oxen and sheep and doves, and also the changers of money, sitting there. And when He had made a scourge of small cords, He drove them all out of the temple, with the sheep and the oxen, and poured out the changers' money and overthrew the tables. And He said unto those who sold doves, "Take these things hence! Make not My Father's house a house of merchandise!"
The Gospel According to John, 2:13-16.

I learned Ferrante Gonzaga was dead when I heard a coyote howl at the full moon. Not long after, a cat screeched. Blood curdling. Then complete silence. I knew the coyote got him. The cat. Not Gonzaga.

But the howl and the cat's terrified scream awakened me. I turned on my 22" refurbished Seiki flat screen TV and saw Ferrante's face with a trailer running underneath. "Local entrepreneur, philanthropist dies while parachute jumping on his 85th birthday."

Ferrante was Aloisia Gonzaga's grandfather, and I was renting Aloisia's guesthouse. I moved from Riviera Beach to Long Beach when I accepted an assignment working for the Diocese of Los Angeles on difficult cases—embarrassing situations the Catholic Church did not want to handle officially and were also 'not ready to be turned over to the police,' as the Chancery's Monsignor Francisco Montoya explained.

Aloisia's cottage was a modest bungalow on 5th Street,

north of Ocean Boulevard, Bluff Park, Long Beach Harbor and the Pacific Ocean. On the wrong side of Broadway, on the wrong side of Bluff Heights. Not a bad neighborhood. Palm trees. Eucalyptus trees. Ocean breezes. Sidewalks. But more crime than you might expect. Mostly petty crime. Some dangerous crime. It was Long Beach.

The real estate people made up a name for the neighborhood, Rose Park South, to try and upgrade real estate values. Then came the Great Recession, and it wasn't easy to get a mortgage on 5th Street. Fortunately, Aloisia already had one. Still, she wanted help with the payments so she decided to rent the guesthouse in back of her cottage and she placed it on Craig's List.

When I saw the listing I immediately went to see her. The price was right, and I hadn't been able to find anything in Riviera Beach. Not for what the Diocese was willing to pay me.

I was pleasantly surprised. The cottage's front yard was planted in drought-tolerant pampas grass. The showy, feathery white-gold flowers swayed in the gentle breezes and draped onto her walkway and the cottage's porch railings. The main house was painted in the neo-1930s revival style— the shingles in Barley Corn Green, the trim Old Brick Red and the shutters Crème White. Cute.

I was greeted by a tall, slim, fair-skinned woman, freckles across her nose. She was in her mid-thirties, standing on the porch, looking down at me. Rag & Bone camel, Nubuck Ankle Boots with 3½ inch heels. Short-cropped curly platinum blonde hair. Tom Ford striped brown, Cat-Eye Fashion Glasses. Etro, purple Classic Capri Pants. Joie Meliana Long-Sleeve Peasant Blouse. No bra.

She studied my weary face, bald pate, white t-shirt frayed around the collar and blue jeans. One of the ones with paint stains on them. "I'm so sorry. I'm afraid I've just rented the guesthouse to someone else," she said.

"Oh…uh, well, good," I said.

"Good?"

"I'm a priest," I said.

"So…?"

"You're an extremely attractive woman." I turned to leave.

She laughed. "I'm a lesbian, Father." Her eyes twinkled through her tinted lenses. She laughed again. "Not that you'd have much of a shot anyway."

I turned back toward her. "Sorry? I didn't mean…"

"Of course you did," she said, but with no rancor. "So, you're a priest? Interesting." She left her porch, joined me on the walkway and extended her hand. I took it and we shook. She had a firm grip.

We talked some more. I told her about my new job with the diocese. I told her I needed a place that could also be my studio. A place where I could paint. She told me she taught Women's Health at Cal State Long Beach, and she ran a Free Clinic in the MacArthur Park neighborhood. She held a Ph.D from Stanford. An M.D. from University of California, San Francisco. We got along.

She told me she lied. She hadn't really rented the place and invited me to have a look.

Her guesthouse was small, 25 feet by 30, not much bigger than my old room in the Jesuit home on Dolorita Avenue in Riviera Beach, but the guesthouse had its own bathroom and kitchen area as well as an entire north wall and part of the south wall constructed from Vistabrik High Performance

Glass Block. Beautiful light. It was perfect.

Two days later, I retrieved my meager belongings from a unit in South Bay Storage, and arrived with my ancient bureaucratic gray metal writing desk, my Herman Miller desk chair with the loose arm, the Baxton overstuffed leather club chair that was losing even more stuffing and my Santa Fe II double-masted studio easel. I opened my MacBook Pro and I was ready for work or creation. I was ready for my new life.

After the cat was murdered, I never made it back to bed. Around 7:00 AM, I was reciting my breviary for the day, Matins, Psalm 18, "The fear of the Lord is holy, enduring for ever and ever: the judgments of the Lord are true, justified in themselves. More to be desired than gold and many precious stones: and sweeter than honey and the honeycomb. For thy servant keepeth them, and in keeping them there is a great reward…" when I saw the lights come on in Aloisia's house. Minutes later, she was tapping on my door.

"Grandfather died." She was barefoot, wearing a flimsy red, black and yellow Japanese Happi coat for a robe. It draped no more than midway down her long thighs. Her eyes were puffy. Her nose pink.

"I know." I said. "But I thought you hated him."

"Mostly, but he was my grandfather."

I took her hand. "Then let's say a prayer for him."

She stopped sniffling. "Maybe…Yes. Well, okay."

There are many prayers for the dead, but I chose a simple one: "O God, in Thy mercy have pity on the soul of Aloisia's grandfather. Forgive him his trespasses; and allow her to someday see him again in the joy of everlasting brightness. Through Christ our Lord. Amen."

She frowned. "I'm not sure about that last part, about seeing him again. I'm not sure I want that." She was thoughtful. "But I do hope God forgives him his trespasses. There were so many." She shook her head.

"The reality of most rich and powerful men…and women." I glanced up to search her eyes for a reaction.

"I'm neither rich nor powerful, Father, despite my name. I have renounced my family. I despise their money. I despise their…values."

"Yet you were crying."

"Yes."

"So, you did love him?"

She sighed. "No. Definitely not." She stared at her bare feet. Wriggled her toes. "Do you have any tea? Black tea, I think, this morning. Strong."

I opened two sachets of Twining's Orange Pekoe. Boiled water in my baby blue Melitta electric kettle. I said, "You know your grandfather was a great supporter of the Catholic Church. A major contributor to the cathedral building fund. Lots of money for the overseas missions."

"My grandfather?"

"Yes. He must have been very religious."

"Hardly."

"Then why would he give all that money?"

"Grandmother. She loved ceremony and incense."

"What about God?"

"Him, too, I guess."

I brought her tea in a Bodum, double-walled glass cup. I added milk and Splenda to mine as I raised a questioning eyebrow.

"No," she said. "Just lemon."

I went for a lemon. "And your grandfather?"

Aloisia looked perplexed. "I told you, he was not…"

"I meant, did she love your grandfather?"

She considered the question. "No, I don't think so. He was not a lovable man."

"But he loved her?"

"He loved what being married to her meant to him."

"And what did it mean?"

"I get my looks from my grandmother." I was amused by her lack of humility, but I knew she had a point. Ferrante was a short, wiry man with thick, course eyebrows, oversized ears and a large beaked nose broken in two places. A slalom run of a nose. He was bowlegged and walked with his chest thrust out. A bantam rooster. If her grandmother was Aloisia's genetic double, then Ferrante had done very well for himself. Very well indeed.

"Then why would she want to be with him?"

"She had a very comfortable life with Ferrante. He bought her whatever she wanted. Then, after my father was born and grandfather had an heir, he left my grandmother alone while he pursued…other interests."

"Other women."

"Yes. Of course. He was a man. But he loved money most of all. If he was generous to the church, it must have amounted to peace offerings for my grandmother."

Aloisia was staring off in the middle distance when her eyes teared up again. Her shoulders hunched. She threw back her head. He robe slipped open as she raised her arms to stretch away her emotions. My eyes went to her pert, perfect, small breasts and her pink nipples. I coughed discreetly.

She realized I was looking at her exposed chest. "Father," she reprimanded me.

"Maybe we need a dress code."

"You're a priest."

"And you're a lesbian, still...." I meant my remark to be humorous, but she didn't take it that way.

"And this is my house, so I will dress as I please..." She grabbed her tea glass, raised it into the air and dropped it on the marble counter. It shattered into delicate, sharp, explosive, expensive shards. "...and...I will do as I please." She stood whirled around and walked back to her house. Her looks might come from her grandmother, but there was plenty of Ferrante Gonzaga blood in her veins.

As I was cleaning up the broken glass and spilt tea, my phone chirped. By the time I found my Galaxy, I'd missed the call. But within seconds there was a voicemail. Monsignor Montoya's flat, unemotional voice had a touch of panic. "Paderewski, call me. Now."

Despite Montoya's sense of urgency, I put off answering him until after my morning walk. I made my way down Temple Avenue to Bluff Park overlooking San Pedro Bay and Freeman, Grissom, White, and Chaffee Islands. Astronaut Freeman crashed in a training flight in a Navy T-38 in 1964. Grissom, White, and Chaffee were astronauts burned to death in the cabin fire on Apollo One in 1967.

The islands are artificial islands their facades designed to disguise the fact they are active oil wells and pump jacks. The disguise doesn't work so well in the harsh light of a Southern California morning. At night, their twinkling lights are actually quite charming. A metaphor for all of Southern California.

The bay was calm. The highly polluted waters were nonetheless blue and beautiful. The joggers who wore either very tight Spandex or very loose baggy running shorts were sweating their way along the path in Bluff Park. Old men walked their big dogs. Young women walked their little dogs. Homeless vagrants slept under the palm trees while BMWs, Audis, Mercedes and Lexuses were cruising Ocean Boulevard. The overwhelming disparity in wealth—another Southern California metaphor.

I thought about my grandson, Ignatius Loyola. I missed him terribly. I prayed for him every morning while I walked on the bluff. Although I was facing China, I tricked myself into believing little Iggy was out there across the water. Which he was in one sense. If my vision went south along the Mexican coast, through the Panama Canal, then into the Caribbean, up along the Atlantic Coast north to the St. Lawrence River. Then down the river to Quebec City. That's where Ignatius lived. With his mother, Angela. Hopefully they were happy. Hopefully they were forgetting the horrors we experienced not so long ago. Hopefully I would see him again. Soon.

Back home, I took a deep breath and called Montoya. "I have a job for you," he said, then just a name, "Ferrante Gonzaga."

"Ferrante's dead."

"Yes. I know. That's why I'm calling you, Paderewski. The Gonzaga Family Trust guarantees a number of loans made by the Diocese of Los Angeles."

"How much?"

"Not on the phone."

"What's the problem?"

"Not on the phone. How quickly can you get to my office?"

I could get there fairly quickly. After taking public transportation or driving beat-up old junkers all my life, the

Diocese gave me a small car allowance that I used to lease an orange Fiat 500e, a tiny little shocking orange electric car tight and frisky to drive. Italian. I was learning, in my late middle age, that driving could actually be fun. If I didn't kill myself. Oh well, 'Nearer my God to Thee.'

I threw on my cleanest white t-shirt, my jeans without paint stains and stepped into my huarache sandals. Then, when I approached my 500e, I noticed a crumpled, discarded bundle of tabby fur near the back right bumper. I looked more closely. It was the poor cat. Her neck was broken. Her entrails were ripped from her stomach. Her eyes glazed in death. Dark bloodstains trailed toward the gutter.

I wondered why the coyote didn't take the corpse with him. Were the local coyotes, well-fed from garbage, simply killing for sport? I went back to the house, grabbed a Hefty kitchen bag and returned to the car. I said a little cat prayer, dumped the body into the bag, and the bag into the large gray plastic container sitting on the street waiting for collection. Not the blue one. Not the green one. The gray one. At least the body wouldn't rot on the street.

Upset over the death of the cat, meditating on greed and regretting my unintended confrontation with Aloisia made me drive even faster than normal. I sped south on Temple onto Ocean Boulevard, then right on Ocean all the way through downtown Long Beach, changing lanes incessantly, scooting between delivery trucks and bloated Mercedes to Shoreline Drive, north through Golden Park, racing up the entrance ramp, passing over the concrete embankments of the Los Angeles River and skidding onto the 710 Long Beach Freeway. A controlled skid. More or less.

The freeway was packed with lumbering behemoths,

18-wheelers loaded with ship containers driving from the port, but they had to maintain some distance between one another so I weaved through the Peterbilts and Freightliners until the freeway became a parking lot where it merged with the Golden State Freeway. I exited onto East Olympic Boulevard and shot through the no-man's land where Olympic becomes 9th Street between the Fashion District and downtown Los Angeles, south on Spring Street to West Olympic Boulevard, then west to Vermont where I turned north again through K-town, Koreatown, to Wilshire and the business offices of the Diocese of Los Angeles. 42 minutes. A new record. For me anyway.

Montoya, Monsignor Montoya, was in a bad mood, despite the fact that the relatively clear day gave his bland office a view that caught a peek of the distant Pacific. His thin brown hair was tangled and his rimless glasses were slightly crooked. He astonished me when he actually made momentary eye contact, looked me over and snapped, "Couldn't you wear clothes more appropriate to the job?" I didn't argue. I apologized. No worries. I was curious to know what had him so frazzled.

Montoya's eyes returned to the beige file in front of him. "I'll cut to the chase." That remark worried me. Montoya never cut to the chase. He was a master of misdirection. Could have been a talented magician in another life. "The Gonzaga Family Trust currently guarantees $357 million in diocesan loans."

"Whew. That's a lot of money."

"We've had a lot of expenses."

"The $660 million to settle the abuse scandal?"

He frowned. "Yes, approximately, as well as other expenses."

"What other expenses?"

"You don't need to know. Let's talk about Gonzaga. At his death, the family trust passes into the control of his heirs."

"And they…"

"That's the point. We don't know anything about them."

"I know quite a bit about one of them. I live with her."

His head snapped back. He raised his eyebrows.

"In her guesthouse. I rent from Aloisia Gonzaga. Ferrante's granddaughter."

"You're kidding?"

"No."

He looked at the file again.

"What's the problem?" I asked to get his attention.

"Well, the family could withdraw their guarantee."

"Who made that deal?" I guessed it was probably Montoya himself.

"As the Bible says, 'Beggars can't be choosers'."

I couldn't stop myself. "Not in the Bible."

"What?"

"That's not in the Bible. It's from the John Heywood, a 16th Century British playwright."

"Thanks for the clarification," he noted sarcastically.

"He was also John Donne's grandfather."

"Who?"

"Heywood, not Gonzaga."

Everyone in the South Bay knew Ferrante Gonzaga. Or at least where he lived. On the bluffs overlooking Santa Monica Bay in Riviera Beach. He was our very own eccentric, our very own mean, rich old bastard.

His house was a rambling white Cape Cod built in the 1920s and never really renovated despite his riches. The paint was peeling. Dry rot was crumbling supporting beams under the overhanging roof. The place was a relic of olden days and one of the few remaining private homes along the bluff. All the others had been destroyed in the 1970s and 80s to make way for luxury, high-rise condominiums. Which weren't really very luxurious. Except in price.

So, after talking with Montoya, on the way back to Long Beach, I stopped in Riviera Beach. I drove by Ferrante's house to see what might be taking place there since his untimely accident. There was one black and white and one unmarked light blue Ford Crown Vic parked out front. I knew the Ford.

I approached the front steps just as my old pal and fellow Polak, Sergeant Stanley Milosz, was closing the door behind him. "Pete," he said, "what brings you here?"

He looked pretty much the same as he did when we watched Iggy's grandmother Lilith electrocute herself. Except he had dropped a few pounds. He had also shaved off his moustache and that made him look younger. But he hadn't gained any hair and he still had that hangdog look as if he carried all the problems of the South Bay on his shoulders.

I said, "Just wanted to pay my respects. Gonzaga gave a lot of money to the church."

"No one here to pay respects to. Good thing. The place is falling apart."

"Guess they'll tear it down. Like all the others." We immediately drifted into the easiest topic of discussion in southern California—real estate.

"Yeah. Sure. The property's worth four or five million even without the house. Even with the recession."

"I suppose if they build something nice, they could get close to ten million for it."

"Have to be. I heard your Jesuits got a bundle for that crummy house where you used to live over on Dolorita."

"I hope they use it to do some good."

"Yeah. Sure. Church money doing good?" He harrumphed to himself.

"They're Jesuits. They might."

He shook his head. He clearly didn't agree. "Money… seems it almost never leads to good."

"I wouldn't know."

"Yeah, but you're not supposed to know. You don't have any."

"And you're an honest cop." He really was honest. And a loyal family man to boot. "Look," I said, "anything I should know about the old guy's death?"

"Other than the obvious?"

"The obvious?"

"That he was stupid?"

"Why?"

"Jumping out of an airplane at his age?"

We bantered awhile longer, but Milosz didn't have any more information about Ferrante, so I headed home.

I ate a small organic free range chicken sandwich and a half cup of Dark Chocolate sorbet. Before I went onto the internet to find out more about Ferrante Gonzaga, I began to recite Sext,, Psalm 73: "O deliver not up unto the beasts the souls of them that confess to thee; / and forget not the souls of thy poor, for ever…" when I heard a loud crash from the main house. I debated whether I should just ignore the noise given my morning's bad experience with a very grumpy Aloisia. But I am a priest. Maybe she needed help.

I hoisted myself up onto her back deck and peeked inside

her kitchen window. She was sprawled on the floor. A very large, sharp Horschner Chef's knife lay next to her. The radial artery in her left wrist was spurting blood.

Crimson red on the canary yellow tiles.

ACKNOWLEDGMENTS

I really do need to thank the Jesuit priests, teachers and scholastics whose lives, guidance and example left me with an enduring respect for their intellect and learning, but also for their very human view of the Catholic Church and the priesthood. The Jesuits are often extremely complex people living contradictory lives, a reality that I pray will continue to influence the Papacy of Francis, Bishop of Rome.

I must also thank all those who took the time to read drafts of *The Innocents* and who offered comments which always led to improvements: my award-winning essayist son Morgan Meis and his wife, the writer and performance artist Stefany Golberg; my tough, no-nonsense defense lawyer daughter Marika Meis and her husband an equally tough defense lawyer, Aaron Mysliwiec; my brothers, Michael Meis and the novelist Vincent Meis; my sisters, Mary, Monica, Marcie; my 92-year-old very literary mother, Ginny Meis; the writer Robert Sam Anson who was for one turbulent year my roommate at Jesuit boarding school; the novelist Peter Lefcourt; Lily Coyle at Beavers Pond; Sabine Huemer; Penny Wales; Jeannie Ringel; Tracy Boatfield-Bell; the artists Charles Cloverdale, Mary Ghesquire and Betty Warner Sheinbaum; and many others, brothers and sisters and friends who are always there with support and encouragement.

To those upon whom the characters in this story are roughly filched, you shall remain anonymous but I am obviously in your debt. Always.

Thank you Margot Farris, a lovely woman at {**pages**} a terrific independent bookstore in Manhattan Beach, California.

And, as always, a nod toward the heavens where my original inspiration, Dr. William A. Meis, Sr. now resides.

CPSIA information can be obtained at www.ICGtesting.com
Printed in the USA
BVOW04s0226200115

384061BV00015B/222/P